THE PERFE

Josephina Trafford was fas[...]
plows, intrigued by the lates[...]
enchanted by a novel bree[...]
life until now was George F[...]
rations of love were infinit[...]
farmers' crop reports.

And as far as her latest suitor was concerned, Josephina found Lord Conniston Venables to be deeply absorbed with the proper knot in his cravat, immersed in the elegant cut of his jacket, and involved in the pleasures of the gaming table, ballroom, and boudoir. And if all that were not sufficiently unbearable, the current lady in his life was the bewitching wife of a local lord, and she was, as rumour had it, just one of many whom he changed almost as often as he did his linen.

Clearly it was impossible that Josephina and the outrageously rakish Venables could ever be together. Unfortunately, it was even harder for them to stay apart. . . .

St. Martin's Summer

SIGNET Regency Romances You'll Enjoy

- [ ] **THE INNOCENT DECEIVER by Vanessa Gray.**
  (#E9463—$1.75)*
- [ ] **THE LONELY EARL by Vanessa Gray.** (#E7922—$1.75)
- [ ] **THE MASKED HEIRESS by Vanessa Gray.** (#E9331—$1.75)
- [ ] **THE DUTIFUL DAUGHTER by Vanessa Gray.**
  (#E9017—$1.75)*
- [ ] **THE WICKED GUARDIAN by Vanessa Gray.** (#E8390—$1.75)
- [ ] **THE WAYWARD GOVERNESS by Vanessa Gray.**
  (#E8696—$1.75)*
- [ ] **THE GOLDEN SONG BIRD by Sheila Walsh.** (#E8155—$1.75)†
- [ ] **LORD GILMORE'S BRIDE by Sheila Walsh.** (#E8600—$1.75)*
- [ ] **THE SERGEANT MAJOR'S DAUGHTER by Sheila Walsh.**
  (#E8220—$1.75)
- [ ] **THE INCOMPARABLE MISS BRADY by Sheila Walsh.**
  (#E9245—$1.75)*
- [ ] **MADALENA by Sheila Walsh.** (#E9332—$1.75)
- [ ] **THE REBEL BRIDE by Catherine Coulter.** (#J9630—$1.95)
- [ ] **THE AUTUMN COUNTESS by Catherine Coulter.**
  (#AE1445—$2.25)
- [ ] **LORD DEVERILL'S HEIR by Catherine Coulter.**
  (#E9200—$1.75)*
- [ ] **LORD RIVINGTON'S LADY by Eileen Jackson.**
  (#E9408—$1.75)*
- [ ] **BORROWED PLUMES by Roseleen Milne.** (#E8113—$1.75)†

*Price slightly higher in Canada
†Not available in Canada

Buy them at your local bookstore or use this convenient coupon for ordering.

THE NEW AMERICAN LIBRARY, INC.,
P.O. Box 999, Bergenfield, New Jersey 07621

Please send me the SIGNET BOOKS I have checked above. I am enclosing
$_____(please add $1.00 to this order to cover postage and handling).
Send check or money order—no cash or C.O.D.'s. Prices and numbers are
subject to change without notice.

Name _____

Address_____

City _____ State _____ Zip Code _____
Allow 4-6 weeks for delivery.
This offer is subject to withdrawal without notice.

St. Martin's Summer

by
Diana Brown

A SIGNET BOOK
NEW AMERICAN LIBRARY
TIMES MIRROR

PUBLISHER'S NOTE

This novel is a work of fiction. Names, characters, places, and incidents are either the product of the author's imagination or are used fictitiously, and any resemblance to actual persons, living or dead, events, or locales is entirely coincidental.

NAL BOOKS ARE AVAILABLE AT QUANTITY DISCOUNTS WHEN USED TO PROMOTE PRODUCTS OR SERVICES. FOR INFORMATION PLEASE WRITE TO PREMIUM MARKETING DIVISION, THE NEW AMERICAN LIBRARY, INC., 1633 BROADWAY, NEW YORK, NEW YORK 10019.

SIGNET TRADEMARK REG. U.S. PAT. OFF. AND FOREIGN COUNTRIES REGISTERED TRADEMARK—MARCA REGISTRADA HECHO EN CHICAGO, U.S.A.

SIGNET, SIGNET CLASSICS, MENTOR, PLUME, MERIDIAN AND NAL Books are published by The New American Library, Inc., 1633 Broadway, New York, New York 10019

First Printing, July, 1982

1 2 3 4 5 6 7 8 9

PRINTED IN THE UNITED STATES OF AMERICA

For Pamela—
dearest daughter, dearest friend

Expect Saint Martin's Summer, halcyon days
　　　—Shakespeare, *Henry VI*, Part I

1

"It's Will, Miss Trafford. He was caught last night—over at Venarvon. He's to be up before the magistrate in the morning, and everyone knows how Squire Ridgeway is about poaching." Bessie Meersham pulled compulsively at the drenched handkerchief in her hands. "I don't doubt it could even go on to the assizes."

With that she burst into tears, causing Josephina Trafford to push aside the heavy ledgers she had been studying before Bessie's arrival and get up to comfort the young woman. Bessie was the daughter of the Trumbulls, longtime Westlands' tenants, and Josephina had known her ever since childhood. She had learned from Mrs. Trumbull only the previous week that the wedding she had witnessed a year ago between Bessie and Will Meersham, was to bear fruit, and had thought that was the matter that had brought Bessie to see her, rather than the unfolding tale of woe.

"He done it, Miss Trafford, he don't deny he done it, but he didn't mean to steal. I mean, well, the way Venarvon is now, no one living there, game running wild all over—it didn't seem like stealing, though I know some as'll call it so. But Will didn't mean to, he wouldn't harm no one, my Will—he's a good man, a good husband, and he'll be a good father, God willing."

Again Bessie broke into a flood of tears, and Josephina, her arm about her shoulders, soothed, "There, Bessie, I know how you must feel. It may be bad, but not necessarily hopeless, and you know I'll do whatever I can. But I refuse to let you talk about it until you feel calmer; then we shall see what can be done. First, I'm going to have Rose bring us some tea."

While Bessie gradually stemmed her tears and they awaited the comfort of tea, Josephina Trafford's thoughts drifted back to the task in which she had been interrupted, the annual settling of Westlands' accounts. The figures she was deriving, despite the dry summer and that disastrous harvest rain, were

1

far better than she had expected; they were, in fact, proving her agricultural ventures correct.

It had come as no surprise to Westlands' tenants when, on Mr. Trafford's death, it was discovered that he had left his estate in its entirety to Josephina, for after a pulmonary ailment had taken his only son, Gerald, from him, he had turned increasingly to his eldest daughter, taking her with him on his rounds, explaining to her the duties of a landowner. She knew all the tenants, their children, the number of their livestock, the extent of their holdings, their sorrows and joys, and a mutual respect had been firmly established between them.

Not unexpectedly, Milvercombe's Squire Ridgeway had heartily disapproved.

"It's a bad thing for the Traffords the boy didn't live, but he always was a sickly creature"—the squire had looked proudly upon the strapping figure of his eldest son, George—"I believe in entail myself, always have and always will. Property left to the distaff side can never survive. Westlands will fall to the auctioneer's block before the year is out, mark my words."

Had Mrs. Trafford had her way, Squire Ridgeway's prophecy would most certainly have been fulfilled. Isabel Mulliner, her sister, and her husband had arrived for the funeral intent upon assisting Josephina to sell the estate and removing the entire family to London, a plan dear to Mrs. Trafford's heart. But Josephina, hating what she knew of the frivolity of London life, was adamant in her refusal to part with Westlands. The estate and the responsibility for its upkeep had been passed to her; she intended to keep it.

It had turned out to be no easy matter, though, for when Frank Ridgeway, the squire's younger son, who practiced law in nearby Torbridge, had read the stipulations of Mr. Trafford's will, it was revealed that Josephina, besides providing for her mother during her lifetime, was required to give her sisters, Prudence and Amelia, upon marriage, settlements of five thousand pounds each, yet the estate was all but bankrupt. Only then had Josephina realized the heavy penalty her father had paid to gain freedom from her mother's sharp tongue by acquiescing to all her foolish extravagances.

Josephina had resolved not only that she would not part with Westlands but also that she would pay off all its debts and make the estate profitable enough to provide her sisters' settlements, though she was relieved that it would be some time before they were likely to marry.

In her resolve, Josephina had committed the unforgiveable sin of not seeking the advice of Squire Ridgeway, nor any of the other estate owners thereabouts, no one, that is, except for old Mr. Bracewaite over at Trentor, and everyone knew he was full of foolish ideas. Look at the way he had invested in those peculiar merino sheep brought to England from Spain by George the Third. He was a mad king and no mistake, and Mr. Bracewaite took after him—never mind that he'd pulled in a tidy profit from the merinos' fine wool, for which the London market, cut off from the source of supply by the continuing wars with Napoleon, was crying.

Mr. Bracewaite, it was, who had spoken to Josephina of Jethro Tull's ideas on tillage and vegetation that had resulted in her purchasing a seed drill of Tull's design, to be followed the next year by a four-coultered plough that turned the earth with such efficiency it threw up grass and weeds so their roots dried, destroying them in the process and allowing the crops to flourish.

The good people of Milvercombe had laughed at such foolishness, but the figures Josephina had set aside on Bessie's arrival were proving that her outlays had been profitable.

Over the years, and over her mother's objections, she had managed to pay off their most pressing creditors.

"It's ridiculous!" Mrs. Trafford had remonstrated bitterly. "Why bother with them? Let them wait, they've waited long enough."

"That's just it," Josephina reasoned, "they've waited long enough, but they won't wait forever. If we don't take care, we may find ourselves without a roof over our heads."

"Nonsense! Why, when I lived in London, no one thought anything of running a few thousand into debt. Tradesmen know they must wait. If they go into trade, they must expect it. I don't know why we simply don't pack up and move back to a civilized life. I'm sure if you and Prudence don't want to, Amelia will be glad to come to London with me."

"But we simply haven't the money now to support two households, Mother. We have nothing except for our land, and we must get the greatest return possible from it, can't you understand?"

But Mrs. Trafford could not understand and complained bitterly and unceasingly that no one had any feeling for her poor nerves excepting her dear Amelia. Josephina wasted money on foolish stuff for the farm, she bemoaned to her friend Lady Netherton, and denied her mother, her only mother, the beautiful cashmere shawl on display at Torbridge's haberdasher's—a mere six pounds. Such a hard daughter Josephina had turned out to be; how she missed her dear husband. While Lady Netherton had nodded sympathetically, she had privately thought that Mrs. Trafford mourned her husband in death far more than she had enjoyed his company in life.

Squire Ridgeway certainly agreed with Mrs. Trafford on the foolishness of Josephina's expenditures, particularly in the matter of the seed drill.

"Ridiculous," he had snorted when first he heard of it, his red face puffed in umbrage, "spending all that money for a machine to do what man's right hand has been doing for centuries. Sowing broadcast is what we've always done; it did for my father, it does for me, and it will do for George after me. Silly waste, if you ask me. Josephina Trafford would do well to get rid of that useless old Winslow and hire herself a bailiff worth his salt. I know the very man for her, but she won't listen to me. Stubborn young woman. Should be married and confining her activities to the house and the begetting of children instead of tromping around barns and fields like a hoyden."

The Trafford girls might be handsome enough, but given their financial state, he was glad when Frank overcame his infatuation for Prudence. If only George would do likewise in his regard for Josephina; the squire might wish her married, but certainly to someone other than his son and heir.

It was one point on which Josephina and Squire Ridgeway saw eye to eye. She liked George Ridgeway, but she had never sought the constant attendance of that stalwart, florid gentleman to be prompted by anything more than friendship.

Josephina, her long brown hair knotted atop her head neatly but without style, her skin unfashionably bronzed by the sun, never noticed the brightness the fresh air imparted to her hazel eyes, nor the fascination of the smile that lit not only those eyes but also her entire face. Indeed, she never thought herself as attracting any member of the opposite sex, nor did that perturb her. It was Prudence, at twenty-three, her junior by two years, who was the family beauty, with her classical features and the soft pink-and-white complexion she had inherited from her mother. Amelia was also lovely, with her flaxen hair and heart-shaped face with its retroussé nose; she was full of wiles that she used to elude her sisters at lesson-time, escaping with her friend Mildred Carew, the rector's youngest daughter, and hiding away in the window seat to whisper of assemblies and balls and waltzes with scarlet-coated officers. As the youngest, she was indulged by her sisters, who would never return from visits to Torbridge without some gift for her, the latest of Maria Edgeworth's novels or a piece of ribbon to retrim a bonnet. Yet even these favours did not satisfy her. Nothing had until Aunt Mulliner had offered to bring her out at the London season; since then, her excitement further inflamed by her mother's reminiscences of her own season, she had spoken of nothing else.

It was as Rose was serving tea to Bessie Meersham that Amelia came bursting in upon them, clad in a China-blue redingote with matching satin bows.

"What do you think of it, Jo? Is it not elegant? There was one almost exactly like it in the *Repository* last month, and Pru copied it, except for the material. It should be velvet, velvet is all the rage. But this wool has a light nap on it that from a distance could pass for velvet. What do you think? I should die in London rather than be taken for a country bumpkin."

Amelia waltzed around the study, displaying the redingote and her lovely Dresden figure, and while her sister admired the sight, she could not put from her mind the multitude of expenses that the visit, notwithstanding her aunt's generosity, must entail. She had sought to put if off for a year, but Amelia's disappointment and Mrs. Trafford's remonstrances had been more than she could bear.

"Well, Jo, what do you think? Do tell, pray."

"I think you are very lovely and that the wool is every bit as fine as velvet. But can't you see that I am occupied? Run along and show Mother."

Amelia's eyes flickered across Bessie in disinterest before, with one final swirl, she swept from the room.

Josephina smiled at Bessie. "Young sisters are a tease. Be glad you don't have any. Feeling a bit better now?"

Bessie nodded.

"Well enough to tell me all about what happened at Venarvon?"

"Like I said, Miss Trafford, Will's no common poacher, but he thought I should be eating well with the baby coming and all. It's been a bad year for most folk around here, with the harvest not what it should be, payment is slow, not their fault, but it keeps us short. Will was starting to feel desperate—that's why he took the two rabbits."

Josephina was in a quandary. As a landowner she could not condone poaching, yet she believed Bessie—Will was no common poacher; if he had caught the rabbits, it was from necessity, not for profit.

"But why didn't Will come to me?" she asked.

"You've done so much for us already, Miss Trafford, and Will is proud. You see, he'd done a job of work at Venarvon, and Mr. Farnsworth kept putting off paying him, no matter that Will told how much we needed the money. Anyway, like I said, he got desperate. On the way home, he caught the rabbits. Mr. Farnsworth had followed Will. He saw everything."

Josephina could not restrain a sigh.

If only it had been anywhere except Venarvon, and anyone except Farnsworth, for with the owner of Venarvon constantly absent, his bailiff had come to regard the huge estate as his own preserve. On the death of the fourth Earl of Venables, who had been a close friend of Mr. Trafford's, the estate had been inherited by his eldest son, Randolph. He had spent most of his time in London, seldom visiting Devon and then only for brief sojourns to hunt for stag on Exmoor or occasionally to ride with Squire Ridgeway's hounds, which he declared poor sport compared to being out with the Quorn. Three years had passed since he had visited the estate, and it had recently been learned that he had been killed in a hunting accident with that very pack, leaving the title and estate to pass to his younger brother, Conniston. Squire Ridgeway had ridden out himself to Westlands to inform the Traffords of the event.

"Called our pack poor sport. Well, he learned his lesson," Milvercombe's squire had pontificated in his usual bellicose manner. "At least we don't go killing off the members of our hunt. Still, he was better than that reprobate brother of his. I've no liking for him, and well he knows it. Don't suppose he'll dare to show his face in this village again after the way he acted."

Josephina knew there had once been trouble between the squire and the younger Venables, though she had paid no more heed to its cause than she did to any other village gossip. Farnsworth had evidently agreed with the squire's speculation that the sixth earl would keep his distance, for the bailiff had been even lazier than usual since he had inherited the property. No repairs were being undertaken and tenants' grievances were seldom redressed unless it happened to be some special favourite of Farnsworth's; even then Josephina did not doubt that money changed hands. She was sure the bailiff was pocketing funds which did not belong to him, but that was a matter for the owner's concern. It was the neglect of the land and the lack of heed to the tenants' welfare which she resented. As the largest landowner in that part of Devon, she felt it incumbent on Lord Venables to set the example. His father had done so, but neither of the sons seemed inclined to follow in paternal footsteps.

She knew little of the present title holder, for he had left Venarvon under a cloud many years ago when she was still a child. She had not understood the circumstances that had caused his departure, except that he had incurred Squire Ridgeway's wrath and that father and son had quarrelled bitterly over the dispute. Little had been spoken of the matter in her presence, and she was not one to listen to gossip. She knew that he had left England and gone abroad, but she had heard he had returned sometime prior to his brother's death. She occasionally read of him as a member of fashionable London gatherings recounted in the *Morning Post*. Her mother, who avidly followed such matters, conjectured that he must be well past his thirtieth birthday, and as no lady bearing his name was ever mentioned, Mrs. Trafford was led to speculate that he had remained unmarried.

When Conniston Venables had first inherited Venarvon, Josephina had thought to apprise him of the estate's condition. She had had many altercations with Farnsworth concerning care of the land, particularly that along their joint boundary, where gates, fences, and hedgerows were allowed to straggle and rot; often her herds strayed onto Venables' property and her men were accused of trespassing after going to retrieve them, forcing Josephina to make repairs that were not her responsibility and that she could ill afford. Her letters to Lord Randolph Venables on the subject having gone unanswered, she didn't doubt that the new owner would prove equally unsympathetic, and she felt that Squire Ridgeway, as magistrate, should approach him. Yet the squire, usually avid in his interest of the affairs of others, was strangely reluctant.

"If the Venables don't want to take care of their property, that's their loss," was all he said in response to Josephina's request.

"But it would be to the advantage of all if the land were well tended, and they have the money to do so, for the Venables are reputed to be among the wealthiest landowners in England," Josephina persisted.

"Let's say they were before the sons got their hands on the fortune. Randolph ran through a pile, and this one will be no better, you mark my words. Why, when last I was in London, I heard tell of a wager he'd made at White's with Lord Cansfield that a certain Miss Anstey, a lady noted for her prudery, mark you, would accept a monstrously huge diamond pendant from him and wear it at Almack's. Asinine, if you ask me, for though he won the wagered five thousand, he was down the cost of the necklace, and from what I heard, it was worth far more. But that's the sort of foolishness I would expect of him. He never was any good." The squire sniffed censoriously.

Gracious! Five thousand pounds, Josephina mused; that would have been enough to buy the merino sheep Mr. Bracewaite was mindful of selling now that age was forcing him to cut back on his livestock; she'd never seen such thick, fine fleece as they bore; there would be a handsome profit eventually for whoever could afford them, and there would have been money over to cover the expenses of Amelia's coming out besides. Yes, she could have made good use of the five thousand pounds Lord Venables had wagered so recklessly. She hated to agree with the squire, but it did sound a silly and extravagant way to dispose of money.

"No, Josephina," Squire Ridgeway continued, "it's not our business if they want their property to go to rack and ruin. I take care of mine, just as you do yours. Can't expect Farnsworth to do much. He says he's kept strapped for money."

"He's not short of anything, from my observation," Josephina retorted acidly.

"Well, and what if he does take care of himself a bit? More fool Venables, I say, if he can't look after what's his."

Josephina doubted that Squire Ridgeway would be any more helpful now if she went directly to him over Will Meersham's dilemma. She could hear him intoning, "Poaching is a crime, my dear, you know it and I know it. We can't let anyone off, it would set a bad example." If it were true, as Bessie had said, that he was referring poaching cases to the assizes, it would be preferable if the matter never reached him.

She smiled over at Bessie with a confidence she was far from feeling.

"I'm very glad you came to me, Bessie, and I shall do everything that I can for Will, though I can make no promises. Mr. Farnsworth is not an easy man, but I shall try to make him see reason. I shall make good the loss and assure him that it will never happen again."

"It won't, Miss Trafford, that it won't," Bessie promised fervently. "It's scared the living daylights out of Will—and me too."

"I know, Bessie. Now, before you go home, I want you to

go to the kitchen and have Mrs. Cooper put up a basket of provisions for you."

"But I didn't come for that, Miss Trafford," Bessie protested.

"I know you didn't, Bessie, but we have far more than we need, and Mrs. Cooper will be glad to get some space in her larder. I shall take up the matter with Mr. Farnsworth, and if I do not succeed there, I shall see the squire. Believe me, I shall do everything within my power to prevent harsh punishment, but I can't promise that I shall be successful."

"Oh, Miss Trafford, if anyone can do it, you can. I think you can do anything. I know you can save him." Bessie's relieved smile embarrassed Josephina, for she did not have such faith in her own ability. She cut short her thanks and accompanied her to the door, instructing Rose to see her to the kitchen and make sure she had a well-stocked basket when she left.

It wasn't going to be easy, she thought, sitting once again at her desk and resting her chin on her hands. If only she knew how best to proceed. Usually she had a liking for significant problems which forced her to consider all approaches, to weigh the pros and cons and to make decisions which must be adhered to after all the evidence had been examined, but her decisions theretofore had not had a life depending on them—or three lives, if she included Bessie and the unborn baby.

She got up and walked over to the window. It would be useless to write to Lord Venables, for by the time a reply were received, if, in fact, it were forthcoming at all, Will would already have been charged and the case in all likelihood referred to a higher authority. Now was the time to do something, before it got that far. Besides, she had no idea where to address him; he was probably at his London house, but she had no way of knowing for sure. No, it must be Farnsworth. If only there were a way to bring pressure on him. Though she was aware that many of his dealings were less than aboveboard, she had no proof of his dishonesty. She supposed she might assert to him that she had such proof, but he was an ugly man to deal with; he would probably discover she was bluffing and become even more belligerent. Appealing to his better nature, reminding him of Bessie's condition, would be of little avail. His ill treatment of his own wife was well known. Poor woman, she was often beaten, particularly after his bouts of drinking, which were common knowledge in Milvercombe. Once she had run away and sought shelter at Westlands; Josephina believed he still bore a grudge against her on that account. She gazed speculatively past the yew hedges that bordered the drive leading to the road which ran to Milvercombe in one direction and to Venarvon in the other. Should she ride over there now, or ask Farnsworth to come and see her? So engrossed was she in the problem that she did not hear the door open, and was startled by Prudence's voice close at hand.

"Lost in thought, Jo, or is something the matter?"

It was possible at a glance to know that they were sisters; both were slightly above average in height and both had slender, well-proportioned figures. They held themselves proudly, owing, no doubt, to their mother's constant admonition to them as children, "Hold your heads up, girls—no, not your chins out, but your heads up. Remember you are ladies and must always so carry yourselves."

Though Josephina greeted her sister warmly, Prudence quickly reasserted, "There is something wrong, Jo, I can see it in your eyes. What is it?"

So Josephina, though she would have preferred to spare her sister, who worried on everyone's account except her own, told her of Bessie's plight.

"Poor Bessie, I saw her in the kitchen and thought she had been crying—no wonder. Of course, poaching is unlawful, I know Will shouldn't have taken the rabbits, but I can understand why he did it. I can't bear to think of them in need, especially now Bessie is with child. What can we do?"

"She has food now, and we can make sure that she lacks nothing. As for Will, I shall write to Farnsworth and request him to call. I had thought of riding over to Venarvon, but it is, perhaps, preferable if Winslow delivers my note asking him to see me at Westlands. He is not such a bully away from his home ground."

"I hate that awful man, Jo, but even more I hate you having to see him." Prudence had been present when Farnsworth had come to reclaim his reluctant wife, and she had been unable to sleep for a week thinking of her suffering. "He's monstrous."

It was the worst thing Josephina had ever heard Pru, who saw good in everybody, say of anyone.

"You don't suppose it would be better to go to Squire Ridgeway, do you, Jo?"

"No, I don't, but if I have no success with Farnsworth, then of course I will go see him. Come, Pru, tell me what you've been doing this morning."

10

"I've been helping Mrs. Cooper in the kitchen with her damson preserves. We put up twenty-four bottles and now she is making some of her splendid apple tart. I wish I could make pastry like hers, but try as I will, mine is always heavy."

"Well, I prefer your jam tarts to hers."

"That's only because jam tarts require a heavier pastry," Pru sighed, "but I must own that I think my maids of honour are superior."

"They are indeed. All this talk of food is making me hungry, and it's hours till four."

"Shall I have a tray prepared to tide you over till dinner?"

"No, I'll wait. But I must get Winslow to carry a note over to Venarvon. It won't take me long to write it. Would you be a dear and tell Rose to have him come and see me as soon as he can?"

With that, Josephina took up her pen to write a note she hoped was at once sufficiently courteous and peremptory to make Farnsworth come to see her without delay.

2

Josephina, awaiting a reply to her note, was glad her mother had chosen that day to visit Milvercombe. Though Mrs. Trafford evidenced no interest in estate matters, she was acutely curious concerning any unusual comings and goings, and would, no doubt, demand full particulars should Farnsworth call.

Mrs. Trafford's avid interest in visitors was not altogether unwarranted, for in Milvercombe, a small North Devon village, the only thing that changed conspicuously was the weather. Situated on the edge of Exmoor, its winters were long and severe, with bitter winds blowing down from the moors to engulf the soft, rolling hills, whistling through the thatched cottages, shaking the barns until worried farmers shook their heads and Mr. Carew, the rector, was called upon to explain why such worthy people should be so afflicted.

Nevertheless, Milvercombe was an amenable place in that unusually warm late autumn, just as it was in summer, when the rich, red land yielded its abundance and workers challenged the very bees in their industry. For those without occupation, however, Milvercombe's only entertainment was the ongoing round of social visits conducted, as Amelia once astutely observed, for the purpose of further dissecting one another. Prudence was so shocked by this statement that she made Amelia learn the entire eighth chapter of Mark by heart. But when Amelia complained bitterly of this to Mildred Carew, she gained little sympathy.

"Only thirty-eight verses, you were lucky! Why, just because I said Lady Netherton was a meddling busybody, I had to memorize the hundred and nineteenth psalm, and that's a hundred and seventy-six verses—actually, it wasn't too difficult, because Mama forgot she had made me do this once before as a punishment, and it came back quite easily."

And the two girls would put their heads together and laugh at the vagaries of adults and parents, a favourite theme, declaring that when they became parents they would never

12

make their daughters do such foolish things, a statement which invariably led Amelia to wondering just who she would marry, declaring there was no one in Milvercombe who was remotely attractive enough, to which Mildred would reply. "That's only because my brother, Charles, is still away at the wars. If he were here, you wouldn't say that."

But Amelia, though she had sense enough not to mention it to Mildred, thought there was little attraction in serving with Wellington's army as a chaplain, convinced as she was that Charles would not be required to wear a red coat to perform his offices, an automatic qualification, in her eyes, for a dashing hero.

In the eyes of other Milvercombe residents, however, Charles Carew had grown to be a romantic figure. His letters home describing life in Spain and Portugal were said, by those privileged to hear them read by his fond mother, to be worthy of publication. Josephina and Prudence were among his most consant admirers, for the letters brought into their quiet lives an element of excitement which, despite their sedulousness, both found sadly lacking. It was many years since they had seen Charles, for though they had played together as children, he had been sent up to Oxford and had then gone on to serve with the Army under the patronage of Sir John Brennan, a wealthy Yorkshire nobleman, a post of which his father was justly proud, though Mrs. Carew worried about his safety.

"You'd think chaplains had to be right there in the firing line, to listen to their talk," Amelia had snorted. "I expect he only says prayers on Sunday and just sits around reading the rest of the time."

But Josephina pointed out to her that the greatest duty of chaplains in the field was to give solace to the soldiers going into battle and administer comfort to the seriously wounded and dying; thus Charles Carew had probably seen more of the true nature of war than had many line officers.

For the past week there had been great excitement in the village, for Charles Carew was returning. Prudence had learned from Fanny Netherton, whose mother had heard it directly from Mrs. Carew herself, that his patron was resigning from the Army and was to sell his commission, thus he would no longer have need of a chaplain. Therefore Charles Carew planned to assist his father in Milvercombe until he found a place, and his day of arrival was anxiously awaited.

"You may be sure we shall celebrate as soon as Charles is amongst us once again," Mrs. Carew had assured Mrs. Trafford, "and we shall count upon you and your daughters being with us, for no party is ever complete without the charming Misses Trafford, you know."

Mrs. Trafford, who understood Mrs. Carew's "Misses" as "Mrs.," bowed her head in acknowledgement and decided that Mrs. Carew was not quite the prig she had previously thought her to be.

It was for the purpose of visiting the rectory to ascertain whether any news of the arrival had been received that Mrs. Trafford had set out that day. On her way she stopped in at Mrs. Tyrrell's general shop but, finding nothing new in her stock, decided the shopkeeper was a poor replacement for the previous owner, Stanley Potter, an ambitious man who had left Devon to try his luck in London and was said to be making a veritable fortune with his linen draper's establishment on Bond Street.

No glance was spared for the boot- and shoemaker who spent his time constructing heavy footgear of ponderous size from bark-tanned leather, studding the soles with row upon row of hobnails. Nor did the village smithy, who stood outside, arms akimbo, warrant any recognition from the worthy widow of Westlands.

Mrs. Trafford did, however, pop in to see Mrs. Fenwick, the lacemaker, who plied her bobbins with such dexterity that people came from throughout the county for her lace, to select trim for the new caps Pru was making for her and to comment upon everyone else's selections while so doing.

Shepton Park, the home of Lady Netherton and her daughter, Fanny, was a usual stopping place. Mrs. Trafford visited there more often than Lady Netherton came to Westlands, which, though situated only three miles from the village, Lady Netherton always described as being out in the country. This was particularly galling to Mrs. Trafford, who sniffed, "To hear her talk, you would think living in Milvercombe were living in town." Nevertheless, in the heart of winter, when the road connecting Westlands to the village became impassable with drifting snow banks and then later with mud in the thaw, the Trafford residence was remote indeed.

But that day Mrs. Trafford passed by both Shepton Park and Ridgeway Hall in favour of the rectory, and she was rewarded by news that a letter had only just been delivered from Charles, announcing that he would be riding down from Yorkshire the following week.

"Riding, mind you, not by post chaise," Mrs. Trafford was to remark later with evident disapproval, though Amelia

14

thought it the most romantic thing she had ever heard him do.

Mrs. Trafford waited only long enough to have the letter read to her thrice so that she might memorize its contents before hurrying away to pass the information to Lady Netherton. It was a treat, for once, to be the bearer of news rather than the receiver, and as she went, she ruminated upon every detail, for she had no doubt that as soon as she left Shepton Park, Lady Netherton would call upon Mrs. Carew to ascertain whether anything had been overlooked.

While Mrs. Trafford proceeded on her mission, Josephina impatiently awaited a response from Farnsworth, but it was well past one before she saw Winslow turn in the driveway and she hurried out to meet him.

"He's all in a pother, Miss Trafford, and I'm afraid it's not good for your business, for he sends his regrets and says he cannot possibly see you today about anything. Seems Lord Venarvon is expected momentarily from London. He gave only a day's notice of his arrival, and that to the housekeeper so that a bed would be ready, with not a word to Farnsworth himself. He's seething with anger and rushing around like a bear in a trap, trying to get the place and his accounts into some kind of order. He had ledgers out all over the table, and from the look on his face, he was worried indeed."

"That might be in our favour. If he's so busy, he won't be able to press charges against Will."

"I wouldn't count on it, Miss Trafford. He'll probably do so just to prove what an efficient bailiff he is. He has little else to show for his services."

Josephina had to acknowledge that to be so, and even if it were not, she could not leave the outcome to chance. She would have to ride out to Venarvon herself.

She asked Winslow to see that Pandora, her chestnut mare, was saddled and brought round, and made to go in to change into her riding habit, but not before she listened once again to Winslow's diatribe on her deportment and the necessity of remembering her station in life. It was difficult to bear, especially that day, so often had it been repeated, but she knew that, unlike the censure of Squire Ridgeway, he had only her well-being at heart. Looking at his brown, wrinkled face, the straightforward gaze of his brown eyes, narrowed beneath tightly knit eyebrows liberally sprinkled with grey, his gnarled hands fidgeting with the reins as he warmed to his subject, she remembered the long service he had rendered to her father and the love and respect in which he held the family. He should have retired long since, but whenever she hinted at it, she had to contend with a hurt look and the nodding of that old head with mutters of, "Past it all nowadays, am I . . . well, it's not what your father would have said," only to know that mention of her father was enough to win any argument with Josephina. Winslow secretly thought that she did a better job of running the estate than her father ever had, but he would never tell her so, grumbling at her innovations as much as any other villager, but Josephina knew that whenever she made a decision, he would carry out the task with unfailing loyalty to the best of his ability.

And, as Josephina expected, he finished his chiding with a reminder of her father.

"I know Mr. Trafford wouldn't approve of your having any doings with a man like Farnsworth, a bad lot and certainly not the sort of person any lady should go near. And then, there is Lord Venables due—from what I've heard, it wouldn't be at all the thing for you to be there alone if he were to arrive. Better let me come along, Miss Trafford, just in case."

"But this is precisely a matter on which my father would strongly approve of my action," Josephina responded gently but firmly. "The treatment of tenants and villagers was something dear to his heart, as you well know. And it is best that I see Farnsworth alone, for if he is inclined to accede to my request, he will more readily do so without a witness to his changed opinion—he would hate anyone to think him bested by a woman. Besides, I need you to look at the fence bordering Venarvon on the east meadow—I hear it's down again. If Lord Venables should have arrived, I shall most certainly mention that matter to him." Seeing the frown deepen on Winslow's face, she smiled. "I assure you I can take care of myself. My father and his were friends. I'm sure he would wish me no harm."

"I don't know about that, Miss Trafford. They say he's a wild one, not like his father. I'd feel a lot better if I was along."

But she steadfastly refused his company, and when he set off for the stables to order her horse saddled, he was still grumbling.

3

As Josephina turned in the great iron gates of Venarvon, she became increasingly aware of the decay and dilapidation which had overtaken the park; it was hard to believe that Capability Brown had once had a hand in its landscaping. Trees were still lying where the winds had tossed them in previous winters. Branches of the elms that lined the drive were untrimmed, so that she often had to lower her head to pass beneath them. Furze had taken over, and its yellow flowers were to be seen throughout the park, crowding out the rose beds that had once been the pride of Lady Venables. Josephina caught the sweet scent of the Devon myrtle that grew in great profusion; if Pru were with her, she would want to stop and collect it for their linen; surely in the confusion of foliage the owner should have been grateful for any clearing.

The long driveway curved before it reached the imposing grey stone mansion, which looked, from the outside, much as it always had, though the mullioned windows lacked lustre and there was a general air of neglect.

As she approached the entrance, she saw a smart black curricle drawn by four beautifully matched roans standing before the wide front steps, and drawing closer, she noticed the black-and-white Venables crest on the front panel. The new owner had arrived, then; so much the better. She called to a groom who was about to lead the curricle away, instructing him to see also to her mount, and climbed the front steps, boldly though not entirely free from trepidation.

Kister, the Venarvon butler, who had served there for as long as she remembered, wore an unhappy expression as he responded to Josephina's enquiry for his master, informing her in mournful tones that his lordship was indeed just that moment arrived and was above changing from his travelling clothes.

"Perhaps you would be so kind as to tell him I am here and that it is a matter of some urgency on which I wish to see him."

17

"Was he expecting you, Miss Trafford?"

"Of course not, Kister, but I must see him and I refuse to leave until I do."

Though Kister seemed reluctant, Josephina's determined look left no doubt that she was intent upon seeing his master, so he showed her into the library and promised to inform his lordship.

Josephina looked around the room lined with glass-covered bookcases, much in need of cleaning. The furniture was shrouded in grey covers and there was dust everywhere, disguising the elegance of the priceless inlaid walnut writing cabinet and the Chippendale clock in the corner with its hands permanently set at a quarter past nine. The room was of luxurious proportions, with high ceilings inlaid with paintings of scenes from Homer's *Odyssey*, from which descended the bookshelves crammed with leather-bound volumes, yet it must present a depressing sight for a homecoming.

She peered through the murky glass, examining the titles of the works: whoever had made the collection knew what he was about. Some of the titles were in her father's library, but she noticed a volume of William Cobbett's *Political Register* that she had long been wanting to examine, and she took it down. Removing the dust cover from a chair by the window, she settled down, to become so deeply engrossed in Cobbett's radical reasoning that she was not aware that over half an hour had passed since her arrival, nor was she aware that she was no longer alone until a resonant voice enquired. "Miss Trafford? I understand you wished to see me. I am Venables."

Josephina got up hastily, setting aside the volume. That she did not recognize the gentleman before her was hardly surprising since she had still been in the schoolroom when he left Venarvon. Though lacking Amelia's intuitive ability to assess the quality of others' mode of dress, she was aware that his coat of dark mulberry superfine fitted his broad shoulders to perfection, that his snow-white neckcloth, while not elaborately tied, had been arranged with care and precision, and that his boots gleamed in a manner not theretofore seen in Milvercombe. His appearance was marked by a mingling of elegance and strength—he had the air of a man who had, at once, seen too much and not enough of the world to satisfy him. For the first time, Josephina was aware of the shabbiness of her own dark-green riding attire.

His piercing grey eyes were now examining her with a

cold, enquiring glance that made her realize she had not acknowledged his greeting.

"To what do I own the pleasure of this call so close on the heels of my arrival?" His frigid tones implied that the visit was less than sought-after.

"I am, indeed, sorry to trouble you so soon, Lord Venables, but there is an urgent matter on which I must speak to you. I had intended to discuss it with your bailiff, but now you are here, it is preferable that I refer it to you directly."

"I don't believe we have met before."

"Excuse me." She extended her hand, smiling. "I am Miss Trafford of Westlands, your neighbour to the west. Your father and mine were good friends in the past."

"Ah, yes, I remember." A veiled expression crossed his face at the mention of his father; then he turned and stripped the cover from a chair opposite the one in which she had been sitting.

"Excuse the state of this room, Miss Trafford. I find the house in awful disarray, and the park in even worse condition. But before we get to your matter, let me call for some refreshments. My father used to have a very fine claret in his cellar, but I suppose you might prefer ratafia."

She accepted the offer of ratafia without relish, but preferring it to the claret, while she examined the earl with interest. His dark hair was short and curled slightly, his face was long with a strong chin, and though lines were etched around the corners of his mouth and eyes, he was, she realized with almost a start of surprise, an exceedingly handsome man. Tall, he carried himself with an easy grace, and his peremptory tone to Kister, who answered his summons with unusual alacrity, gave evidence that he was a man used to commanding and being obeyed without question.

Turning back to her, he asked, "If your groom has attended to your horses, perhaps he can find some refreshment in the kitchen."

"I rode over alone. I have no groom with me."

He raised his eyebrows, but it was not until Kister had left the room that he questioned, "Quite alone, Miss Trafford, to see me or to see my bailiff. Was that wise?"

Josephina felt her colour rise at the implication of her lack of conduct.

"My lord, it is a matter of some urgency on which I come, and there is little time to spare for the niceties of propriety and fashion that may be of importanace in those circles in which you move but have little meaning here in the country."

"Was it always so, Miss Trafford? I had it rather harshly impressed upon me, as I remember, that a young lady's reputation was equally as important here as in the world of fashionable society. Perhaps times have changed. It is some years since I have resided in Devon."

There was no ignoring the bitterness in his tone, which seemed to apply to something beyond her own lack of conduct, yet Josephina was stung by his remark.

"I do not feel my conduct is your affair, Lord Venables, and though I am a lady, I feel it is unnecessary to point out that I am no longer a young lady. I am quite used to going out alone, nor is it considered unusual that I should do so. It would be impossible to go about my business had I always to wait upon someone to accompany me. Besides, those employed at Westlands have better use for their time than to follow me around."

"But you cannot have reached your majority, surely."

"I am five and twenty, my lord, quite past my majority. Now, having settled the questions of my age and conduct, perhaps we may proceed. A man's life and the well-being of his family are at stake, and you can assist them if you will."

"Indeed!"

Josephina began to feel that it would be no easier dealing with Lord Venables than with his bailiff: she was also beginning to feel quite unsure of herself: yet having come with a purpose, she refused to leave until she had done everything within her power to achieve it.

Kister brought in the wine, and she noticed that Venables conspicuously examined the glasses before it was poured. The Kisters were in for difficult days ahead, she conjectured without great sorrow: they had had an easy time of it with no master at hand to care whether they performed their duties.

Satisfied at last, Venables sat back, holding the stem of his glass in his long fingers with their square-cut nails, the heavy gold of his signet ring, set with carved jade, gleaming on his right hand.

"Pray do go on, Miss Trafford. I had not expected to discover a Cheltenham tragedy awaiting me on my arrival, but it may be diverting."

For all the world Josephina wished she might have dashed the glass of ratafia into his mocking smile and left Venarvon, never to see his handsome face again, but she could not yield to her impulse. It was not on her behalf that she was there, but on behalf of those who had turned to her for help. Her face was expressionless, though her voice was icy when she spoke.

"I hardly consider it diverting, but it may be that you will find it so, for what is tragedy to one may be diverting to another, especially when those involved are not personally known."

"And who is involved?" he prompted.

"Will Meersham, a young lad born in this village. He is a hardworking fellow and has many times been employed at Westlands during planting and harvest. To my personal knowledge he is industrious and honest. Early this year he married the daughter of tenants of mine who have long farmed here." She stopped, conscious of the look of disinterest in his eyes.

"And just what can I do for this esteemed couple?" His drawled words, forcibly reminding her of his own lack of interest in Venarvon and the well-being of his own tenants infuriated her. What could he care for the tenants of others?

No longer weighing her words or attempting to hide her contempt, she burst forth, "I might have expected that tone, sir. The want of care for your own land could not be more apparent, nor have I patience for one who would leave his tenants to suffer under the vagaries of a rascal like Farnsworth, though I should have thought you would have called a halt to his misdeeds, if only for the sake of your own purse—that your tenants' buildings are rotting and no repairs are ever made will be your loss eventually. No help is ever given to them, but let them be a day late with their rents, and they are threatened with eviction. I know, sir, for I have observed this and much more firsthand. But it is not their case I plead, but for a lad and girl I have known since they were children. This has been a hard year for everyone here in Devon, first the drought and then rain close to harvestime. Landowners have suffered, but it has been even worse for those who toil on the land for so little reward. Many have not been fully paid their just due, and Will Meersham is among them. Had I known he and his wife, who is with child, were short of food, I should have seen it was supplied to them, but foolishly they did not come to me first, only now, after Will has been caught on your land by Farnsworth with two rabbits—"

She did not finish her sentence, for he gave a sudden shout of laughter. "So *that's* it, Miss Trafford, you come to plead the cause of a poacher, a common poacher."

She took a deep breath and clenched her fists to prevent herself from slapping his laughing face. She had never before

21

been so incensed. "That is unworthy, sir; this is no laughing matter. I plead the case for a young couple starting out in life and off to a very unfortunate start. I know just as well as you do, possibly better, that poaching is a crime, and that it is a crime which should not go unpunished, but that is precisely what I am asking of you in this instance. I have little time or patience with those I know to be inveterate poachers and who pride themselves on freely availing themselves of game belonging to others; there are many such in this neighbourhood whom I could but will not name, men who do not get caught because they are too clever or because they work in conjunction with rascally bailiffs, paying them off for the privilege of poaching on land of absentee landlords. . . . But I have said enough. I would not plead for those men, for they are, indeed, common poachers, but Will Meersham is not such a man. He was driven to his act by necessity and desperation. It was a mistake that he will never make again; you have my word on it. If you bring charges, it could mean a long prison sentence—even transportation and a wife and child forced on the parish. I am asking you not to press those charges before the magistrate tomorrow."

She finished, her face flushed, her breast heaving, to find Venables' look of irony replaced by one of interest, even admiration.

"Miss Trafford, I do not know your Christian name, but to me you will always be Portia. You are most eloquent—I must confess to find myself thoroughly moved by your argument."

"Then you will not prosecute Will Meersham?"

"No, I shall not claim my pound of flesh, but I am not sure that I may not claim something in return. Do you know that your eyes become quite green when you are angry?" He leaned forward in his chair, and by gazing into those green eyes, caused her to blush furiously. "I see that they are really hazel flecked with green, but they completely change colour when you are aroused."

Josephina turned from him in confusion. Nobody had ever spoken to her in such a manner. She should have let Winslow come with her. Though she had won the day, she had never felt less at ease, less sure of herself. She made to rise from her chair, but he protested,

"Pray don't leave me now, just when you have piqued my curiosity. Tell me about yourself. Let me refill your glass . . . but you're not enjoying that ratafia—I don't blame you, it's awful stuff. Let me ring for some sherry . . ." And, in answer to her protest that she must leave, "No, no, it's a poor guest that refuses to drink with his host."

Having called for Kister, he settled back.

"Now, tell me, why did your father not come to me on this matter, or does he not feel as you do about it?"

"My father, sir, has been dead these past seven years, but I can assure you that if he were still alive he would feel exactly as I do. In my actions I am always conscious of what would have been his desires and wishes; they continue to influence my own."

He looked at her with keen interest.

"You, too," he said, half to himself. "But I seem to remember your father had a son, did he not, a little fellow when I was here."

"My brother, Gerald, was nine when he died. There are now three of us, myself and my two younger sisters, and, of course, my mother."

"And you run the estate?"

"Since my father's death. He willed it to me, on condition that we all partake of its benefits, of course."

"That is no job for a woman. You should be busying yourself with shopping, and balls, and the latest gossip, and lovers. At least, that is what the ladies of my acquaintance seem to enjoy."

"I care little for any of those things."

"Any of them?" His glance was quizzical.

"Any of them," she reiterated firmly. "I find them shallow and worthless and would not care to pass my time in such a manner."

"On most of the pursuits I named, I must admit I would agree with you, though not, I confess, all." His smile was mischievous.

Again Josephina felt ill-at-ease, and the gentleman did nothing to alleviate her discomfort, seeming, rather, to enjoy it.

"Undoubtedly most people enjoy balls, but for my part I find them a waste of time," she rallied.

"It was not that pursuit to which I referred, but no mind." He picked up the book she had been reading and saw the title. "You *are* a serious young lady! Cobbett's a radical pamphleteer if there ever was one, though his ideas are not entirely without merit. But I had thought to find you reading one of Richardson's novels of those virtuous young ladies, Pamela or Clarissa."

"I'm afraid I always found them a bore."

"So did I. I must say that I always had a sneaking regard for Lovelace, not at all the author's intent, I'm sure, though Lovelace could never replace Tom Jones as my ultimate hero."

Josephina knew that the conversation was turning to paths she preferred not to follow, and she reached for her gloves.

"No, don't run off—just when I'm getting to know you."

"It must be close to our dinnertime."

"So early?"

"We dine early in the country. By this hour we have already put in a good day's work."

"Ah, another jab at us poltroons, no doubt. I fear I shall be quite full of wounds before you leave, Portia."

Then he added earnestly, "But I do not mean to tease you. Tell me, what has been happening here in my absence? You referred to some misdeeds of my bailiff, and I should like to know more before I have him in. You see, I am not current with what has led to the state in which I find Venarvon. I had not expected to inherit either estate or title."

Joesphina began to offer condolences on the death of his brother, but he stopped her, saying, "I cannot pretend we were close in life, so I would be hypocritical to mourn his death, though I would to God he were still alive. I did not desire the title and I particularly did not wish to inherit Venarvon. Its memories are not happy . . . but that is another story. Tell me what has been going on since my father died."

And Josephina told him of the hardships suffered by the tenants, of the acreage left fallow, of the difficulties she had suffered over want of care of their joint boundary, and she concluded, "When people are hungry and need work, and good land which could be productive is allowed to remain idle, it is for the landlord to take remedial action, especially in those cases where there is wealth as well as acreage. For my own part, I wish there were more I could do, but much is not yet possible."

"Left with a parcel of debts, were you?"

She flushed at his perspicacity.

"I am convinced my father did not know the extent of the estate's indebtedness, otherwise he would never have . . ." She broke off, realizing that she had never before discussed her father's will with anyone outside the family.

"Never have what?"

"Nothing. Just a matter of marriage portions for my sisters."

24

"Were they of large amounts?" he asked.

"Five thousand pounds each." Then, remembering the squire's story of Venables' wager over the diamond pendant, she added quickly, "I realize that may not be a great sum to you, but when one does not have ten thousand pounds, it can be a fortune indeed."

"Surely it was unfair . . ." He broke off, then added ruefully, "The vagaries of parents, there's no accounting for it."

The phase so forcibly reminded Josephina of Amelia's constant complaint that she could not prevent herself from laughing.

"Oh, do excuse me, but you sounded quite like Amelia. She is my youngest sister and is constantly complaining of the vagaries of adults, especially when we demand she do her lessons. I assure you I did not mean to laugh at you."

"I must admit to being unused to being compared with sisters, particularly younger sisters. Perhaps I should take some issue with you over the likeness, but I cannot do so when you smile so prettily. Laugh at me as often as you wish, so that I can see your eyes light up in that fashion," he declared.

Josephina rose, certain she should prolong her visit not a moment longer.

"Sir I am not a flirt, nor am I knowledgeable of your world, but I am quite sure that enough comments have been made on my eyes for one day. I must take my leave."

"My remarks were intended only to compliment a most attractive young lady, but if you truly dislike compliments, you are indeed unlike others of your sex," he responded in rising.

Chastened, Josephina thanked him for hearing her out. "In truth I am glad you were here, for I must admit, despite all, that I would rather deal with you than Farnsworth."

"I suppose I must be content with being preferred to my bailiff," he said in mock dejection.

"I meant that he is a difficult man who will often refuse to listen. You, however, have listened to the case and made a decision, and one which I consider fair."

"That is because it is the decision which you sought. Perhaps, after all, you are not so different from other women," he asserted.

"No, not just because it is a decision I wanted, though I did indeed want it, but because it is the decision I considered to be the right one. There is a vast difference," she argued.

"There is indeed. If you must leave, I will thank you for providing a lively beginning to my visit. I'm sorry if I was

25

abrupt when I arrived. It was simply that I had wondered what my reception here might be like. I hadn't expected my first encounter would be with anyone as delightful as you. Your matter will be attended to, and you may tell those involved that no charges will me made. You have my word on it." He put out his hand, and she clasped it, only to have her hand enfolded between both of his.

"You are a charming young lady, Portia. If I get into any trouble here, I hope I can count on you to defend me—or do you defend only the poor and downtrodden?"

"I shall help you if I can." She was acutely aware of his hands around hers in that strong but strangely caressing hold.

"In what way would you help me?" he asked, ignoring her attempt to extricate her hand from his grasp.

"I shall see that you are not maligned."

"Now, if you can prevent me from being maligned in Milvercombe, you will, indeed, be an extraordinary advocate. But tell me, how is the good squire?"

"He is well, busy and active, always . . . settling the affairs of others."

"Meddling in the affairs of others. I believe we are of one mind on that issue, at least. He has not changed, then."

"I really must go now," she repeated.

"Then I must not detain you."

"But . . . my hand." She tried again to extricate it.

"Oh!" He laughed mischievously, looking suddenly very young. "I am sorry. It fitted so well between my own, I quite forgot I still held it." And he swiftly released it, but not before raising it to his lips.

"Allow me to see you out, Miss Trafford."

He called for her horse and waited with her on the front steps while it was brought around, remarking on the fine October.

"They used to call this St. Martin's summer when I was a boy, because it usually held till St. Martin's Day or beyond."

"They still do," she replied.

"I'm glad, then, to find some things don't change," he said, looking around at the wilderness of the park.

Pandora came, led by the groom, but before Josephina could mount, Venables had taken hold of her around the waist and lifted her into the saddle with an astounding ease.

"I trust I may turn to you for advice from time to time," he said. "I believe I may be in great need, for it is so long since I have lived here."

She looked down at him, unable to determine whether he was still teasing or was serious in his intent.

"I shall do whatever I can to help you," she promised solemnly.

"Thank you, fair Portia." He smiled. "I can ask no more."

4

Josephina was late for dinner and Mrs. Trafford was upset. Tardiness always upset her, for, she said, there could be no reason justifying it other than serious accident or death; therefore, to be late signified that one or the other of these catastrophes had occurred. Mrs. Trafford was waiting at the window of the front parlour as Josephina arrived back from Venarvon, dusty and dishevelled, with Pandora in a lather, for, realizing she was late, she had spurred the mare into a faster pace than that to which she was accustomed. She hurried into the house, apologizing, and begged that they would all sit down, declaring it would not take her a minute to change, but her mother was adamant in preserving the social graces, always insisting no meal be served until everyone was at the table for the saying of grace, so Josephina rushed to throw off her dusty riding habit and pull on the faded blue cambric gown she wore at home, straightening her hair as best she could. Had it been possible, she would gladly have forgone dinner altogether, but to do so would raise more comment than would her present lack of appetite. Five minutes later she found herself faced with her favourite dish of stewed mutton and walnuts, which that day, in her flurried emotional state, she found strangely unappetizing. Each mouthful she took stuck in her throat, and she was forced to consume more than her usual amount of wine and water to be able to swallow the food and thus make a small dent in the amount on her plate. She moved the meat around so much in an attempt to make it appear she had eaten more than she had that Pru finally asked if there was something wrong with it.

"No, indeed, it is really delicious, but for some reason I am lacking my usual appetite."

"You should have a larger appetite than usual after the pace at which you came up the driveway. I do wish you wouldn't caper about the countryside in such a wild manner,

28

and alone too, it is so unladylike. I've mentioned it before, but you never listen to me."

Josephina looked sharply at her mother. If she had not known better, she would have thought her in collusion with Lord Venables on the state of her conduct. It was really too much to be borne, to be censured twice in one afternoon on the same subject.

"Mother," she protested, "you know we cannot spare anyone from the house or the farm to accompany me wherever I go. I think it is quite ridiculous that people should expect it. As long as I behave in a ladylike manner, I see no reason why I should be treated otherwise."

She had not realized the vehemence of her protest until she found three pairs of astonished eyes fixed upon her, for her mother had done no more than repeat a frequent admonition to which Josephina usually paid not the slightest attention.

Josephina, for her part, was at a loss to understand what there could have been in her conduct to make Lord Venables act toward her as he had done. She must have appeared willing to accept his advances, for otherwise surely he would not have spoken to her in such a manner. She blushed, thinking of his voice and his hands holding hers, so firmly yet so caressingly; looking down at her right hand holding her dinner knife, she remembered the swift kiss he had placed upon the back of it. He was not the sort of man she should encourage in any way, and she had no wish to be classed as a country wench, free for the taking. Perhaps he believed his advances were welcome to any woman; if that was the case, he was most certainly mistaken, and she would make that abundantly clear should she meet him again.

"Well, I didn't mean to upset you," her mother exclaimed. "You usually pay me no heed. Are you sure you feel quite well?"

"I do have a little headache, but it is nothing. I'm sure it will go away," Josephina lied.

Prudence looked at her sister with genuine concern. Josephina never suffered with headaches; even during the worst of the family crises she had never experienced any emotional setbacks or complained of the *mal de tête* that so frequently attacked their mother.

"Would you like to go upstairs and lie down for a while, Jo?" Prudence ventured. "Mrs. Cooper can keep your dinner warm if you would like to have it later."

There was nothing that Josephina would rather have done, but she knew that to do so would raise endless comment from her mother, so she squared her shoulders, selecting another morsel of food carefully and assuring her sister that she was perfectly well and was, in truth, enjoying the meal but intended to save some of her appetite for Mrs. Cooper's apple tart.

"Where were you coming from, anyway, in such a rush?" asked her mother.

Josephina sighed to herself. Her mother never knew when to leave well enough alone. However, she might as well tell her about Venables' arrival rather than wait until later, though she knew, once told, there would be endless questions she would have preferred to avoid, but there was no escaping it. If she made no mention and her mother discovered later that she had known all along of his arrival at Venarvon, there would be bitter recriminations for robbing her of the opportunity of bearing the news throughout the village. There was nothing in life her mother relished more.

"I had to go over to Venarvon this afternoon on a matter concerning one of our tenants. I had intended to see Farnsworth, but he was busy, and as Lord Venables had just arrived, I spoke to him on the matter instead, and he was able to resolve it. I was delayed, however, as I had to wait for him—he had only just arrived and was changing from his travelling clothes when I got there. That is the reason I was late, and I hurried in order not to delay the meal any longer than necessary."

Mrs. Trafford did not hear her excuse; she was transfixed at the news of Lord Venables' arrival.

"Oh, you sly girl. Why did you not tell me immediately when you got home that Lord Venables was arrived? I did not even know he was expected. To think that he has come back. I did not expect he would after all . . ." She hesitated, seeing her daughter's eyes questioning her, then went on, "I mean, I didn't know he would come so soon after his brother's death."

"But it is not soon," Josephina argued. "I thought he should have come long since. Surely he should have been here ages ago to survey conditions at Venarvon. God knows somebody should."

"Josephina, I have asked you before to refrain from breaking the Third Commandment, and yet you continue to do so. It comes of mixing with riffraff from the stables. If you were younger, I would request you to wash your mouth out with soap; however, at your age, I doubt it would be of any avail."

"If you prefer, I will leave the table, Mother." Josephina

30

pushed back her chair with an air of relief that was, however, short-lived.

"No, you will stay at the table until we are all finished. In polite society, people get to the table on time and they stay until the meal is over. Even though you have not had the benefit of a London coming out, I feel that you should have had at least the rudiments of well-mannered behaviour instilled in you by this time."

Josephina reflected that if members of London society worried more about their morals and less about their manners, they might all be better off. She knew her mother would approve of Venables' manners but wondered what she would think of other aspects of his behaviour, spoken and unspoken. But perhaps that was how all members of the *haut ton* behaved.

"But tell me," her mother continued, "what does he look like now? Is he married? I have heard nothing of it, but since he was so long out of the country, it is possible. Did he mention a wife? I imagine the Kisters are in for a time now. They've been sitting there doing nothing except eating well. The amount of food and supplies that have been ordered for Venarvon, I heard from Mrs. Tyrrell, is incredible—you would think that the family had been in residence all along. Shameful, I call it, but I imagine there'll be some reckoning now. Tell me everything, Josephina. What did he say? What did he do?"

There was no missing the coaxing tone Mrs. Trafford employed when she wanted every detail, every minute detail, of gossip. It would all be passed along to Lady Netherton, who would see that it would reach Mrs. Ridgeway without delay, who would, in turn, tell her husband, and the whole village would then know, with some embellishments, whatever Josephina said about Lord Venables. Josephina, little aware of the ways of London society matrons, often thought that the only benefit of living in town would be that of anonymity and freedom from gossiping tongues.

"He seems a pleasant enough man, Mother. He is tall and dark and quite pleasing to look at." She remembered the lines around his mouth and the bitterness she had caught in his eyes when his father's name had been mentioned. "Well, perhaps 'pleasing' is not the word to describe him, but he is well-mannered." She thought of him leaning forward and gazing deeply into her eyes; *that* was hardly well-mannered. "I mean, he is courteous," she continued, until she suddenly remembered his drawling reference to "this esteemed couple" and felt once more the wrath it had incurred. She looked at her mother's expectant face. It wouldn't do to tell her what she really thought of him; it was best to describe him as her mother would wish.

"Josephina," her mother snapped, "sometimes you exasperate me. Here you have been all afternoon talking to this gentleman and you can't give a simple description of him. It is too provoking of you."

"Well, Mother, Lord Venables is taller than George Ridgeway, and less . . . less robust. He is dark and carries himself proudly, and he has a thoughtful aspect. I suppose he might be accounted quite handsome. He has the manners of a gentleman"—that covered it well—"and he heard out the matter on which I was concerned with polite interest and resolved it satisfactorily. He invited me to take a glass of sherry, and he asked after life in the village and at Venarvon in his absence, and he asked after the squire."

"Are you sure he mentioned the squire?" her mother pressed.

"Yes, I distinctly remember that he did. He remembered Papa and Gerald also."

"But what did he say about the squire?"

"Only that he wondered whether he was as busy as ever."

Her mother looked disappointed.

"And what did he say of his own life?"

"Very little. We mainly discussed the matter on which I had approached him. Oh, yes, we spoke of Cobbett, and a little of Richardsons' novels."

"Cobbett and Richardson!" Her mother did not attempt to hide her exasperation. "But what about him, what was he wearing, at least you must have noticed that?"

"Yes, he was very handsomely attired. His coat was of a dark red colour and made of a very fine material and it fitted him extremely well. He had an equally handsome neckcloth and his boots had silver tassels and an incredible shine. I must admit he was altogether elegant."

Amelia was transfixed at the thought of his attire, and now she spoke for the first time.

"I'll bet he uses champagne."

"No, he drank claret," Josephina disclosed.

"I meant for his boots, that's what I once read Beau Brummell's valet uses on his boots."

"Amelia, I wish you would not say 'I'll bet.' It sounds so unladylike."

"Yes, Mama."

Her mother turned again to her eldest daughter.

"But is he to settle here, what did he say about that, and did he have anyone with him?"

"He did not mention the length of his stay, and I saw no one else there, nor did Kister mention that he was accompanied."

"But surely you remember something more. Did he say or do anything out of the ordinary? Where did you talk to him? Josephina, I have to drag every tiny piece of information from you. Surely you remember something of interest."

There was a pleading note in her mother's voice and Josephina wished that she could have obliged. She imagined the impact of saying to her mother, "He held my hand between his for the longest time and then kissed it, and he talked to me as no man has ever done before," but said instead, "That's all I remember. We talked in the library, and I must say the place was very dusty and dingy. I don't think Lord Venables was too well pleased about the condition of the house, he seemed quite put out about it in fact, and more so about the park. I suspect heads may begin to roll."

"Josephina, that is a particularly hideous expression in view of the awful days of the guillotine, which are well within my memory. It should not be used around the nobility. I hope you will remember that in London, Amelia, there are so many French emigrés there, you never know to whom you may be talking."

"Yes, Mama."

Prudence, who had followed her sister's account of her visit thoughtfully, made no comment except to say that she was glad all had been resolved for the Meershams.

They were almost finished with their dessert when Mrs. Trafford suddenly remembered that she had promised Lady Netherton her recipe for mead and she might just as well take it down to her.

"But, Mama"—Prudence could not contain her surprise—"I thought you said you would never let her have your recipe."

"Well, I shan't tell her quite everything, but she has been so insistent of late, I think I shall give it to her so that she will stop asking me. And would you put up a basket of those apples you showed me today. Mrs. Ridgeway doesn't have any of the pippins in her orchard and she does so enjoy them. Since I am going in, I might as well take them. Amelia, would you like to come with me, for I don't believe you were finished looking at Fanny's new copy of *La Belle Assemblée*

33

this morning, and you might see a design for your ball dress. Would you girls like to come also?"

The invitation to her elder daughters was halfhearted, and Mrs. Trafford showed no sign of regret when Prudence said that she would prefer to stay and that she was sure Josephina would also. Josephina had been about to remonstrate with her mother for going out again so late in the day, but she caught a warning look from Prudence and merely asked her mother to convey her regrets to Fanny and to tell her to come and see them soon.

Lady Netherton's sharply arched eyebrows rose and the nostrils of her ample nose flared in disbelief at Mrs. Trafford's proffered mead recipe as an excuse for her second visit of the day. She sent Amelia and Fanny to the next room to go over the fashion magazines and ordered tea for Mrs. Trafford and then sat back to await her news.

Though Mrs. Trafford was bursting with her tidings, she waited until tea was served before imparting them to Lady Netherton; then, as she stirred the sugar in her tea, sipping it and savouring the sweet warm liquid and the thought of yet undisclosed revelation, then and only then did she say. "Only think, Lady Netherton, we have two new arrivals in the neighbourhood. Such excitement for this little village. Of course, I know Charles Carew is not yet with us, but his arrival is certain."

"Two, Mrs. Trafford? But who is the other?" Lady Netherton exclaimed, unable to conceal her curiosity any longer.

"Why, Lord Venables. He is at Venarvon now, and kicking up quite a dust at the state of the place, from what I hear."

"Lord Venables here? But are you sure, for I heard noth-.ing of it and I saw Mrs. Ridgeway only this afternoon. She did not mention that the squire knew anything of it."

Mrs. Trafford half-closed her eyes; she had conjectured that Lady Netherton would have gone to Mrs. Ridgeway with the news she herself had brought about Charles Carew. She would certainly see to it that she would be the first to tell the squire about Lord Venables' arrival.

"Well, I plan to stop in and see her shortly before I return home. I have some of our pippins for her, she does so enjoy them. With this warm weather, it is hard to keep them from spoiling, so I thought I should bring them with me, since I was coming in with the mead recipe."

Lady Netherton accepted this palpable lie with all the equanimity she could muster, but she was determined that she would be there when Mrs. Trafford delivered the news to the

34

Ridgeways. It would be most interesting to see their reaction; she would not miss it for the world.

"Since you are going to the Hall, I might as well accompany you, for there is no point in your telling your news twice," and fearing Mrs. Trafford, who was not at all averse to telling her news twice, ten or even a hundred times, was about to object, she added, "I believe I left my gloves when I was there this afternoon, and it will give me a chance to retrieve them. We can go in my carriage."

Before Mrs. Trafford could make reply, she sailed from the room to get her bonnet, leaving Mrs. Trafford fuming, for Lady Netherton missed no opportunity to remind her that she kept a carriage while Mrs. Trafford must be content to travel by gig.

Amelia was in Fanny's room examining the new bonnet she had purchased the week before in Exeter, when Lady Netherton popped her head around the door to say that she and Mrs. Trafford were going to the Ridgeways'. It was a lovely thing, a cottage bonnet of pink satin, with a raised crown, trimmed with puffed ribands of a darker rose, and Amelia, trying it on her blond head, primped before the mirror. In truth it suited her fair beauty better than it did Fanny, who was small and dark-haired and dark-eyed. "Nondescript" was the unkind word Mrs. Trafford often used to describe her, proud of the looks of her own three daughters. She was never allowed by Lady Netherton to forget that Fanny had been presented at court, unlike her own daughters.

"A lot of good it did her, though, for she still didn't catch a husband, despite the amount that was spent on her. I hear it ran well into four figures."

Prudence, who was particularly fond of Fanny, would not allow a word to be said against her.

"If she did not find a husband, it was only because she did not meet anyone she liked. Fanny is well provided for and has no need to be forced into marriage."

Mrs. Trafford, knowing that Fanny would bring at least ten thousand pounds to the man she married, could not deny that it would be a tempting figure, nondescript looks or not.

Squire Ridgeway and his wife were no less surprised to see the ladies descend upon them than Lady Netherton had been to see Mrs. Trafford half an hour earlier. They were at tea, though tea for the squire consisted of his favourite port. His corpulent frame was ensconced in an armchair by the fire, the warming task of which was assisted by the large glass of wine in the squire's hand. The firelight danced across his rubicund face, turning it to a shade of red even deeper than usual. Mrs. Ridgeway, tall and thin, her iron-grey hair almost completely hidden beneath one of Mrs. Fenwick's lace caps, sat at her tambour frame with her interminable embroidery. Josephina conjectured that she must, like Penelope in the *Odyssey*, undo her work each night to restitch it the following day, so little was the progress noted for the time employed.

George, their eldest son, was engrossed in the *Exeter Journal*. He was of stocky build, a younger version of his father excepting he had not yet achieved his girth, nor was his face of the same floridity, though the ruddiness of his complexion was emphasized by sandy-coloured hair and pale blue eyes fringed with blond lashes.

Mrs. Trafford, over her second cup of tea of the evening, wished that Lady Netherton had not accompanied her so that she could have had the pleasure of passing along to her the Ridgeways' reaction to the news. On the other hand, however, she consoled herself with the reflection that it would be interesting to compare notes later. She wondered when to drop her little gem of intelligence and how to extract the most from its revelation, but, fearing Lady Netherton might rob her of her prize, she suddenly blurted out haphazardly, "I understand Lord Venables has arrived in Venarvon."

There was complete silence, broken only by the crackling of the fire in the heavy iron grate. George Ridgeway put down his paper. The squire, about to raise the glass of port to his lips, stopped midway. Mrs. Ridgeway ceased her industrious stitching to look up at Mrs. Trafford and then over at her husband, and say, "Oh, dear, no."

"The devil he has," the squire expostulated. "Why, the impudent young puppy—not that he's young anymore. I didn't think he would be showing his face around here, not after his behaviour. Not a word to me about it, but of course he would hardly dare to write to me. Of course, it's his property now, and he has a right to visit it," he allowed generously, "but I doubt he'll stay around here long. He needn't expect me to receive him. No, indeed. I had my say to that young man once and for all, as all of you well know. But are you sure he is here, for I heard nothing of his arrival from Farnsworth?"

"Oh, yes, indeed. Josephina saw him only this afternoon. She had to visit Venarvon on some matter, and Farnsworth was busy, so she saw Lord Venables instead. She said he was quite affable and settled the matter without delay."

"What matter was it? She should have come to me if she

has something to be settled, not take matters into her own hands. It's not the sort of thing she should be doing, Mrs. Trafford—I know we have spoken of this before," she squire admonished.

"I know, squire, and I told her about it when she got home, but you know she doesn't listen to me. She's quite headstrong and likes to have her own way. I don't know where she gets it from." A significant look passed between Mrs. Ridgeway and the Lady Netherton. "But anyway, she said he was very gentlemanly and dressed in the first stare of fashion, from her description."

Before the ladies could ask for further particulars of his appearance and dress, George interrupted, "You don't mean to say that she saw this man completely on her own. Wasn't Winslow with her?"

"No, he wasn't. I made the same comment to her, George, for I agree that it was the height of impropriety, and I don't know what Lord Venables thought of it."

"It's not a question of what he thought of it, but it must be impressed upon her that she can't call upon him just as she might upon me, for instance. Josephina may not be aware of the type of man he is, for she was still in short skirts when . . . when he left Venarvon, and I know she is not one to listen to tales."

"She is not indeed," said her mother, unable to keep the regret from her voice.

"But since she did see him, we might as well learn what he is like now, especially if we are not to receive him." Mrs. Ridgeway directed another meaningful look at her husband.

"But, Madge, surely you don't want that man in the house," the squire bellowed.

"No, indeed, I didn't say that I did. I merely thought that since he is the largest landowner hereabouts, and since you are the squire, that perhaps it would be odd not to receive him, though I know he does not deserve to be received by us. I would not go so far as to say that there should be the slightest degree of intimacy between us, but not to receive him at all reflects, somewhat, on your position."

"You may receive him if you wish, but I want nothing to do with a man who treated our daughter in such a shameful manner."

The argument continued, and Mrs. Trafford sat back, delighted with the outcome of her visit. She wouldn't have missed it for the world. Squire Ridgeway drank yet another glass of port, getting more lugubrious as the evening wore on.

Mrs. Trafford would gladly have stayed to take a bite of supper with them, as she was invited to do, had not Lady Netherton reminded her that the girls were expecting them back. Mrs. Trafford, in her turn, quite unkindly reminded Lady Netherton that she had come for her gloves, and Lady Netherton said that now she thought about it again, she remembered stuffing them into her reticule—they must still be there.

The squire thanked them for their courtesy in letting him know of Venables' arrival.

"As I said before"—he swayed unsteadily on his feet as he spoke—"he should have informed me himself that he intended to come to Venarvon, but no doubt he was ashamed to approach me—understandably so. I shall take pleasure in cutting him dead at the first opportunity that presents itself."

George Ridgeway accompanied the ladies to the carriage.

"A fine St. Martin's summer we're having this year. From the almanacs it must be the warmest we've had in this century, certainly the longest, though they do say there was one in 1787, or was it '97, that must be it, for it was about twenty-five years ago—anyway, that one is reported to have lasted almost till Christmas. I doubt we can count on this one continuing much longer, though, for I noticed drops of sweat on the smithy's anvil this morning—big as donkey's ears they were, that usually portends a heavy rain, so I advise you not to go too far in your gig without some weatherproof garb, Mrs. Trafford. Tell Josephina I'll be out to see her in the morning."

"Such a pleasant young man," Lady Netherton purred as the coach pulled away, "and quite interested in your Josephina, I've always thought."

Mrs. Trafford did not reply. She was still fuming about George's reminder on the gig. Why would Josephina not let them own a carriage? It was such a pointless economy. A carriage was a necessity for a gentleman's family, not a luxury.

While Mrs. Trafford was out braving the hazards of the night air, Josephina and Prudence sat by the fire in the small back sitting room. Prudence was mending linen while Josephina sat reading in the *Lady's Magazine* of that novel and daring dance, the waltz. How would it feel, she wondered, to be whirled around the room, a man's arm about her waist? Gazing into the fire, the gentleman she saw holding her so was not George Ridgeway, her usual partner, who had difficulty with even a morris dance, but Venarvon's owner, whom she had met only that afternoon.

So carried away was Josephina by the image in the fire that she was not aware Prudence had been trying to get her attention until her sister's voice at last broke through her thoughts, saying, "Where are you, Joe? I've asked you three times whether you would like tea now, and can get nothing out of you."

"Sorry, Pru, I just feel awfully tired today. Yes, a cup of tea would be very nice."

Pru said nothing till Rose brought the tea; then, as she poured it, she asked hesitantly, "Did anything happen to upset you this afternoon, Jo?"

Josephina flushed slightly, wondering whether to tell Pru of Venables' conduct. They kept nothing from one another as a rule, but in this instance she felt unsure of herself and her own conduct.

"Nothing happened, really. I just haven't met anyone quite like him before."

"Lord Venables, you mean?"

"Yes, he was quite outspoken."

"In what way do you mean?"

"I mean that he was quite flirtatious. I am not used to compliments, and I find it embarrassing. At my age it seems silly, but I don't know what to say."

"He's not really the kind of man to be encouraged, Jo," said her sister with a worried frown.

Josephina scrutinized her. It was one of the few occasions on which she could remember her sister saying anything remotely unpleasant about anyone.

"Do you know why he left, then, Pru?"

Prudence, like her sister, despised village gossip, but unlike Josephina, she did not refuse to listen to it, though she rarely discussed it. She had heard Lord Venables' story many times when visiting Fanny, for it was one of Lady Netherton's favourites, but she would never have thought of repeating it, nor that Josephina would ever ask her to do so.

"He quarrelled with his father."

"Well, I know that, Pru, but why did he quarrel with him?"

"I believe he is said to have compromised Lucy Ridgeway."

Josephina was astounded. She was well acquainted with Lucy, now a matronly woman married to an attorney friend of Frank's with four, or was it five, children. She had settled near Exeter but visited the Hall often. She had never seemed the sort to have a tragedy attached to her, nor could Josephina conceive she was of a type Venables would prefer. Of course, she had been young then, but she must always have been a bore.

"Did Lucy say he compromised her?" Josephina asked at last.

"I believe she denied it, but the fact remains they were gone all night."

"Oh!" The silence was broken only by the sound of the clock on the mantelpiece and an occasional crackle from the fire.

"How did it happen?"

"It was when he was down from Oxford. Lord Venables, his father, was then quite friendly with Squire Ridgeway—not that he liked his company as much as he did father's, but their children, being closer in age, played together often. Lady Netherton says there was some speculation, or at least aspiration on the squire's part, for a match of their eldest child, Lucy, with Lord Venables' second son—Conniston, the present earl. Everyone said that though he would not inherit, he would be well provided for because his father liked him so—it was said he preferred him to Randolph, his heir. I suppose, too, that the squire might have thought he was aiming too high if he promoted an alliance with the heir himself.

"Anyway, when it happened, the Venables family had accompanied the Ridgeways to Exmoor for a picnic; somehow the two young people became separated from the others. A sudden summer storm came up and the party was obliged to return home without them. The young pair had, it transpired later, taken refuge in a farmhouse, and that is where they spent the night. Conniston Venables rode in early the next morning to get another mount for Lucy, for her horse had lost a shoe. Anyway, Squire Ridgeway insisted that his daughter's honour had been compromised while Conniston Venables was equally insistent that all propriety had been observed and that nothing . . . nothing untoward had occurred. Lord Venables sided with the squire against his son, saying he was honour-bound to marry Lucy, but he refused to do so. They quarrelled bitterly and his son left home forever, telling no one where he was going. I think it broke his father's heart, for as you know, the family left Venarvon not long after and never returned. The matter was hushed up as much as it is possible in this village, but with no great success, as you can see."

Josephina had listened intently to her sister's account that gave new meaning to some of Venables' comments that afternoon.

"But Lucy never complained of his conduct," she said at last.

"No. Of course she was awfully young at the time, barely sixteen, and he was less than twenty. There was no denying, however, that they had been away from home all night together."

"You must think there was something more in it, Pru, if you warn me against him. Not that I wish to see more of him, for he was, in some respects, quite odious."

"I don't know, but even if he were innocent then, there can be no doubt he is far from so now. Fanny heard some wild tales of his conduct in London. He gambles excessively and has many . . . paramours."

Josephina laughed at this word on her sister's lips and her manner of saying what was so evidently distasteful to her.

"Oh, I know, Jo, I sound just like Lady Netherton repeating such awful things. It is just that you will never listen to any of it, and sometimes it is better to be aware, that's all."

Josephina gave her sister's hand an affectionate squeeze.

"There was really no danger, I assure you, but consider me now truly forewarned."

5

Warning followed warning, for Josephina had not yet left the house for her usual morning round when George Ridgeway arrived.

"What a grand morning it is, George," Josephina greeted him, determined to get in the first word about the weather. Sometimes she and Prudence counted the number of references George would make to the weather during a single conversation. Josephina wondered whether his addiction to the whims of the elements was brought about because they truly intrigued him or to cover his lack of other topics. It was probably a little of both, for George Ridgeway was not a man of great conversational powers, but he prided himself on being able to predict the weather, no mean feat in their part of Devon, where their proximity to the moor and the Bristol Channel made for constantly changing conditions. One year Josephina had kept a record of his predictions, discovering that he was right about half the time, less than exact the rest. Had it been possible to determine one from another, he might have performed a useful service, but being totally incapable of such discrimination, she disregarded all, sometimes to her disadvantage.

That morning, however, George did not respond to her greeting with his usual meteorological monologue, muttering only that it was fair enough for the time of year as he lowered his sturdy frame into the large chintz-covered armchair near the fireplace in which he always sat on his frequent visits, declaring it more comfortable than any chair at the Hall. Josephina wished that she might have made a present of it to him for his use there, for she felt its comfort helped to prolong his visits, at times to inordinate length.

She glanced now at the clock on the mantel, showing almost half-past ten; she sighed softly, wishing that she had hurried a little more that morning so that she might already have left the house before his arrival, but she had felt unusually languorous.

42

For the first time Josephina found herself observing the ill-cut of George's serviceable brown cloth coat and the unkempt appearance of his heavy boots. She discovered herself contrasting his attire with that of Venables and immediately chided herself for being no better than Amelia. She tried to make up for her unkind thoughts by searching for a subject of conversation he might enjoy.

"I hear the stag are really running on the moor now. Are you planning to hunt there soon?"

"Haven't given it much thought."

She tried again.

"I went over to Trentor to look at Mr. Bracewaite's merinos again last week. The wool is of unbelievably fine quality—I heard it fetched the highest price at Exeter last year. I am still of a mind to invest in a ram and a few ewes. I know the price is forbidding but the gain can well make up for it, especially if they do well in lambing season."

"That's just what I wanted to talk to you about, Josephina."

Josephina detected an argumentative note in his voice, but she queried frankly, "The merinos? Don't tell me your father is showing some interest after all. He's been chiding me all along for even considering what he calls a foolhardy investment."

"No, not that. I agree with him they're far too dear." His voice was definitely exasperated. "What I mean is . . . well, it's about your jaunting around all over the country. You shouldn't do it, you really shouldn't."

"To go over to Trentor to see Mr. Bracewaite, such an old friend of Papa's. Why ever not? What's got into you, George?" Josephina stared at him in astonishment.

"It's not about your going over to Trentor, though even that's a ride of close to ten miles, and if I know you, you probably went without Winslow. It's about yesterday. Your mother came last evening and told us you had been up at Venarvon and had been . . . been entertained by Venables—Conniston Venables."

"Ah, so that's it," she retorted. "I don't believe it is any concern of yours, but it is true that yesterday I rode over there on a business matter to see Farnsworth and talked it over with Lord Venables, who had just arrived, instead. We reached a solution and I returned home. I owe you no explanation, George—however, that is just what happened."

He ignored her frozen glance and plunged on. "But that's what I mean, you went jaunting over there quite on your own to see a man who is a reprobate and a rogue. You are much too trusting. Can't you see it is unwise to be alone with a man of that character?"

"I really think you are making far too much of this, George. I did not go with the intention of seeing him, alone or otherwise, though as it happened I was glad that he was there, for he was far easier to deal with than Farnsworth."

"I imagine he was."

"Would you please explain what you mean by that remark and that tone of voice," she snapped.

"I don't believe Venables makes any secret of his preference for women, particularly pretty women."

Josephina was taken aback. George had never referred to her looks before, and the compliment sounded odd on his lips.

"I've never spoken of this to you before, Josephina," he confided, "but I have little love for the man who ruined my sister."

"Ruined Lucy? I thought she was perfectly happy."

"She is happy now, but no thanks to him. He caused her name to be blackened when she was just a young girl, and then, like the cad he is, he refused to marry her. It is an ugly story and one I would not burden you with except that you have been exposed to him and I fear with your trusting nature you might come to some harm."

"You make him into a complete ogre. Could not the matter with your sister have been one of misunderstanding rather than intent?"

"There, you already begin to argue for him. Is it a misunderstanding to stay out all night with a young girl on the moor? I don't want to discuss it any more, but surely now you can see he is not the sort of man you can associate with."

His possessive tone annoyed her. They had long been friends, but she feared at times he assumed more from that friendship than was intended. She would have liked to set matters straight on that score, but she found it difficult to discourage a man from matrimonial pretensions who has never made a marriage proposal, and her veiled or even overt hints of disinterest did little to deter his continued attentions. She knew that the squire did not favour her as a future daughter-in-law; he knew to a penny the amount of indebtedness of her estate and would prefer to find an heiress for his son. He had often attempted to turn George's attention toward Fanny Netherton, but though George had known Fanny as long as he had known Josephina, he assumed no proprietary air over her. Josephina wished that he would, for she felt Fanny would not be half as vexed over it; in fact, there were even times she believed that she would welcome it.

"Thank you for the advice, George," she said stiffly, "but I cannot allow you to run my life for me."

"But, Josephina, I only wanted to protect you from possible harm."

"Well, don't."

It was at that moment, as they glared at one another, that Rose came to announce Lord Venables.

"What is that fellow doing here?" George exploded just as Venables came in. He seemed to fill the room with his presence and Josephina wondered why she felt such perturbation in her breast, though she greeted him with outward calm.

"I expect you remember George Ridgeway."

The two men bowed stiffly to one another.

"Yes, of course. I hope I am not disturbing anything."

"No, indeed," Josephina assured him a trifle too vehemently for George's liking.

"I am glad," he said calmly, ignoring George's malevolent stare. "I noticed that you were deeply entrenched in Cobbett yesterday and thought you might like to borrow the volume to see whether you find yourself in agreement with him. I suspect you will not, though he is an interesting man in many ways."

"I should hope you would not," George interrupted, and turning to Venables, he said, "I wish you would not encourage Miss Trafford to read such dangerous stuff."

"Oh!" Venables raised an eyebrow. "Am I to take it, then, Ridgeway, that you select Miss Trafford's reading material for her? I find myself surprised."

"No indeed, neither George nor anyone else does that," she interposed heatedly, but not without noticing that her reference to George by his Christian name had caused Venables to direct an intent glance one to the other. "My father allowed me to read as I wished. It would be foolhardy now for anyone to dictate to me on that subject. Though I may listen to the advice of old friends, I cannot be counted upon to follow it."

George showed his irritation at being dismissed as an old friend by firmly planting his feet apart and clasping his hands behind him in a stance to indicate he meant to outstay Venables. Josephina relieved the tension by inviting them both to be seated and asking Rose to bring refreshments and to call Prudence to join them. She was unaccountably glad that her mother had chosen that morning to go into the village again. George said little, but Venables conversed readily until Prudence joined them, flushing slightly on learning the visitor's name and looking prettier than ever. Josephina noticed Venables' admiring glance, though during the remainder of his visit she had to admit that he concentrated his attentions upon her more than Pru, much to George's annoyance, and it crossed her mind that he might be doing it purposely. At last he rose, but not before asking a favour of her.

"My sister and her husband and a party of friends arrive from London next week, and I must take immediate steps to make the place habitable. I will need a veritable army of labourers and gardeners to clear the park, and an equal number of people for the house. I wonder whether you could assist me by recommending good people. I am willing to pay well, but I am not interested in shovel leaners or dustcloth gossipers. I think your long experience in hiring the workers of this neighbourhood could be an invaluable help. I would deem it a great personal kindness to have your recommendations."

Josephina readily acquiesced, pleased that he had turned to her, remarking that people thereabouts would be happy to get work at this time of the year; she promised to draw up a list without delay and send it over to Farnsworth.

"Please send it to me directly," Venables said. "I believe Farnsworth is at this moment in the throes of packing his belongings prior to leaving Venarvon for good. I gave him twenty-four hours' notice yesterday and would hope that he has already left. As you indicated, he has done far more harm than good during his tenure."

At the door he turned back to say, "Don't forget to put that fellow on the list—Meersham, was it?" and then he was gone.

"Well," George leaned back in indignation, hardly waiting for Venables to get out of earshot. "So you've been advising him on how to run his estate."

"I merely told him some of the things that I had previously asked your father to draw to his attention, to no avail," Josephina declared.

"You can't expect my father to save that man's bacon, can you?"

"I can say nothing on that score. All I know is that a well-

46

kept and well-administered estate, especially one as significant as Venarvon, cannot but benefit all of us."

"What's this about Farnsworth leaving? And what did he mean about Meersham? What were you talking to him about yesterday?"

But Josephina had had all she could allow for one morning. She rose abruptly. "I am sorry, George, but it is almost noon and I have not yet accomplished anything. I hope you will excuse me."

"Oh, very well, if you don't wish to discuss it. Don't forget, you dine with us Friday."

Josephina assured him she had not forgotten. How could she, when they dined at the Hall regularly every second Friday of the month? Their round of engagements had assumed a regularity that so small a social acquaintance might predict. There were times when she wished they called on and received no one, but she realized these obligations were a duty; they were obligations observed by her father and his father before him, and though she might know exactly what Mrs. Ridgeway would say as they sat down at the table, or how many mistakes Mildred Carew would make at the piano until she got her piece right, she concealed her boredom and tolerated the visits as yet another responsibility to be undertaken.

When they were alone, Prudence turned to her sister to commend Venables' gentlemanly appearance and manners; that unaccountably pleased Josephina.

"After seeing him, I can well believe he may have broken many hearts," Pru said, "though he somehow seemed very kind. It was awkward that George should have been here when he called, but it was inevitable that they should meet, and it was not as difficult as I thought it might be. With so much work to be done at Venarvon, it would appear that he is planning on settling there for some time."

Josephine feigned an indifference to his actions, merely asking her sister's aid in supplying her with names of those who would make good maids and footmen, and she devoted the rest of her day to compiling a list of suitable labourers for the park. She derived more enjoyment than she would have thought possible from such a task, and put down her pleasure to the benefits the villagers would gain from employment after the harvest was over. Before dinner she had the list ready and sent it with a brief cover note to Lord Venables.

The Traffords saw little of their neighbour in the next week, although there were great comings and goings along the road that ran past Westlands from Milvercombe to Venarvon. Certainly nothing else was talked of in the village except the great renovation taking place on the hill.

It was not until mattins on Sunday that Josephina saw Venables' head looming above the high-backed pews that served to preserve privacy in prayer. It was strange to see the Venables pew occupied at last, and many were the enquiring glances turned on its occupant as he joined in the service and after as he stood talking with Mr. Carew in the vestry. Venables bowed in acknowledgement to Josephina and stood aside to thank her for her astute recommendations. Work was proceeding apace, and he hoped to have some kind of order there by Wednesday, the expected date of arrival of his sister and the rest of his friends.

Josephina presented him to her mother, who was later pleased to pronounce him as fine a looking man as she had seen for many a moon.

There was no lack of people waiting to shake Venables by the hand and to wish him well. Though caustics might assert his favourable reception to be occasioned by the money he was pouring into the village, Josephina observed more sign of genuine pleasure. Squire Ridgeway, always the first to leave the church after service, was unusually reticent in entering the vestry, but when he came abreast of Venables, he greeted him with outward affability, not choosing to carry out his threat of cutting him dead at the first opportunity. Venables, for his part, returned the squire's greeting with civility, if not with warmth, and the meeting, so long anticipated by many of Milvercombe's residents, passed off without incident.

Excitement continued to run high in Milvercombe, for the next day Charles Carew rode in from Yorkshire. Lady Netherton was the first to see him, and though he was obviously tired and merely bowed in response to her greeting, she considered it sufficiently important to warrant a drive out to Westlands early that afternoon to inform Mrs. Trafford, who, in turn, hastened to the vicarage the following morning with both Amelia and Prudence in attendance in hopes of meeting him. They were not disappointed.

Charles Carew was sitting with his parents and sisters when they were announced, and an "I-told-you-so" glance passed from mother to son. Nevertheless the visit went surprisingly well. Mrs. Trafford smiled upon Carew's slender, well-proportioned figure, close-cut brown hair, and thin face set off by deep-set, thoughtful eyes, deciding that, for a clergyman, he had the air of a man of the world; no doubt it was occasioned by his serving so long with the armies in the Peninsula. Carew sat next to Prudence, explaining the more desirable aspects of camp life and comparing the scenery of Portugal with that of Devon. Prudence, listening intently, was enchanted to meet the writer of the letters she had long appreciated and to discover that he was as eloquent in speech as he had been in writing. He, in turn, found himself talking far more than was his wont because of the unfeigned interest and intelligent questions of his fair listener.

So deep were they in conversation that neither noticed that Mrs. Trafford had risen to leave till she called quite sharply, "Come along, Prudence, we really must stop at Mrs. Tyrrell's before we return, for Amelia still has to choose the silk for her ball gown. I do hope we shall find something halfway suitable, else it will mean going to Torbridge or even Exeter, and I am sure I am not up to trotting all over the countryside for a length of material, though, of course, I do want her to look her best."

Prudence rose hastily, dropping her reticule, which Charles Carew retrieved and handed to her with a smile and a soft wish that they would soon meet again; and Mrs. Carew, after assuring Mrs. Trafford that whatever Amelia wore, she was sure to be the belle of the ball, promised that they would dine at Westlands the following week.

"I do wish you two had not been talking in such low tones, for I found it most difficult to follow what was being said, Prudence," her mother scolded.

"I am sorry. I really didn't realize that we were so apart. It was unintentional, but truly, Mother, his stories of Peninsular life are so interesting."

"Then I, too, should have liked to hear them. I do hope that when they dine with us he will favour us all with the benefit of his intelligence."

Mrs. Trafford's humour did not improve by finding that Mrs. Tyrrell did not have a single piece of material she considered suitable for Amelia, not though she turned out her entire stock of silks, muslins, and taffetas, holding each piece up to Amelia in turn for Mrs. Trafford's inspection. None would do.

"You would think she would keep more selection." Mrs. Trafford's peeved tones were well within earshot of the belaboured shopkeeper. "I know Mr. Potter always had a good stock to choose from, but of course now he is in London making all that money waiting on society folk, we can't expect him to come back to supply our needs. Come, girls, I can see we shall have to go to Torbridge after all."

So she continued as they left, despite Pru's admonitions to lower her voice, deploring the fact they must now get James to take them to Torbridge without delay, for with the assemblies due to start, supplies there would soon be depleted. If only they lived in London, they would have a hundred establishments from which to choose.

As they stepped into the high street, a smart travelling chaise bearing a coat of arms on the door passed by carrying a modishly attired lady and gentleman.

"Well, Lady Francesca is here, Lord Venables' sister, and that must be her husband, Sir Hugh Lanyon."

This chaise was shortly followed by another, carrying an equally elegant couple unknown to Mrs. Trafford.

"More of the Venarvon party I suppose. I thought they were not due till tomorrow. Well, girls, Torbridge must wait; we should first see whether Lady Netherton has received a new issue of *La Belle Assemblée*," and without listening to Amelia's protest that they had received one only the previous week and since it was a monthly magazine there could not possibly be another so soon, Mrs. Trafford got into the gig, ordering James to drive immediately to Shepton Park.

6

But merely seeing Sir Hugh and Lady Lanyon in their travelling chaise was a poor fillip compared with the plum that Mrs. Trafford was able to offer Lady Netherton a few days later.

In preparing Amelia's London wardrobe, Prudence had been unable to finish her sewing for the poor of the parish, and with the distribution date only a week away, she pressed her mother and sisters into assisting her at the task. They were busily engaged at their work in the back sitting room when the sound of wheels was heard upon the driveway.

"That is probably Lady Netherton," Mrs. Trafford commented. "She said she would be over with some of her black-currant jam. I assured her we had so much damson of our own we didn't know what to do, but she says no one makes black-currant jam like Smith. She will have it so."

It was not Lady Netherton, however, but Lord Venables, accompanied by his sister, Francesca, who entered with a waft of fragrance of violets, modishly attired in a lemon-yellow sarcenet dress trimmed with embroidered roses. Her dark hair was loosely curled beneath a Lavinia chip hat, tied under her chin with a broad yellow sarcenet ribbon. Amelia could not take her eyes away from her.

Mrs. Trafford put aside her work in a fluster to welcome the company.

"We should adjourn to the front parlour. We are quite squeezed in here," Mrs. Trafford fluttered, but her visitors insisted they were comfortable as they were and bid the ladies not to stop their work on their account.

"It is nothing, really, but one must do these things for those less fortunate. I am sure most of our time goes in tending to the poor," Mrs. Trafford, who rarely participated in such endeavours, explained.

Josephina, after greeting the newcomers, said little, though she was aware of Lady Francesca's eyes upon her with such a look of curiosity and appraisal she believed she must have been the subject of discussion with that lady.

51

Lord Venables sat down next to her, apart from the others, commenting, "So you sew, too, Miss Trafford. Your talents are endless."

"It would be an odd woman who did not sew, my lord," she replied, bending over her task.

"But you are an odd woman," he exclaimed; then, seeing her enquiring gaze turned on him, he hastened to add, "I do not intend the use of that adjective in a sense which could be construed as pejorative, but merely that you are out of the ordinary."

"I feel particularly ordinary this morning." Josephina smiled, glancing down at her faded blue cambric frock. "You and your sister are positive birds of paradise, compared with my guinea hen."

"I do not believe what you wear signifies in the least. And, what is even stranger still, I do not believe it signifies to you, either. That is why I use the word 'odd' to describe you. You are not like others."

Lady Francesca turned to Josephina. "I understand from my brother that we have you to thank that we find Venarvon in as good a condition as it is. He assures me that when he arrived it was all quite horrid, but the people you found for him have made some order from the chaos. I remember it when my father was alive, the smooth lawns and trim rose beds. Time is a destroyer, as we women well know."

Josephina wondered whether the reference to their father would affect Venables, but he looked upon his sister with an affectionate smile.

"Time does not seem to affect you, Francesca. I believe that like everything else, you take it in your stride and organize it."

"You make me sound such a managing woman, brother. I am not sure I like the image."

"You are not managing enough this morning, though, for you have quite forgot the purpose of our visit."

"Why, to be sure," and turning to Mrs. Trafford, she very prettily invited them to dinner the following evening. "Apart from our own party, the Carews are also to join us. Their son is just returned from Spain. He was chaplain to a neighbour of ours in Yorkshire, Sir John Brennan, and I believe he is known to Colonel Underwood, an old friend of my brother's who is with us from London. I cannot promise what may be the quality of the repast served from our kitchen, though Conniston assures me it is daily improving. From my observation, improvement over an entire year would not bring matters to rights."

"Just because your toast this morning was rather too brown for your liking, Francesca, don't tell me you are still fussing about that," her brother laughingly responded.

"Too brown! I like that, Conn. 'Burnt' would be my description of it."

"The trouble with you, Francesca, is that you have never had to rough it. If you had been with me in the Indies, you would have considered this morning's breakfast admirable."

From the badinage between sister and brother, their close bond was apparent; Venables talked as freely to his sister about his exile from England as on every other matter.

"You know you are quite as fussy as anyone else when you're at Blenhasset," his sister responded.

"At Blenhasset, yes, that is different—that is my estate."

"Well, so, too, is Venarvon." Lady Francesca turned to Mrs. Trafford. "But I am afraid we bore with our family patter, you must excuse us." Then to her brother she reminded, "We should go, for you have promised to ride with Hugh this afternoon, and despite the warmth, we must remember it is autumn and the days are short."

For Mrs. Trafford's part they could have continued their family patter all day, so much did she enjoy it, but despite her entreaties that they stay, they made their adieus. Mrs. Trafford thanked them effusively for the invitation and Venables promised that his carriage would be there for them at six; the realization that he was acquainted with the fact that they did not keep their own carriage took some of the glow from Mrs. Trafford's smile.

Nevertheless, when the vehicle drew up to collect them the following evening, she was the first to luxuriate in the opulence of its beige velvet-and-leather-lined interior and the gleam from the black-and-white crest on the door.

"Even in London," she assured Amelia, "you will not see many to equal the splendour of this carriage. Do hold yourselves up, girls, and don't be intimidated."

But it was Mrs. Trafford who was intimidated by the opulence, and Josephina who was amazed at the change in Venarvon. A veritable transformation had taken place since her visit there little over a week ago. The fine polished oak glowed in the light of myriad candles fluttering throughout. A fire burned merrily in the hearth of the great saloon into which they were conducted, where awaited them, along with Lord Venables and his sister, Francesca's husband, Sir Hugh

Lanyon, a distinguished gentleman some years senior to his wife, with a fine head of silver hair and a long Roman nose.

But the one who drew the eye of every member of the Westlands party was an exquisite, shapely beauty with hair of burnished gold, clad in pale blue gossamer silk that floated around her like the merest wisp of a cloud. The dress became her to perfection, emphasizing her comely figure and graceful movements. The lady, of a pale complexion, with delicate features and high arched brows over large, thickly lashed blue eyes, was introduced to the Westlands party as Lady Eliza Coningsby. Her husband, Sir Harlan, stood talking to a tall, military gentleman, the Colonel Underwood whom Lady Francesca had mentioned the previous day. Sir Harlan was short and unprepossessing and uncompromisingly plump, with heavy bags under his eyes and far more chins than the requisite one. Judging by the colour of his complexion, particularly startling in his bulbous red nose, he was not averse to imbibing. Josephina wondered how so beautiful a creature as Lady Eliza could have chosen to be joined to such a gentleman, but a glance at the diamonds gracing her slender neck and hands decided the reason. Surprisingly, Sir Harlan made few demands on his wife during the course of the evening, leaving her to the company of Lord Venables, a company to which she was plainly not averse. Josephina became aware that whenever Venables addressed her for any length of time, Lady Eliza would seek him out to insist that he repair to another part of the room to settle an argument on the exact date they had attended the Carlton's rout, or to see whether she might have left her shawl on the terrace where they had been sitting, and she concluded that, husband notwithstanding, Lady Eliza and Lord Venables must indeed be close friends. She felt the pang of an emotion previously unknown to her; whatever it was, it made her conceive a dislike of Lady Eliza without understanding why. Could it be jealousy? But jealous of what? She certainly had no claim on Venables' attention.

She spent most of the evening before dinner with Colonel Underwood, a sensible, well-spoken man who said he had known Venables since his days in the West Indies. Charles Carew joined them, for he was overjoyed at finding a colleague from his days on the Peninsula. His attentions, however, were divided, for his singling out of Prudence could not escape Josephina's notice. Pru's blond beauty was enhanced by the high-waisted blue crepe gown she wore, trimmed with Mrs. Fenwick's finest lace; though her attire was not opulent, it set off her own style of grace, and Josephina felt proud of her. Mrs. Trafford was, for the most part, far too busy taking in details of the evening for relay to Lady Netherton the next day to say anything too embarrassing, though her constant references to London society in her day grew wearisome in their repetition.

The gentlemen did not sit long with their port after dinner, but soon followed Venables, who had been the first to join the ladies, into the saloon.

"What do you think of the place now?" he asked Josephina.

"You have simply done wonders. I must congratulate you on the transformation, for I did not believe it possible in so short a time."

"There is still much to be done, new curtains, new carpets, some of the furniture to be replaced, though I mean to keep it much as it was. I am, I fear, a sentimentalist," he responded wryly.

He was a curious man. It was not a word which Josephina would have used to describe him, but he was not a person to be understood in a few brief meetings. She watched his face now, reposed in thought, the sharp lines etched around his mouth and eyes softened in the glow from the fire, and his long fingers closed around the saucer of the delicate teacup in a relaxed but firm clasp. She flushed suddenly, realizing she could never look at his hands without feeling them about her own, and he caught her look and demanded, "What did you think of just then?"

"Nothing, nothing at all. Just some nonsense." But the smile in his eyes made her think he knew exactly what the nonsense was.

"I believe I can guess——" he began, but before he could continue, and somewhat to Josephina's relief, Lady Eliza joined them, so that Venables rose immediately to offer her his chair.

"So you are the Miss Trafford, that paragon of virtue of whom I've heard so much," Lady Eliza began.

"I assure you I am nothing so stuffy as a paragon of virtue," Josephina protested, "but I am Miss Trafford. I live at Westlands, one of the estates bordering Venarvon."

"But you don't simply live there, do you, you are far too modest. I hear you run the whole thing practically on your own. Why, just the thought is positively exhausting," and Lady Eliza raised her bejewelled fingers to her cheeks in mock horror. Had she not been so pretty, her gesture might

55

have been ridiculous, but as it was, she made a perfect picture, the diamonds glowing in the firelight and her soft mouth partly open to reveal straight white teeth. Josephina saw Venables looking down at her, chuckling, and again she felt that pang of emotion.

"Come, Eliza, enough of your theatricals. If you insist upon any more of that, I, in turn, shall insist upon playing charades."

"Not charades, Conniston, but if you want to get up a table for faro, I shall be glad to join you."

"Not faro tonight, perhaps a pool of quadrille. Let me see what are the desires of the others."

And he wandered off and was soon in deep conversation with Charles Carew, to whom he had taken an immediate liking.

"But doesn't a young lady like yourself find it terribly dull down here, buried in the deepest wilds, day in and day out? For myself, I find it fascinating for a short period of time. I can't wait to explore Exmoor, because Conniston has told me so much about it. But I could not live without London society for very long."

"Then it is well that it is my lot to live here and yours only to visit. Ours is undoubtedly a quiet life, but never having known any other, I find it quite to my liking."

"Never having known any other! Do you mean that you have not been brought out, not had a London season?"

Josephina had to confess to both these glaring omissions.

"My dear, how positively primitive!" Had Lady Eliza's voice not been so delightful, the remark was a cutting one, but Josephina could not help but laugh at the extremity of her tone.

"How can you ever expect to find a husband?" Lady Eliza demanded.

"Oh, people do marry, even in the country, and even those who have not come out, strangely enough. However, for my own part, if I am unable to find a husband to suit me, it will not be the end of the world. My life is fully occupied as it is."

"What a peculiar thing for a woman to say."

Josephina observed that this was the second time in as many days that she had been called odd or peculiar. She had never thought of herself as being different from others and wondered if it could really be so.

Lady Francesca joined them. "I do believe Conniston is firm on giving a ball for the local . . ." She broke off, notic-

56

ing Josephina, then went on, ". . . for the local gentry. He has already decided to entertain Venarvon's tenants on the tenth of November, and now I hear him with Mr. Carew deciding on St. Martin's Day, the eleventh, as a suitable date for a ball here."

"Then he is intending to stay longer than we expected." Lady Eliza looked over at Venables thoughtfully. "I hope he does not delay too long, or else we may miss Christmas with you in Yorkshire. We should not leave it too late in setting out for the north—by mid-December the roads are often impassable."

"Conniston has not missed a Christmas with us since his return. I am sure he will not this year. The children so adore his visits."

A table for quadrille was now set up, at which Sir Harlan was the first to sit down. Venables had not been altogether in favour of cards, and as the London party sat down, Josephina, who stood behind a chair occupied by Lady Eliza, understood why: though they played with counters rather than coins, it was obvious the stakes were high.

"Do come and join us." Lady Eliza inched over her chair.

"No, thank you. I am not a great one for cards," Josephina refused, moving back to sit by the fire, where she was joined within a few minutes by Venables.

"Not playing?" She smiled.

"Not at cards," he countered.

"What, then?" she asked.

"Oh, I might play a little speculation, or perhaps try my hand at fortune-telling. May I read your palm?"

"No certainly not."

"Have you never had your palm read? I know the gypsies come around often, for I remember them camping on the moor and coming in at revel time. Oh, the stories you could buy for a shilling, tales of love and conquest and high adventure, I've never had more for my money. Tell me, do you ever do anything just for the fun of it, or is life all work, for I have observed you doing nothing else since my arrival."

"This is not work tonight, and we visit many families in the neighbourhood. For myself, I like to read."

"Ah, but what heavy stuff you do read. And visiting the Ridgeways could hardly be called fun. What else do you do?"

"I like to lie in the grass and look up at the sky and watch the woodlarks nesting in the oak trees."

"Now, that could be fun, especially if it were not done alone. Do you always do so alone?"

She ignored the question, saying, "But fun is only one aspect of life."

"An important one."

"An important one, perhaps, but one meant only to offset the main part of life, which is duty or responsibility. Perhaps I should ask how many of your activities fall into that sphere."

"Now you are turning the tables, and I am not sure I will allow it. But if you insist, I can assure you that I spend as little of my time as I possibly can in onerous tasks. Life is short and I am still young enough to enjoy its gaiety. Time enough for duty and responsibilities when I no longer . . ." He smiled mischievously at her. ". . . when I no longer savour its pleasures."

"I fear by that time, Lord Venables, it may be too late," was her laconic reply.

He reached over and, under the pretence of taking the empty cup she had been nursing from her hand, grasped that hand briefly and caressingly.

"Oh, my little pedantic one, what, I wonder, would it take to relieve your brow of its sobriety and make your eyes turn green again."

That night at home, as Josephina sat brushing her long hair, she gazed at herself long and critically in the mirror. She saw she was no longer in the first bloom of youth, but passingly handsome. Was it her high, wide brow that gave her a pedantic air, she wondered, or was it nothing to do with her looks but with her demeanour? Why had he so described her? She didn't like it.

She pulled her hair back and draped it around her head, wondering how it would look in the soft style worn by Lady Eliza, then let it drop. No matter how she tried, she could never look like Lady Eliza. She looked down at her strong fingers with their squared nails. Even if they were loaded with diamonds, they could never imitate the flutter of that lady's delicate hands. There could be no question that Lady Eliza enjoyed life, enjoyed it in the terms laid down by Venables. Josephina believed that they might be enjoying it together, and again there was that pang she now acknowledged must be jealousy. Why did Sir Harlan sit back and allow his wife to behave so? she wondered. Such a marriage was beyond her comprehension. Surely he could not approve his wife's overt preference of Venables to any other man in the room, and Venables himself made no effort to disguise their intimacy. Even his sister appeared to approve! It was a strange world, a world entirely alien to her own.

She was still staring at herself in the looking glass when Prudence came in to bid her good night. Her sister was excited, for they had been invited to accompany the Venarvon party on a picnic in Exmoor the following morning, and Charles Carew was to call in at Westlands so that they might ride over together to Venarvon to meet the rest of the party.

Josephina, abashed at having been discovered examining her own reflection, said hastily she felt she had something in her eye, though when Prudence offered to help her remove it, she blinked several times and turned from the mirror saying the irritation was gone.

Josephina looked over at her sister, sitting in the window seat in her voluminous flannel nightgown, her arms curled around her knees, staring out into the night.

"You like him, don't you, Pru?"

"Who?" Prudence did not turn around.

"Charles Carew, of course, who else."

"Yes, I do." She turned slowly and looked back at her sister with a slight, shy smile on her lips. "I think he is the most wonderful man I have ever met. He is quiet and well-spoken, yet he is not afraid to speak his mind if the matter is important to him. And despite all he has seen of the world and of the horrors of the battlefield, his faith is unshaken. I think he will make a wonderful leader of a parish and hope he will soon find a living, though it will mean we shall lose him."

"If he knows you at all, he cannot help but think as highly of you as you think of him."

"He does not seem . . . indifferent."

"He cannot be. Come, we must get to bed, for we break-fast early, and despite all your beauty, you know that pallor and wanness will not suit, they are out this season."

"Since when did you study the fashion to discover what is in or what is out?" her sister demanded.

"Since I saw that charming concoction Lady Eliza Coningsby sported this evening. Its cost must have run into three figures, I would not doubt."

"And if you had it, you would probably end up wearing it down to the stables to care for a stricken horse or to chase after a loosened bull."

"Those events would be forgiven as extenuating circumstances, Pru. I should, otherwise, wear it only on the second Friday of each month at the Ridgeways'."

7

Everyone agreed it was the finest St. Martin's summer in memory. The air was warm, and the brightness of the skies belied the brown and gold leaves of the oak and birch, and the woodthrush remained long past his normal departure date for the south.

The party, as it gathered in the great hall at Venarvon to partake of punch before the day's ride, was filled with enthusiasm. They were to picnic at Ashcombe Hill, and the servants had already left to find a likely spot and set up the provisions in readiness for their arrival.

Venables was clearly elated at the thought of seeing the country again, as was his sister, reminding her brother that their father had taken them there as children at just such a time of the year.

"Where is Eliza?" Venables made no effort to conceal the impatience in his voice. "She doesn't need to be done up like a bandbox for a picnic."

But he gave her a forgiving smile when at last she tripped down the staircase and gave his arm an affectionate squeeze, saying only, "I just couldn't decide which would be best, my silk cottage bonnet or the straw, so I took neither and wore this gypsy hat instead. Will it do?"

"Of course it will. But we are already almost half an hour late in starting, thanks to your millinery quandary. Let's not waste another moment in explanations and compliments. Take it that you look as lovely as ever."

With that he helped her onto her horse before turning to see whether Josephina was already mounted. She had swung herself up and was now gently rubbing Pandora's neck and deciding firmly that she was not going to spend the day watching Lady Eliza and Venables. Her own green riding habit, the better of the two she owned, was less than stylish, but she knew it would be warm should the day turn windy on the moor.

Venables, passing her on his way to his horse, stopped

briefly to ask if everything was all right, to which she nodded assent.

They started out, Josephina riding beside Prudence and Charles. They were soon joined by Colonel Underwood, and the first hour of the ride passed merrily with exchanges of experiences between the men on their days on the Peninsula and many questions from the sisters of life and customs there. Josephina listened to all they had to say with interest. A man's life always fascinated her; compared with her own, it was so free—men seemed able to embark on adventures at a whim. She had often wished to be able to travel, to experience just the sort of things they were speaking of, the strange foods, the warm climate, the bright colours, the exotic fruits. Prudence listened with admiration, especially whenever Charles spoke, occasionally encouraging him with a smile or shaking her head when he paused for fear he might be boring them.

"No, indeed," Josephina concurred. "Far from it, for it is as different from our lives as can be imagined. It is just like reading a novel from the subscription library, except the things you are telling us really happened, and happened to people we have the good fortune of knowing."

Lord Venables and Lady Eliza had drawn abreast of them, and Venables leaned forward in his saddle to call out, "It sounds as though the ladies in this group have definite literary leanings. But did I hear you speak of novels, Miss Trafford? I didn't realize you read anything so frivolous."

"You are determined to make of me a bluestocking, and I am just as determined that it should not be so," she responded.

"Are you indeed? Well, perhaps if you read novels you may also read poetry. How does Byron appeal to you?"

The lane in which they were riding narrowed, and as Sir Harlan had just claimed his wife's attention, Josephina found herself riding beside Venables.

"His poetry is romantic, but vastly overrated, in my opinion. I wonder if he himself enjoys all the fuss made over him."

"Let me assure you he does. You do not share the view of the majority of your sex in your views, but then, I find you seldom do. Tell me, whose poetry do you most admire."

"I think I find all I desire in John Donne."

He laughed aloud. "I might have known you would respond with the unexpected. You have indeed chosen a romantic, nay a passionate poet. Would you describe yourself as a romantic, Miss Trafford?"

"I have never so described myself, nor thought of myself as such."

"Yet to recognize the beauty of Donne's poetry you must indeed be a romantic."

"Perhaps I am, in the same sense as you describe yourself as a sentimentalist. That is not a word which I should choose to describe you, yet it is obviously a characteristic you feel to be yours."

"It is, indeed."

They were passing through Radworthy, and the blue line of the wild, open moor lay ahead of them. Their path had widened and Venables called out to her, "Come along, let's spur our horses and outride the others. We'll watch for the paths where the heather grows, then we can be sure not to get into a bog."

Josephina nodded and pressed her heels to Pandora, who, though no longer in her salad days, seemed inbued with the thrill of the expedition and charged forth. Horse and rider became one, speeding over the rough ground, through the heather and whortleberries and over gorse-covered knolls. Tendrils of hair escaped to blow across Josephina's face, but, exhilarated with the speed of Pandora's pounding hooves, with the touch of the cool wind whistling past her ears, with the smell of the bracken and gorse, and with the song of birds not yet departed for warmer climes, she allowed her hair to fly where it would. Venables rode beside her, not letting his horse have his head for fear of outdistancing his companion, and, noticing her face, flushed and smiling, her cheeks glowing, her eyes sparkling, he discovered there a zest for life, an honesty he had so often found lacking in the opposite sex.

At last they slowed their horses to a trot, and then to a walk, side by side, bridle to bridle, alone, far from the others.

"I hope they know the way," Josephina said, glancing back.

"I don't care whether they do or not. I know the way and would not object if we picnicked alone, in fact I should enjoy it. I seldom get an opportunity to be alone with you. Who knows, we might even linger over wine at lunch and decide to go no farther, just as Paolo and Francesca in the *Inferno* closed the book and that day read no further—do you remember the line?"

"Yes, but for my part I prefer not to live in a whirlwind for eternity."

"Must life always be so quiet for you to enjoy it?" he asked seriously. "I thought I heard you telling Underwood that you longed for excitement."

"I may long for excitement, but not for life in a whirlwind, to which Paolo and Francesca were condemned. If we snatch at excitement in life, we must not forget that all our actions have consequences. When I was young, my father taught me chess to impress upon me the importance of realizing that each of my actions has a consequence, that I must think *before* I act, not after, for once the move has been made, I cannot change my mind and go back."

"Then do you never act spontaneously, from feeling?"

"Rarely."

"How sad!" He studied her for a moment and then asked, "And what do you think may be the consequence of your riding with me towards a lonely destination on the moor?"

"Why"—she turned hearing horses' hooves behind them—"I believe the consequence will be a fine lunch in pleasant company and altogether a splendid day."

An excellent luncheon they did have, for when they arrived shortly after noon at the foot of Ashcombe Hill, it was to find a sheltered spot selected and cold meats laid out together with cheeses and a variety of fruits, homemade breads, and cakes. A light wine was ready to be served in the finest crystal, all of which had been carefully packed and transported there. Josephina had never seen such an elegant repast in such a bucolic setting.

She sat between Colonel Underwood and Sir Harlan Coningsby, the former paying assiduous attention to her every need, the latter concerned almost exclusively with his own.

Their talk turned to the land, Colonel Underwood remarking on the fertility of the Devon soil, though Josephina explained he was not seeing it at its best because of that year's drought. She spoke of her use of Tull's seed drill and the gain she had realized in yield, and was surprised at Sir Harlan's gleam of interest—he even stopped eating to note that he had not only heard of it but also knew how it had been devised by altering and adapting parts of an organ, a wheelbarrow, and a cider mill. He mentioned his own estate in Cheshire; though he did not spend a great deal of time there, as his wife did not care for life in the country, it was admirable land that he was sure could be persuaded to yield greater profit.

"Not only your own farming lands could be improved," Josephina emphasized, "but those of your tenants also. Why, Coke of Holkham managed to raise his rents tenfold in less than four decades, and all because he turned mediocre land into productive acreage. If yield increases, then worth of land increases to tenant and owner alike. I have followed Townshend's four-course system of crop rotation using wheat, barley, clover, and turnips, and I've found it profitable indeed. There was good reason to call him Turnip Townshend." she concluded, referring to the second Viscount Townshend, who had been an agricultural enthusiast in Norfolk and whose favourite topic of conversation had been the rural improvement to be derived from turnips.

Hearing Townshend's name mentioned, Sir Hugh Lanyon joined them, noting he had been intrigued by the man's devotion to the cause of agriculture, yet while there was no doubt that he had made unprofitable land profitable, he wondered whether new methods were not often overrated, causing people to set aside tried-and-true practices.

"But it is not just a case of old versus new. There is a tendency here in Devon to downgrade any new invention, a tendency to prefer one way of doing things simply because it was good enough for our fathers. That is not the argument. Rather it is what will produce the most for the outlay involved." Josephina warmed to her topic.

"Bravo, my dear young lady!" Sir Harlan nodded. "Allow me to congratulate you on your good sense. So few people, let alone ladies, for if I limit my compliment to ladies I shall fall short in my praise of you—there are no ladies of my acquaintance who know anything at all about farming the land; but so few people look at innovation in these essentially practical terms. So often they take something up merely because it is new, in which event it all too often fails, leaving others to scoff. But, as you say, that is precisely the only consideration: will it do a better job and what will it cost."

"Excellent, Miss Trafford," cried Venables, who had overheard the discussion and now joined them. "I have long tried to gain a point with Coningsby, but here you are, and in five minutes you have him saluting you."

Privately Josephina thought that if Venables made fewer points with Sir Harlan's wife he might stand in better stead of gaining points with the husband, but she merely smiled, making no response.

"But I will not allow them to monopolize you with their agricultural dialectics. I have been looking for a companion to

64

climb with me to the brow of the hill, and I am sure you have the fortitude. Come along."

He set off, leaving her little option but to follow him, and they started up the steep path to the summit.

"God, I had forgotten how beautiful the countryside here can be," he said, halting suddenly to look about. "It is years since I was here. My father brought us once, and we picnicked in just about the spot where we have stopped today. I remember it as a particularly happy occasion; it was my mother's birthday we were celebrating. We all seemed so happy then, or is it only because it is in the past it appears that way?"

"Time mellows, but I doubt it really changes one's feelings apart from enhancing them. It is impossible for any number of years to make a truly unhappy occasion into a happy one."

"I wonder. I loved my parents deeply. I had great respect for my father. He was a good man and taught me a great deal about life, neither overlooking its hardships nor overemphasizing its delights. He was a practical man who taught his children to be practical also. You know that I was born a second son, and truly a cadet does not have the opportunities and advantages of a firstborn. My father obeyed those rules in my upbringing and I accepted them. From Oxford I was destined for regimentals, the choice was not mine, it was made for me but I accepted it, or would have done had circumstances not dictated otherwise. I could not obey my father in a certain matter . . ." He paused as though deciding whether to continue, and then went on, ". . . a matter in which I felt that my actions had been without fault. He, though believing me, was forced by the rules of propriety to demand of me an act I felt then and still believe would have led to great unhappiness for all involved. We quarrelled, but despite it all, I believe he loved me. I know that I loved him."

They were walking slowly and he was lost in thought, seeming to be with someone else at another time. In that moment Josephina felt very close to him, as though she had long known him. She touched his arm softly.

"I had never before considered the similarity in situation between the lot of a second son and that of a woman. Both have a lack of choice and must often sublimate their own desires to the wishes of others, though a man has infinitely more options. When you had difficulties and left home, it was possible for you to set out and see the world. Had I disobeyed my father, I could not have done the same thing. Had

I gone anywhere, it could only have been the home of some elderly relative, left there to reconsider the past. I would not have had the opportunity of seeing fresh scenes and meeting new people, as you had."

"Has there ever been a time when you wished to leave?"

"I have a natural curiosity to see the world, and I would like to see it as you did, freely, not chaperoned and taken only to the 'right' places. But if I ever wanted to leave, it was prompted by wanderlust only. My father and I were the greatest friends, and no similar incident arose in my life to make us quarrel. I don't know what I should have done if it had."

They had by this time reached the brow of the hill on which were the remains of a menhir, a series of large upright stones half-buried in heather, indicating either an ancient burial site or a prehistoric dwelling or a mark of buried treasure; archeological theory and superstition did not agree on its origin. Venables stood resting his foot on the granite boulder, while Josephina shaded her eyes from the sun to look out over the rolling expanse of the moor with its deep-cleft valleys, gorse-covered knolls, and wooded dells. In the distance lay the cluster of cottages and converging of paths which marked Simonsbath, the hub of the moor.

"Well," she said at last, looking up at the cloudless sky, "it looks as though the rain George predicted for this week is slow in coming. The sky is clear as far as I can see."

As soon as the words were spoken, she regretted them; it was neither the place nor the time to mention the Ridgeways.

Venables smiled wryly. "If it had come today it wouldn't be the first time I have been drenched at a picnic. You must have heard all about my so-called misdoings with Lucy Ridgeway by now."

She wished she could have feigned ignorance, but replied in all honesty, "I have heard something of it, but only recently."

"From Ridgeway, I suppose," and seeing her flush of acknowledgement, he went on, "I thought he would wish to warn you of me, though I'm surprised he waited till now to talk of it. In looking back, I realize I might have expected it of the squire, to try to saddle me with that young girl—she not yet out of the schoolroom and myself not much older—merely because we became detached from the rest of the group and one of those drenching moor rains set in. While searching for shelter, her horse lost a shoe, and when we did find one of those little cottages such as you see yonder, she wouldn't be persuaded to leave it. We could have both got back to Milvercombe on my mount, but she was frightened and refused to go. I had no choice but to stay with her; I spent the night in the stable. But all my explanations were of no avail to the squire. His daughter was compromised and I must marry her. I refused, for I had done nothing to harm her and I had no wish to tie myself to her for life. She was a sweet little thing, but even at that age I knew she was an irksome bore, just like the rest of the family. Despite my assurances, which, to give Lucy her due, I am sure she corroborated, that all propriety had been observed, that we had not even spent the night under the same roof, he would not listen. I might have expected it of him, but what hurt me was that my father sided with him, insisting that I should marry the girl, for I was a gentleman and it was a gentleman's duty to observe propriety. It made me think gentlemen must be fools to ruin their lives for what—to preserve a good name? I have hated the word 'gentleman' ever since. To live a miserable life but preserve a good name—the stupidity of it."

There was no mistaking the bitterness in his voice; then he shrugged and reached over to gently brush back a lock of hair the wind had blown across her face. "I was very green then, and, I must confess, not tempted. I cannot promise that were we to become lost here today that I would be content to spend the night in a stable, but then I did. My father was very angry when I refused to comply with his wishes, so I packed up and left home. I had a little money in my own right, enough to book passage first for Canada, and then, finding that beastly cold, for the West Indies. There I found that even the second son of an earl was regarded with some esteem. I also found that those who do not mix drinking with their gambling could often walk away from the tables with their winnings in their pockets. In this way I became owner of a large sugar plantation, fired with enthusiasm, determined to make a fortune and boast to my father that I had. Make a fortune I did, but when I returned to England, it was to find my father on his death bed. That made my gains seem paltry indeed, those years wasted in amassing a fortune. For what? To show an old man that I had done it, to prove that I could. If I had made the money for its own sake, it would have meant more to me. When he died I resolved not to go back and never again to work. I bought a house in London and a property in Gloucestershire and decided to enjoy every penny that I had, and that is what I have been doing until now, when I find myself saddled with a title I don't want and property I had no wish to inherit."

Josephina did not reply immediately but stood looking out to the point where the moor met the sky, moved by his explanation, pensive.

"Many might envy you your wealth and position," she said at last.

"Would you?"

"I might," she mused. "Imagine having all that power."

"Power!" He laughed. "I've never thought of myself as particularly powerful."

"That's because you don't have to think about it. You are powerful. Everything you do affects others, even others you may not see or know. A vast amount of that acreage"—she pointed in the direction from which they had come—"is yours. People live and die on it, and they depend on you. There are people also in the West Indies and in Gloucestershire depending on you. You have a voice in Parliament that can affect even more people, and even while you are spending your money, perhaps then most of all, you affect all the people you buy from, or gamble with, or employ. Money has rights and a power of its own. It is impossible to be rich and powerless."

Again he reached over to brush the hair back from her face.

"And my power over you—how is that? I feel, my fair Portia, that it is not the strong, virulent force I should like to wield. but a rather sickly, feeble thing."

"You are changing the subject now," she retorted. "We were talking of the power bestowed by money and property. Now you speak of something else."

"Do you mean to tell me," he said with mock solemnity, "that there are things which cannot be bought."

She laughed. "I do, my judge, I do." Then, fearing that their absence from the rest of the party must cause comment and feeling unsure of herself in the turn the conversation had taken, she urged, "Come, I am sure the others are getting ready to leave by this time. I'll race you down the hill."

"Are you sure you wouldn't wish to become lost with me on the way home? I assure you I know all the best cottages in these parts."

"Dear sir, I am much too old to be compromised." She laughed.

"I wonder."

"Anyway, I am glad you begin to see the funny side of this

tragicomedy. It is lucky that life always has those two sides; even on the darkest days, there is something to laugh about. Come, let's race. But you must give me a start, for I have these long skirts to hamper me."

And she started off down the hill. He stood for some time watching her slim, agile figure skipping over its rough surface, light and surefooted, her green dress blending with the green grass. He so relished the scene he might have waited until she reached the bottom had she not turned halfway down to see how close behind he was; then he started to run, catching up with her as she neared the rest of the party.

Both Lady Eliza and Lady Francesca had been watching their progress down the hill, and the meaningful look they exchanged did not escape Josephina, making her suddenly feel guilty, she knew not why.

"There you are at last. We had quite given you up." Lady Eliza put her arm through Venables' possessively. "Do you know that it is almost three?"

"No, but I do know that you have finished all the wine while I was gone. It's not much of a picnic when the host is left without wine. I think we should all return to Venarvon to slake our thirst."

Josephina demurred, and Prudence agreed they must go directly home, Charles Carew offering to accompany them. The ride back passed without incident. The pace was slower than it had been in the morning, and by the time they reached Milvercombe, dusk was already in the air. Venables waved as Josephina turned in at Westlands. She thought of him often that night.

8

Milvercombe was agog the following week with conjectures on the two gatherings to be held at Venarvon: that on Tuesday for the estate's tenants, for which it was said a cistern of punch was being prepared and two pigs killed for roasting; and the ball to be given the following night for the gentry of the neighbourhood.

Lady Netherton said she could not remember anything like the comings and goings of tradesmen to Venarvon. Smith had told her that pandemonium reigned in the kitchen until the arrival of Pouncett, the majordomo from Blenhasset, Lord Venables' Gloucestershire estate, to whom Kister had resigned all authority. Smith had heard that the newcomer was a veritable demon for work and would permit no slacking with two such large feasts to be prepared.

Squire Ridgeway, meeting Mr. Trummock, one of Venables' tenants, the day following his feasting at Venarvon, was told by him that the present Lord Venables was much more like his father than his brother had been, and he was well pleased with him—it seemed he would be a reasonable gentleman. The squire sufficed himself with commenting that these were early days yet. He himself had toyed with the idea of refusing Venables' invitation when it came, but his good lady would not hear of being the only family among the gentry not to be present. She insisted that the time had come to overlook the past, regrettable though it had been. Lucy was happy, and perhaps Venables, despite his wealth and position, would not have suited her nearly as well as the man she had chosen.

So the Ridgeways, along with the Nethertons, the Carews, and other families from Milvercombe and surrounding towns and villages, found themselves arrayed in their very best, drawing up before the front steps of Venarvon that Wednesday evening. It did not go without comment that the Traffords were transported thither in his lordship's own coach, over which Mrs. Trafford had come to assume a proprietary air that deserted her as soon as she entered the mansion, for

70

she still stood in awe of the brightness and glitter of these London folk, "So different from society in my time," she said, "so . . . so forward, but so very elegant."

The scene that greeted the guests was a positive floodlight of candles, causing the brightly polished interior to gleam and sparkle and literally come alive. The heavy chandeliers, the doors, the staircase, the furniture, the floors, the sconces, the chimneypieces, even the very fire irons bore evidence of repeated polishing and cleaning. Those walls that had not been repapered had been washed, and new draperies of rich deep blue velvet hung in the main saloon, where Lord Venables and his sister were greeting their guests.

Josephina wished that she could rid herself of feeling like a schoolroom miss whenever she saw Venables, but just when she most wished to maintain her composure, it would abandon her, leaving her as blushing and flustered as a sixteen-year-old rather than her usual collected self. In a strange way, it was a pleasant feeling, yet it was disconcerting, for she, who had never had difficulty in exercising self-control, lost it when she most needed it.

Mrs. Trafford had insisted on new gowns for the occasion, and for once Josephina had raised no objection. They had gone as far as Ilchester to find cloth to satisfy Mrs. Trafford, but the results had been worth it, for even among the most expensively dressed, the Misses Trafford made a splendid showing; Amelia in white book-muslin over a pink silk slip, with a long, broad sash and bows on her sleeves of deep rose satin; Prudence wearing a chemise dress of white embroidered lawn; and Josephina in an Empire dress of pale green crepe trimmed at the hem with gold braid.

In reply to her greeting and comment on the beauty of the room, Venables pressed her hand to observe that the room was only a fitting setting for her that evening; Josephina, fearing his appraising glance would arouse her mother's notice, made no response.

George Ridgeway approached her immediately to claim the first two dances, which she allowed with as much grace as possible. Whenever she attended an assembly or ball, infrequent though the occasions might be, George had a way of always being there to claim the first two dances. She could never think of a gracious way to refuse, but once they were on the dance floor, she always wished she had been more brutal in her response, for he approached the challenge like a hunter running down its quarry, cautiously at first, then, warming to the task, with increased pace and enthusiasm, finishing with an éclat that demanded a rousing hurrah. Josephina had grown used to his style, but she suspected it would cause comment among the Venarvon party, and she caught sight of Lady Eliza's raised eyebrows and gesticulating fan as they passed the place where she stood talking to Colonel Underwood. Lord Venables had opened the dance with his sister, and apparently since he was engaged, she had found no one else with whom she wished to dance. It could not be for want of being asked that she stood aside from the dance floor, for she was truly a vision of loveliness, the burnished gold of her hair topped by a wreath of diamonds and her dress of soft white muslin clinging to her shapely figure, set off by a gold sash tied under her bosom. Prudence was dancing with Charles Carew, and Amelia had been discovered by a young officer, a friend of Colonel Underwood's who had come from Exeter for the party.

Josephina was glad, when the dance finished, to be joined by Fanny Netherton, always a source of comfort when George tried her patience, for Fanny would listen for hours to his tales of amazingly accurate weather forecasts he had made, though some, he was forced to admit, might have been rather late in fulfillment. His knowledge of weather lore was phenomenal, even Josephina was forced to admit that, and Fanny would ask just the right questions to draw him out on his favourite topic, listening to his pontifications with an air of interest that made it difficult to believe she had heard them scores of times before. Josephina wondered whether Fanny could possibly be enamoured of George, but apart from her patience with him, she gave no outward indication of it, and George paid her no special attention when Josephina was at hand. Fanny never mentioned him to Josephina, though Prudence said she had once remarked that he was a fine figure of a man, not a phrase that ever came to Josephina's mind on those infrequent occasions when it turned to him.

That evening Josephina had more to think of than George Ridgeway. She was delighted by the gaiety of the scene, greeting people she seldom saw. She danced with Mr. Wilberton, a landowner from the adjoining county of Somerset, and then the following two with Colonel Underwood. But as she was parting from him, she saw George bearing down upon her again and hastily escaped into an adjacent room that had been set up for cards.

There her mother, at a table with Lady Netherton and Mrs. Ridgeway, was looking for a fourth for whist.

"Josephina," she called, "do help us out and take Mrs.

Carew's hand until she returns. Mildred tore the hem of her dress, and her mother is attending to it. I'm sure she won't be long."

"We shouldn't take you away from dancing," Mrs. Ridgeway protested, but Josephina slipped hastily into the vacant chair, remarking she was completely exhausted with the pace of the last set and would be glad of a respite. The game continued, but Mrs. Carew did not return and Josephina thought she would be confined to the card table until supper, for the ladies were engrossed in the game, making it impossible for her to leave.

Just as another dance was about to begin, she felt a light tap on her shoulder and looked up to see Venables standing with Mrs. Rathburn, wife of the squire of the neighbouring parish of Litchford.

"Miss Trafford," Venables addressed her, "I wonder if you would object to giving your place to Mrs. Rathburn. She has been most anxious to get in a hand of whist before supper, and if you are not engaged elsewhere, perhaps you might honour me with the next dance."

"Perverse girl," Venables teased as he led Josephina onto the floor, "I have been looking for you everywhere. Why do you come to a ball looking so ravishingly beautiful and then seat yourself with the dowagers in the card room? It took great ingenuity, I will have you know, to pry you from their clutches. I have been searching this past half-hour for someone to take your place."

"There is an explanation I could give you so that you would not condemn me as a complete sobersides; however, this is not the place for it."

"Would you prefer to go out on the terrace?" he asked hopefully.

"No, I would not," she rebuked, immediately directing her comments to the pleasure he was giving to the neighbourhood. "We have not been half so well entertained in my memory," she concluded, "and I understand your party yesterday was also a great success."

"It was," he declared. "Too great a success, I'm afraid. I awoke with a sore head and found Pouncett threatening to leave because of the condition of the house. I suppose I should have let more time intervene between events. We found people sleeping under the stairs, and even this morning there was a young man discovered under the dining table when we were at breakfast. He joined us and proved a most likeable lad."

"And how did you prevent Pouncett from leaving?"

"Alas, I regret to admit it to you after our discussion of last week, but you are right, money does do a lot of things, and thanks to filthy lucre, precious Pouncett is with us still. Otherwise we would not be able to eat tonight. While we are on that subject, may I take you in to supper?"

George had already elicited this promise from her earlier and had twice reminded her of it, so she smiled ruefully. "I'm sorry, but I promised George I would sit with the Ridgeways at their table."

He looked thoughtful for a moment, then ventured, "Well, that's not an insurmountable problem. Perhaps I can persuade the Ridgeways to join us."

Josephina gasped, "I hardly think so."

"Well, there's no harm in trying. That fellow is dogging your footsteps enough as it is."

After the dance ended, she saw Venables approach Mrs. Ridgeway, who smiled at him amiably while he spoke to her; then she approached her husband, who looked considerably less amiable at the news she imparted. Nevertheless the assembled guests were soon treated with the sight of Mrs. Ridgeway being led in to supper by Lord Venables, who had also contrived that Josephina would sit on his other hand. Two large tables had been joined, Venables making sure that his own party intermingled the Ridgeway group. Thus Lady Eliza sat beside Squire Ridgeway, who fixed her with such lugubrious fascination throughout the meal that Josephina wondered what she could be telling him to obtain such rapt attention. She was, it transpired, describing the clothes worn at a rout she had recently attended in Mayfair, but it is not at all certain that the squire accurately followed the descriptive details, for a large part of his time was spent retrieving Lady Eliza's table napkin that kept slipping from her muslin-covered knees to the floor below. Each time he lowered his staunch frame on its courtly mission, he was not to be faulted that his eyes were lowered across her exquisitely exposed bosom, nor was he untowardly upset to find that his glances had not escaped their object's notice. As they got up to leave, Lady Eliza presented him with the table napkin, remarking she thought he had had more use of it than she. He was, she added laughingly, a veritable rogue.

Josephina was conscious that George had been upstaged by Venables at supper, and by way of recompense, she acceded to his request to dance again after the repast, but positively refused to stand up with him again.

"To stand up with you three times in one evening would lead to comment, George," she rallied, pleased to have a plausible excuse.

"Hang comment, perhaps we should give them something to comment about," and Josephina, fearing her remark might lead to dangerous ground, was glad to be led to the floor by Sir Harlan Coningsby.

He spoke little during the course of the dance, except to remark that she was an excellent little stepper and quite a woman, both comments she received as she believed them intended, as compliments. Despite his bulk, he was surprisingly light on his feet, nor was his conversation taxing, until, with a waft of port-laden breath, he observed that it would be a lucky man who won such an exceptional woman, a comment overheard by Venables, then passing them in the set with Lady Eliza, who leaned over to remark, "You must, indeed, be exceptional, Miss Trafford, to get Coningsby out on the dance floor—I fancy this is the first time I have seen him grace it this evening."

Sir Harlan's eyes followed the pair as they went down the set, Lady Eliza speaking softly, intimately to Venables and he receiving those remarks in a manner that showed him no stranger to them, but all he said, enigmatically, was, "You are, indeed, an exceptional woman."

"Your wife . . . you are friends of long standing of Lord Venables?" Immediately Josephina regretted her slip; Sir Harlan might be a weak, even a stupid man, but he was not to be insulted, yet she, who never pried into the affairs of others, found her curiosity had been insatiably aroused over the relationship between Lord Venables and Lady Eliza.

"You were right—my wife is a friend of long standing of Lord Venables," he replied flatly.

Didn't he mind? she longed to ask, but she had already overstepped the bounds of propriety. Instead, she found herself growing angry at Venables. How dare he so openly court Lady Eliza before her husband? Lady Eliza was clearly used to getting what she wanted, and what she wanted was obviously Venables, yet he was not at all averse to the idea. If these were the ways of the London society so heartily endorsed by her mother, she wanted no part of them. She found herself vexed over the matter, and she took herself to task for allowing the behaviour of others to upset her. It was their concern, not hers, and she should not allow it to ire her, but once again they passed Venables and Eliza in the set, and once again she found herself wrought with anger.

She saw Prudence dancing again with Charles Carew—what a handsome couple they made; she had never before seen two people so obviously destined for one another. Happiness radiated from Pru's face, while his eyes beamed with contentment. Such affection made her sigh, and she had not realized that it was an audible sigh until Sir Harlan asked if she were tired, and realizing she had been silent, she searched her mind for something bright to say.

"I enjoyed talking to you the other day at the picnic. Your knowledge of the background of Tull's seed drill was impressive. I hope we may have another opportunity to exchange views on that subject," she ventured.

"And I also, Miss Trafford. I wish you could visit my estate in Cheshire sometime. I should very much like your opinion on our ways of farming. I have a charming little place there, and Eliza hardly ever comes. We could be alone to . . . to talk."

Josephina knew not how to reply. She was flattered at having her opinion requested, an unusual circumstance, surrounded, as she was, by criticism rather than commendation; however, his implication that she should visit him at his home and in his wife's absence was most improper. She was unsure whether to thank him or to administer a sharp rebuke, and was glad when the dance ended and she could leave him, saying that she had to find her youngest sister.

She had no need to prevaricate, for she realized that she had not seen Amelia since supper, when she had sat with a party of rather boisterous officers at the end of the room. Josephina had attempted to keep an eye on her, trusting she would not be tempted to taste any of the champagne that poured so freely, but noticing her absence, she feared the worst.

She caught up with Prudence and asked her whether she had seen Amelia.

"She was here after supper, dancing with the young man I had seen her with earlier, Captain Williams. I was about to caution her on spending too much time with him, but I think she may have realized my intention, for she disappeared, and then Charles asked me to dance and I presumed she was also on the floor."

"Dear Pru, if you were dancing with Charles, it is no wonder you lost track of her." Josephina gave her sister's hand an affectionate squeeze. "But we must find her. I do hope she didn't indulge in the champagne and become sick."

"No, far from it, she seemed in the best of health."

The sisters crossed the room towards the terrace doors.

"Do you suppose. . . ?" Josephina suddenly hesitated. "She can't have gone outside with him, can she?"

"Oh, no, Jo. I would surely have noticed that."

"Nevertheless, we should make sure. Perhaps you could look in the card room, though I doubt she would be there. I believe there is an anteroom across the hall you might also try, while I look out on the terrace."

It was a bright, clear night, almost full moon, and still warm. The air was delightfully fresh after the stuffiness of the ballroom, and Josephine walked to the edge of the terrace and leaned against the balustrade. Suddenly she became aware that she was not alone, for at the far end she caught a glimpse of a lightly clad figure standing close, far too close, to another, dressed in regimentals. She realized, with horror, that the pair were her sister and her red-coated admirer.

"Amelia!" she gasped in fuming tones.

The figure started back, extricating itself from the officer's embrace, but making no move to leave him.

"Amelia, what are you thinking of!" Josephina was shocked. Was this what they might expect of her in London? It was shameful. Had she no sense of propriety?

As she crossed towards them, Josephina saw the look of defiance on Amelia's face. "I'm sorry, Miss Trafford, it was my fault . . ." began Captain Williams, but Josephina ignored him.

"I think, Amelia, that you should bid this gentleman goodbye without delay and get your pelisse. We are going home."

"Oh, no, please, Josephina. We are all having such a good time," Amelia pleaded.

"You are having much too good a time. Your conduct is deplorable. I think this gentleman can leave us. I have nothing at all to say to him. His conduct is his affair. If that is how you led him to believe he can behave, he will undoubtedly take whatever advantage he can. I cannot say it is the conduct of a gentleman. Are you aware, sir, that my sister is not yet eighteen?"

"Miss Trafford, I want most desperately to apologize. I cannot excuse my conduct except to place some of the blame on the excellent champagne, the fullness of the moon, but most of it on the beauty and charm of my companion. It may seem worse to you than it was, but honestly we merely came out for a breath of air and were standing talking when suddenly it just seemed the natural thing to do to kiss one another."

"That is so, Jo, that is what happened. I didn't mean to, and I know I shouldn't have let him." Amelia sniffed, about to cry.

"And I know I shouldn't have kissed your sister, if only she weren't quite so enchanting," Captain Williams continued.

Fearing the young captain's continued compliments would only serve to further infatuate her sister, Josephina determined to bring an immediate close to the conversation.

"If you will go inside now, Amelia, I shall find Mother and we shall all leave," she decreed.

"Leaving so soon, Miss Trafford, when there are many more dances to be danced, and I know there are young gentlemen anxious to find partners. That would be a bitter disappointment." It was Venables, approaching slowly and casually across the terrace. She had not heard him come out and wondered how much of the scene he had observed.

"I am sorry, but we really must go." Josephina directed a firm gaze at her sister. "Go and get your pelisse now, please."

Amelia ran from the group, crying, followed by Captain Williams.

"Now look what you've done. That was no way to handle the matter," Venables objected.

"And what do you know of it?" she demanded.

"I know nothing except that I find Captain Williams, obviously seeking respite from the crush inside, and your sister, who probably did likewise, and you berating them. If some little flirtation did take place, I see no need to make a mountain out of it. Rather I think that it should be treated with the frivolity with which it most obviously occurred."

"I might expect you to champion light behaviour, Lord Venables, since you seem a past master of it, but I venture to say it is not the behaviour that has prevailed in my family," she fumed.

"It may not have, though that is not to say that a little light behaviour from time to time might not be an improvement," he commented dryly.

"I really don't wish to hear your opinion." She turned to leave, and then stopped. "I should think even you would understand that my sister is not yet eighteen and has never been out in the world. Even you should see that she should not be here alone with a man."

"In some ways I believe your sister to be better able to take care of herself than you, Miss Trafford. Age is not necessarily the criterion of worldliness." His voice was gentler now.

"But there is such a thing as innocence."

"Again, I believe you to be the more innocent. Your sister, though young, knew what she was doing and, in fact, what she did caused no harm—no harm, that is, until you came bellowing upon her like a banshee and informing half the assembled guests that she was here with . . . with a friend."

"Did I raise my voice that much?" she demurred.

"I heard you, though that may have been because I saw you walk out onto the terrace and followed you."

Josephina ignored the veiled implication of his remark. "By your standards, whatever conduct takes place is permissible as long as it is not discovered," she asserted, not concealing her anger.

"I made no such statement. I merely said that you did harm by possibly making her conduct known. If she ran in crying, it will obviously cause comment. But I did not imply that concealment makes any conduct acceptable. I am disappointed that you would lay such a shibboleth at my door. There is conduct that is reprehensible in itself, known or unknown. Such conduct I do not condone, far from it, I have fought too many battles over it. But a kiss stolen on a moonlit night does not, in my estimation, fall into such a category."

Josephina turned and grasped the balustrade with both hands, looking out at the trees silhouetted in the moonlight.

"But Amelia must know that she cannot conduct herself so. She is to come out this season, my aunt in London will conduct her to parties and gatherings where she will meet many people—people who have been out in the world far longer than she has. If she cannot control her behaviour on an occasion such as this, with her whole family present, what may we expect of her conduct in town?"

"Your aunt may have her task cut out for her, but I do not think that if Amelia is a sister of yours she will go far astray —that is, unless you come down on her too hard over this peccadillo. She is pretty, but in London she will find there are many pretty girls. She may not be as tempting or as tempted as in this more closed environment. Then, too, there will not be one ball to go to, but many; the diversions will keep her occupied, for if I do not mistake her, she appreciates entertainment and fine clothes more than her sisters."

"You seem to know her well." His perspicacity surprised her. She had not realized that he had observed her sister so closely. "But it is also her love of fine clothes and entertainment that worries me. The amount of money I have for her presentation is not large, and her spending will be limited. I trust that her desire for finery will not lead her into any imprudence."

He laughed and put out his hands to grasp her shoulders and turn her to him. "Come, now, what are you suggesting, Miss Trafford? I am sure your aunt will look after her better than that. I believe you are going to extraordinary lengths to worry yourself on her behalf. Why don't you worry a little more about yourself? I think you should, for if you don't, I shall have to. Somebody must do it."

"It's all very well for you to talk"—she frowned—"for you don't have a seventeen-year-old sister about to be loosed on London. I daresay it does seem a light matter to you, but if any harm befalls her, it is my responsibility. I think that this evening I did not chaperone her well enough, for had I done so, she would certainly not have ended up on the terrace alone with a gentleman."

"Here you are preaching, and yet you yourself are alone on the terrace with a gentleman. Does not the oddity of it strike you?"

"Really, do be serious," she retorted, while realizing that he was right—she had inadvertently laid herself open for comment by staying and talking to Venables for so long a time.

"I am perfectly serious, but I think you are far too serious, and just to make you feel less grave and to help you understand your sister a little better . . ." He bent down and kissed her swiftly on the lips.

"You see, it can happen to anyone." He smiled. "Now I'm going inside to tell Amelia that you will leave when the ball is over and not before, and I want you to remain on the terrace for a short while—I do not wish our presence here alone together to be the cause of gossip." His eyes twinkled down at her. "After that, I think you can safely come in, for the music of the dance continues, and when I left, George Ridgeway was going through his gyrations with Miss Netherton, and I fancy he is still concentrating, for it is a quadrille. I promise not to breathe a word to anyone of our clandestine meeting as long as you promise me the next dance."

9

The day following a ball is almost as diverting as the event it-self, for then the minutiae of the evening can be examined, dissected, scrutinized, studied, challenged, reconstructed, and savoured at leisure. Thus the sole topic of conversation in Milvercombe's breakfast rooms the following morning was the Venarvon ball.

Lady Netherton enthused over the fine clothes she had seen, particularly those on the ladies from London, though she thought Fanny had shown off well in her pink satin chemise, edged with ruches, which the new dressmaker in Exeter had made for the occasion. She wished that Fanny had danced more often with gentlemen other than George Ridgeway, for he had spent most of the evening following Josephina Trafford around like a lapdog. It infuriated her, for it was obvious to everyone, except George, that she did not care a fig for him.

Charles Carew was unusually silent at the breakfast table, thinking long about a pair of bright blue eyes. He also pon-dered the subject of the matter Lord Venables wished to dis-cuss with him, for as he was leaving he had caught up with him and asked that he call at Venarvon that afternoon to see him. His mother, noticing his silence and conjecturing its cause, did not chide him when he did not respond to her offer of more tea.

Mrs. Ridgeway kept up an incessant monologue, to which neither her son nor her husband contributed, on the vast changes that had been made in the condition of the park and the mansion at Venarvon, the splendour of the new draperies, the immaculate state of the interior, the lustre of the furni-ture—her own servants never produced such a shine, she must get the names of the people Venables had employed and try to get them at the Hall.

Squire Ridgeway wiped his mouth with his linen napkin and set it down on the table, fondling its smoothness. It reminded him of Lady Eliza's voluptuous bosom.

"All very well to crow about last evening, but it's our little girl should be sitting up there now, you seem to forget that," he flung at his prating wife. Lucy was close to thirty, but she remained always their little girl.

"Well," she asserted, with a hard look at her husband, "I'm not sure that I approve of that flighty-looking woman there that you seemed to find so amusing, or her relationship with Lord Venables, she looked up to no good to me, blatantly chasing him in front of her husband that way—and other men too." Her glance left no doubt as to her implication. "Lucy has a good, steady husband, there's something to be said for that."

"Who was that?" George inquired, a large forkful of meat en route to his mouth.

"Oh, George!" His mother was exasperated. "You never notice anything except Josephina Trafford."

"I thought Fanny Netherson looked very pretty last night," his father prompted. "That dress, whatever it was"—he tried to remember what she had worn but couldn't—"anyway, it was very becoming to her, and she acted very prettily, unlike the Trafford girls, that youngest one making all that commotion, and Josephina pushing herself next to Venables at supper, even though you took her in. You could look a lot further and not find a woman who would make a better wife than Fanny Netherton."

George continued to munch on his bread and cold meat, oblivious of his father's broad hints. He'd never seen Josephina looking quite as radiant as last night in all the years he had known her. She'd outshone all the London folk.

The object of his admiration sat silently at the dining table at Westlands wondering just what she should say to Amelia when she talked to her later that morning. Was Venables right when he cautioned her not to come down too hard on her? If only Amelia would learn to consider her actions, to think before she acted. Josephina got up from the table. She was to drive her mother to Shepton Park to spend the day with the Nethertons, and she would talk to Amelia when she got back; by then she would have decided what to say to her.

At Venarvon, Lady Eliza, looking lovely even at the ungodly hour of eleven, prattled on at their repast, pronouncing herself to have been vastly amused the previous evening. She had found the country manners and the styles of dress quite beyond everything.

"My dear," she said to no one in particular or anyone who cared to listen, "I would simply have ruined my new gold slippers if I had danced with any of them. There were one or two especially I remember on the dance floor cutting such strange figures, one might describe their step as a gallop, or perhaps more properly a prance. I have never seen anything to equal it, even in remotest Cheshire."

"Don't care what you say, I enjoyed it," her husband put in. Since he rarely commented at all on social events, his remark drew more attention than the words themselves warranted.

"Did you, indeed," said his wife, narrowing her eyes. "I did see you out on the dance floor, now I come to think of it, with Miss Trafford, wasn't it?"

"Yes, and a nice little stepper I found her to be." But that was all she got out of her husband that morning. She turned away; really, she didn't care what he thought, but she was concerned that Venables had not yet spoken. He was usually the first to share her amusement, noticing odd foibles often before she did, but this morning she was forced to ask him how he had enjoyed himself.

"Excessively," was the only response she could elicit, and she found the look that accompanied his terse reply disconcerting.

He got up soon after, announcing he had to drive over to the Trummock farm that morning to settle a dispute.

"Do you want company?" Lady Eliza enquired.

"I really don't think you would enjoy it," was the response, and he was gone.

"I do think we should see what can be done about getting Conniston back to London, or even Blenhasset," she said to his sister after the others had left the table.

"Any particular reason, or are you just bored with Devon?"

"I think he is showing far too much attention to that Trafford girl."

"You know Conn," his sister mollified. "He's always interested in some girl, but he's not serious about any of them. I don't disapprove, since our little Philip is his heir. It's nice to have a second son so well taken care of. Of course, now he has inherited the title, I've had so many mamas approach me with obvious interest, but I don't think Conn is anxious to establish a dynasty—goodness knows he's had enough opportunities to do so. Anyway, he's ordered me to keep both mamas and daughters away from him, so it sounds as though he intends to carry on much the way he always has."

She sipped her coffee without looking directly at Lady

Eliza, who had held the place of Venables' boon companion for almost a year now. A long time for him, Francesca had mused, wondering how long it would be before he would be buying some superbly expensive piece of jewellery and asking her to drop the hint that his attentions were engaged elsewhere. Lady Eliza, she felt, unlike the others, would not be ushered out quietly. Francesca neither approved nor disapproved of her brother's amours. She appreciated the fact that Philip would remain her brother's heir only as long as he had no children of his own, but she would not have begrudged his marrying on that account as long as the social connexion would be superior. Francesca enjoyed her position in the *haut ton*, and any connexion that would serve to strengthen her repute in that august body would not come amiss. The Duchess of Danforth, whose daughter was recently out, rich and a pretty girl into the bargain, had mentioned her brother as a suitable prospect. She might approach Conn on the matter if he was becoming in any way involved with Josephina Trafford for *she* wouldn't do at all—too respectable for a mistress and too lowly-connected for a wife.

She looked across at Lady Eliza. Francesca would miss her steady companionship, for she was amusing; that was probably what had attracted Conn to her in the first place and kept him by her side for so long, for beauty alone would not do it.

"I have a feeling that this girl is different, and it's only a feeling, but I don't like it," Lady Eliza mused.

"She is a country girl with no social graces and no beauty to speak of. I quite like her open, frank way, but I think I can assure you that Conn just finds her something different to amuse him while he's here. He has seen quite a bit of her, but we'll be leaving soon and that will be an end of it," Francesca consoled her.

Conniston Venables, however, thought he had not seen nearly enough of Josephina, and was wondering how he could correct that omission when he came upon her driving the gig back from Shepton Park.

"I am in luck," he said, reining his curricle as she approached. "You are just the person who can assist me, Miss Trafford. Trummock has asked me to stop at his farm this morning to settle some kind of dispute, and it would help me exceedingly if you would come along. You know these people so much better than I do, and I'm sure your skill in arguing a case is equalled only by that in hearing one. It is probably something which should be attended to by my bailiff, but I think Trummock approached me because Belding is new. I

84

agreed to go, but I've been regretting it ever since I started out."

Josephina readily agreed to accompany him, and he helped her into his curricle, instructing his groom to return her gig to Westlands.

She noticed how comfortable it was compared with the gig, riding smoothly even on the bumpy country lanes. She observed, too, his skill at handling the reins, rounding the corners without hazard even at the fast pace at which they were travelling.

"Do you ever race?" she asked.

"I used to, quite often, and I enjoyed it, but it has palled on me lately. That's the trouble with amusements, you know"—he looked at her, his grey eyes laughing—"they pall after a while and then become a bore. Not that duties are any better—they're the worst bore of the lot, like this thing this morning."

"You're looking only at the surface if you say that; you fail to see the human drama. I find settling disputes intriguing, not because I wish to know the intimacies of other people's lives but because it makes me realize that people, whatever their rank in life, have basically the same wants and desires."

"Then I'm very glad to have you with me this morning. Tell me, did you enjoy yourself last night?"

"I did, immensely."

"You admit, then, that balls can be enjoyable?"

"Yes, if they are as spectacularly catered as yours, and if they happen equally as rarely. I should hate to be going to a ball every night."

"So should I, and no more do I. I thought you looked radiant."

"Thank you." His words and the look accompanying them made her feel distinctly uncomfortable. "What is the nature of Trummock's problem?" she asked, changing to a subject on which she felt on firmer ground.

He grinned at her manoeuvre, but merely answered, "I'm not exactly sure. He did talk to me briefly about it when they were all out on Tuesday, truth to tell, but I can't remember. He'd been drinking, and so had I. We'll soon find out, though, for this is their farm, if I'm not mistaken."

They drew in at a wooden gate set into a wall of large granite blocks entirely surrounding the farm. The farmhouse was a long, low building of rough, warm-coloured stone, with massive walls and a heavy thatch deeply overhanging the whole. Doorways and windows appeared to have been positioned by the dictates of fancy rather than by design, but they combined to make a pleasing picture. The windows of the front parlour, into which they were escorted, looked out onto a neat garden bordered by tall, sweeping hollyhocks and robust dahlias. Beyond was the large barnyard and the barn in which hay could be seen neatly stacked. It was a farm that showed care and hard work, just as did the interior of the farmhouse.

Mr. and Mrs. Trummock awaited Venables, dressed in their Sunday clothes. A fire was burning in the hearth, even though the weather continued warm, and refreshments had been set out on a small table. Mrs. Trummock bustled about serving her guests. Josephina had noticed her look of surprise on finding that she had accompanied Venables, and she wondered whether she had been wise to do so, for though she attended to the disputes of her own tenants, the Trummocks might wish their difficulties known only to their own landlord.

Venables sat at ease in the largest of the armchairs, his long legs stretched before him, drinking the Trummocks' good homemade cider and munching on one of Mrs. Trummock's freshly made tea cakes. He was asking Mr. Trummock's opinion of his new bailiff, and Mr. Trummock, greatly flattered, for he was unused to rendering opinions on any subject, was pronouncing Belding a great improvement over Farnsworth, an opinion in which Mrs. Trummock heartily concurred.

"Miss Trafford was the first to point out to me Farnsworth's iniquitous behaviour," Venables explained, "and she has been of invaluable assistance in helping me in other matters. That's why I asked her to come along this morning."

Mr. Trummock, mollified at having her presence explained, pronounced that she was doing a right good job at Westlands and asked her about her seed drill, listening to her comments politely but with obvious disapprobation.

At last, with a deep sigh, he said, "I suppose, my lord, you would like to see the unhappy pair?"

"Yes, indeed," said Venables cheerfully, "though they may not, in truth, be so unhappy."

"One of 'em's not," Trummock said vindictively, "but my poor girl is, I can assure you of that. I'll not let her forget it, either."

"Come, let's have them in and talk to them. I really think it best if I see them alone," but noticing Josephina about to rise, he motioned her to remain. "No, you stay, of course, Miss Trafford."

Elsie Trummock was about the same age as Bessie Meersham, and Josephina knew her quite well. She was decidedly ill-at-ease as she entered with a young man of about the same age, brawny in build with a shock of yellow hair, who kept his eyes downcast, seeming to find great interest in his heavy boots. Josephina usually saw Elsie at church with the Trummocks on Sunday, but she had missed her there lately; seeing her now, she understood the reason why, for she was close to her term in pregnancy. The import of the dispute Venables had been called in to adjudicate was immediately clear, and Josephina felt her presence there with him was unpardonable. Though pregnancies out of wedlock were not unusual—she often had to deal with them among her own people—they were not the subject of discussion among the gentry, particularly those of the opposite sex. She would not have spoken of such a matter with George Ridgeway, let alone Venables.

She got up abruptly to leave, but Elsie chose that moment to burst into tears, and she went over and conducted her to a chair, not before casting a speaking glance at Venables, which he studiously ignored.

He was talking easily to the young man, saying he had observed him handling carthorses in the field and thought he had done a fine job of it. The young man continued to study his boots, but from the manner in which he rubbed his hands across the rough worsted of his breeches, it was obvious that he was pleased at the compliment.

"Now, Ned," Venables went on, "the fact of the matter is that Mr. Trummock has called me in because his daughter is expecting a child in the near future and he insists you are the father of that child."

"I may be and I mayn't." His Devon drawl was thick and slow. "Fact is, he's looking to gain me for cheap labour and I ain't having any. If I marry her, he'll work the living daylights out of me for scarce any pay and I'll have a wife and child to feed besides. I like what bit of freedom I got. I won't say I didn't touch her, but I won't say I were the first."

"Oh, Ned!" There was a renewed burst of tears from Elsie.

Josephina directed a wrathful glare at Venables, but he continued, oblivious of her chagrin.

"Well, Ned, perhaps you can tell us just what did happen."

"Is that really necessary?" Josephine intervened swiftly, not wishing for the lurid details of the rural romance.

"I believe it is, if we are to get to the root of the matter," was Venables' laconic reply.

"Well, it was this way, me lord. We were getting the fields ready for planting this spring. The ground was awful hard and it weren't easy, I can tell you. Anyway, we finally got the job done and they sent out some cider and bread and cheese from the farm, and she brought it out." He nodded his head in Elsie's direction. "We sort of got talking like, and I drank a bit and she did too. I weren't drunk, mark you. Anyway, it sort of got dark and we were sitting by the hedge on the grass, and I went to get up, and . . . well, I sort of fell against her like, and . . ." His voice trailed off, and he cast a doubtful look in Josephina's direction.

"I think we've heard quite enough, Ned," she said firmly. "You do not in fact deny your part in this business."

"Miss Trafford," Venables observed disarmingly, ignoring her flush of anger, "I do think Ned should be allowed to tell his side completely. We should not put words in his mouth."

Ned looked from one to another with even greater dubiousness, but he continued slowly, "Well, we sort of fell, and there she were and there I were, sort of on top of her like, and it were dark and then she didn't seem to mind and . . . well, one thing led to another . . ." His voice trailed off again. "Well, me lord, that's about it, but what I'm saying is that I don't know that I were the first."

"Oh, Ned!" Elsie's sobs were renewed at a louder pitch. Venables answered Josephina's indignant look with an innocent smile.

"Is it his baby?" Josephina demanded of Elsie.

"Yes, miss," she replied between sobs.

"Well," Venables said, getting up, "I don't think this is any insurmountable problem if you young people like one another at all."

Ned allowed as how he liked Elsie quite a bit, and Elsie, on hearing this, nodded, her head still in her hands.

"I take it your main concern, Ned, is that Trummock should not take advantage of your labour by paying you insufficiently, isn't that so?"

"That, me lord, and the fact there's no place to live. I certainly don't want to move in here."

"If I should arrange for you to have a cottage on my estate and for you to work for me and be paid a reasonable living wage, with the understanding you will be free to help Trummock a specified number of days at planting and harvest, could we then wish you joy?"

Ned smiled for the first time that day. "Couldn't you just."

Even Elsie stopped crying and got up and went over to Ned. Venables shook them both by the hand and called for her parents to come back in.

Their joy was unconcealed. Mr. Trummock shook Venables' hand several times, pronouncing him to be just like his father, and said he would see the parson without delay. They were pressed to take a glass of wine, but Josephina protested, saying she was needed at home. Venables, however, insisted on drinking the health of the young couple, and he even helped select a date for the wedding and promised a christening gift for the child. Then, advising Ned to see Belding, Venables helped Josephina into his curricle, ignoring the fact that she sat as far away from him as she possibly could and flicked her skirts with impatience.

"A fine young couple," he said cheerfully as they drove off. "I think they'll be happy, at least as happy as that father of hers will allow them to be. Poor Elsie, I wonder if these are the hedges where she met her downfall."

It was all too much for Josephina, the embarrassment of the morning and his cheerful attitude. She felt so angry that she was close to tears.

"Lord Venables, your want of conduct in asking me to accompany you on such a mission is unpardonable. This was no matter to be discussed before a lady . . . or a gentleman . . . well, what I mean is, with both of us. It was wrong. It should not have been discussed before me while you were in the room. You knew what the matter was, yet you insisted I come. It was a matter you could handle perfectly well yourself, in fact you probably have great experience in such affairs, and despite your protestations, you seem to get along famously with your tenants. I have no idea why you asked me to come, except to embarrass and humiliate me."

"Well, well, well!" He seemed nonplussed for a moment. "I thought you were disturbed, but I didn't know you were quite so angry. In truth, I had forgotten what Trummock wanted when I asked you to come, but even had I remembered, I should still have asked you, so it doesn't signify. I find it hard to believe that this is not a matter for your ears, for Mr. Carew tells me that the majority of village brides come to his altar in such condition, and you must have to deal with it often yourself. It is unlike you to hide behind the epithet 'lady.' You freely discuss fertilizing the land and cross-breeding of stock. Why is this so different?"

"It is different and you well know it." Her eyes were gleaming with anger. "I am sorry if my past conduct has led you to think of me other than as a lady. I am a gentleman's daughter and should hate to be supposed otherwise. I am afraid my emancipated way of speaking has given many wrong impressions. I gathered as much from Sir Harlan last evening."

"What did he say to you?" he asked quickly.

"He only extended a veiled invitation to his estate in his wife's absence."

"The devil he did." His mouth was set in a straight line; then he continued slowly. "I have never questioned your being a lady. I merely said that you should not hide behind the word as a code of conduct. You can be yourself completely, and no one can doubt that you are a lady.

"But in bringing me here to listen to this . . . this rural courting in your presence, I was embarrassed and demeaned. You would not have asked a lady of rank—Lady Eliza, for instance—to accompany you on such a mission."

"No, I would not have asked Lady Eliza to come, though I assure you she would have been quite willing to do so. I would not ask her, but not for the reason you give—because she is a lady of rank—but because she lacks understanding. Well, I have wondered what it would take for you to lose that precious composure of yours, and now, I suppose, I have found out." He reined the horses and held out his hand to her. "I am truly sorry if I offended you. Come, let's be friends again."

But she refused her hand, turning her head away, and he leaned over and put his hand under her chin, drawing her face around towards him and looking into her troubled eyes. Then he said slowly, "Well, if you insist on being treated like Eliza . . ." and he took her swiftly and forcefully into his arms and brought his mouth down upon her with great deliberation. She struggled against him initially, but against all her wishes an unexpected emotion gripped her with such force that it made her forget everything but his lips moving softly but insistently from her mouth, across her closed eyelids, over her brows; then, pushing back her bonnet, he kissed her hair, loosening it till it fell like a shawl around her. As he kissed her lips again, earnestly and demandingly, she felt a passion such as she had never known before. Without knowing what she did, her arms encircling his body, she pressed him to her and returned his kisses without restraint.

It was not until a rustle in the hedgerow startled the horses, making them stir, that he released her to tighten the reins and calm them; then he turned back and took hold of her shoulders caressingly, his eyes holding hers.

"We can never be just friends, you and I." He ran his hand softly over her hair. "Do you know your eyes are quite green again?"

She said nothing, at once aware of her dishevelled appearance, her quickened heartbeat, and the blood still racing through her veins. She vividly recalled not only his kisses but also her own as she attempted to put her hair in order and smooth her dress. She must have been mad.

"Would you please take me home." Her voice sounded oddly small and distant.

"My dear one . . ." He took her hand, but she pulled it away.

"I am not your dear one. Will you please take me home—now." She picked up her bonnet and put it on, tucking in the recalcitrant locks impatiently, not daring to look at him. He, however, kept his eyes upon her thoughtfully for a time; then, without further argument, he started the horses at a slow trot.

They were silent till he asked, without looking at her, "Tell me, was that the first time you have been kissed?"

She thought of George Ridgeway's fumbled attempts under the mistletoe at Christmas; they seemed unrelated to what she had just experienced.

"In such a fashion, yes, it was," she replied.

"My God! What is wrong with the stalwart Ridgeway? He is even more of a fool than I thought."

"George," she said primly, "is a family friend and has been since my childhood."

"I believe he considers himself something more, judging from the way he hung around your skirts last night."

"He may think . . ." She broke off."I really don't have to discuss George Ridgeway with you. At least he does not take me for a country wench. His conduct is that of a gentleman at all times."

"I have told you before what I think of a gentleman's code; you should not expect it of me now. If he cares for some artificial set of values, that is his affair, but how dull! I didn't kiss you taking you for a country wench, but because you are exceptionally charming. You should be so kissed, and often."

Josephina felt her colour rising again. She was conscious of her own behaviour as much as his, perhaps more so. The shock of finding herself capable of such uncontrollable passions was unnerving. Realizing they were advancing towards Westlands at a snail's pace, she admonished him, "This team moved fast enough this morning, my lord. Can they not go at a sprightlier pace now?"

"They may have overtired themselves." His eyes twinkled mischievously. Glancing up at the cloud formation in the sky, he suddenly put out his hand. "Dear me, I do believe we may be in for a little rain—that is, if the wind continues in this direction—southeast, I think. Let me see . . ." He licked the tip of his finger and extended it to feel the current of air. "Ah, I was right, it blows from the southeast. However, should it change and move in a northerly direction . . ."

Josephina laughed despite herself at his imitation, but reproached him, "You are being unkind."

"I know I am. I intended to be so. I do not like him, you know. I find him excessively dull and it irks me that he should hang around you as he does."

"That is no concern of yours."

"Not now, perhaps," he replied, and was silent until they neared the driveway to Westlands; then he turned and said, "Perhaps I should not have taken you with me this morning, but I am glad I did. I would not for the world have changed it."

"I found your conduct totally reprehensible," she said stiffly.

"It was," he agreed.

"You behaved no better than Ned Wade," she scolded.

"And you responded in much the same way as Elsie Trummock, and it was beyond all delight, and proves you were right this morning when you said we all have the same wants and desires."

She had invited such a comment, but felt no less angry when it came.

"You take me for a country hoyden, sir."

"I take you only for what you are, an attractive, intelligent, and very desirable woman."

They were now before her front door, and she jumped down without waiting for him to alight and assist her, with a terse "Good day to you, sir."

"Don't forget, Miss Trafford, you are engaged to play cards at Venarvon this evening. I shall send my carriage at seven."

But she had swept into the house and slammed the door shut behind her, and he was left looking pensively at the brightly polished door knocker swinging vigorously back and forth.

10

But Josephina did not play cards at Venarvon that night.

When she arrived home she went straight to her room to fling herself across her bed, allowing the tears she had so long held back to flow, until a light knock at the door signalled Prudence had heard her, at which she assured her sister she was all right and would soon be down. But though she got up, she did not go downstairs; instead she stood staring at her tear-drenched face and swollen eyes in the looking glass. Her eyes were dark, deeply troubled, her brows drawn tightly together, while an occasional sob broke from her parted lips. How long she stood looking at herself, she did not know, but at last she put a cool, wet cloth to her eyes, then slowly removed her dress and hung it in the cupboard, pulling on a loose robe.

She stood at the window brushing her long brown hair, wondering what had happened to her that morning, what it was that had possessed her to act in such a fashion. It was beyond all reason. She had behaved like a woman possessed. She felt the emotion again and shuddered. How could she have been so wanton, so careless, so . . . so free?

Though his behaviour had been unconscionable, it was her own that mortified her. Had she resisted him, she would not now feel the remorse from which she was suffering. It was the fact that she had surrendered herself to him—no, not just that she had merely surrendered to him, but that she had actively sought him, returning his kisses with a passion she did not know herself to possess; it was that which caused her anguish. She had never before felt such emotions and she knew not how to deal with them. She was convinced that she never again wished to see the man who had caused them, conscious, even as she made the vow, of his palpable presence in her thoughts. Again she felt the texture of his coat under her hand, and beneath it the powerful muscles of his arms and shoulders, the demanding pressure of his lips on hers. Would it never go away?

She sat down in the window seat, the window open and the breeze billowing the chintz curtains around her, gazing down at the apple orchard that lay behind the house, neatly pruned, awaiting next year's blossom and abundant harvest. She clasped her arms around her body, quiet now except for an occasional heavy sigh. She ran her hands down her arms, across her breasts, down her flat stomach to her thighs and knees. She had never paid much attention to her body, apart from being aware that it must be fed, cleaned, and clothed. Now it had assumed a new perspective with capacities of which she had never dreamed, a living essence in its own right.

When next Pru came, shortly before dinner, Josephina was dressed, and though pale and drawn, she managed a smile in an attempt to remove her sister's worried frown.

"I'm sorry, Pru. I just seem to have an attack of nerves or something. Perhaps it's this long spell of warm weather that has upset me. I'm just not feeling myself."

This did nothing to alleviate Pru's worry; in fact it increased it; had it been her mother talking, she might have believed the explanation, but not from Jo. She made no comment, realizing her sister did not want to talk, and she caught the appreciative glance Jo gave for her unquestioning acceptance of her palpable lie.

"Are you sure you are up to coming to dinner?" Pru asked.

"Yes, as long as you promise to serve me only a morsel. I would rather come than bear mother's catechism."

Prudence put her hand to Jo's forehead.

"You are deathly cold, Jo. I really think you should be in bed. Let me call Rogers in to see what he thinks."

"I don't need the apothecary, I assure you. I shall feel quite myself soon, and I shall retire after dinner. Pru, please put that frown from your face. I'm all right, I assure you, though I won't deny there have been days when I felt better."

The two sisters descended the stairs together, Josephina leading the way, feeling a sinking sickness that contrarily seemed to come from her mind rather than from her churning stomach.

Mrs. Trafford was full of her day at the Nethertons' and all the comments that had been made about last night's ball.

"And going out again tonight, I told Lady Netherton that we are in a positive social whirl. She has taken a great preference for Lord Venables and I'm sure now she wishes she were as close to Venarvon as we are, for there was not a single remark today about the fact that we lived so far out in the country. She thinks he is the handsomest man she has seen, and you know she was with Fanny in London for the whole season two years ago. She thought he showed quite a preference for you, Josephina?" There was no ignoring the pliant, questioning tone; it hovered in the air, not to be dissipated until a response was made.

"Did she?" was all Josephina would allow. The meal was turning into another agony. If she ever had children, she resolved she would never make attendance at meals compulsory. Without hunger it was a diabolical ritual.

"Yes, she did." Her mother was not to be put off.

"Well, she is such a perceptive woman, I fear she observed more than is there." Josephina endeavoured to keep all emotion from her voice.

"She told me that you were out on the terrace with him?"

Amelia's eyes flew to Josephina's. She could not understand why neither of her sisters had yet taken her aside for the wigging she was sure was coming. Josephina paused to reflect, for the first time, that she had, herself, indulged in the very same behaviour for which she had so heavily censured her younger sister.

"That is true," she told her mother. "I was there with Amelia and Captain Williams. Amelia felt slightly faint with the heat, and Lord Venables came to see if we needed anything, as any good host might."

She surprised herself by the way the lies rolled from her tongue, and studiously ignored Amelia's grateful expression. It was not so much the untruths that disturbed her, though she had never made a practice of lying, but it was the ease with which she uttered them. They must have sounded more plausible than the truth, for there were no further questions on that topic from her mother, who returned to a discussion of clothes, commenting that with their limited wardrobes they would have no difficulty deciding what to wear that evening.

Josephina braced herself for an argument.

"I am afraid I do not feel well. I cannot go to Venarvon this evening. I have been unwell for most of the afternoon and plan to go right to bed after dinner. I trust you will convey my apologies."

Prudence hastened to add her corroboration of Josephina's state of health, but her mother's protests had already begun.

"But you must go, Josephina, you are expected. I daresay they have tables set for cards; to be one short will put them out."

"I am sure they will be able to manage. They can play another game, or someone may not wish to play. I don't believe my absence will upset their arrangements."

"They may think it rude. After all, you were perfectly well last night. Now, don't be missish. Go and lie down for an hour and I'm sure you will feel better. I'll send Rose for my vinaigrette, and I have a little of Rogers' tonic left, I think. Don't bother to finish your meal. Go up now and I'm sure you will soon be all right. The carriage will be here at seven."

Josephina thankfully left the table, but she was adamant in her refusal to stir from the house that evening, despite her mother's pleadings, entreaties, and threats.

Prudence came in before she left to see whether her sister needed anything.

"See if you can sleep, Jo. You'll feel better in the morning."

Josephina could not sleep, nor did she feel better the following morning. She toyed with the idea of staying in bed, but she could not give in to such indolence. She did, however, wish to keep away from anyplace where she was likely to meet Venables. She decided to ride over to Trentor and see Mr. Bracewaite.

It was peaceful to be in Mr. Bracewaite's company; he reminded her of her father, a scholarly, gentle man, though he was much more practical than her father had ever been. Now over seventy, he had the stride and bearing of a much younger man. Together they went again to look over the merinos, and for a time she forgot her personal feelings in speculation of the profit that might be derived from a sizeable flock. It was little over ten years since the first merinos had been brought into England by George the Third, but they had not become popular in time of war, when sheep were being raised for their mutton yield rather than the quality of their fleece. The market for fine wool continued to exist, however, and there were few to supply it.

"These are now almost three years old," Mr. Bracewaite said as they watched them grazing. "They mature a little later than our cheviots, but they have the advantage of increased longevity, and though they may not be as prolific breeders, they counterbalance it by breeding to a greater age. This is the type I would recommend you to choose—that is, if you decide on them."

He indicated a ewe and pointed out her head, smaller than that of the ram, but broad above the eyes and wedge-shaped.

"The back should be wide and straight and the neck short

and fat," he said. "Look for short, strong legs and long hind-quarters. Feel the wool on this one."

The fleece was dense and smooth under her hand, the wool about two inches in length, even over the entire body.

"I really want to get them, Mr. Bracewaite," she said earnestly.

"What you should do after a season or so is to cross-breed. Lots of experiments have been made in selective breeding. What we're after is greater size and weight of fleece; the one on that ram weighs maybe twelve pounds, maybe a little more. That's more than twice the weight of one from our breeds. If you decide to try it, I'll put you in touch with people I know in Leicestershire and Norfolk. You know that Robert Bakewell of Dishley bred such a tremendous ram, the Two-pounder they called him, that he could let him for a thousand guineas and upwards a season, and he had people standing in line for his use. It could be done here."

She returned home that afternoon having committed herself to the purchase of the sheep. She would raise the money somehow. Her mother greeted her with the news that Venables had called and waited almost an hour for her that morning.

"Why didn't you say you were going to Trentor? I felt most uncomfortable—first you are too ill to go out of the house and then you stay out all the next day. You do provoke me. Are you hiding something from me?"

"No, Mother, of course not. I felt much better today. Last night I made the decision to buy Mr. Bracewaite's merinos and I went over to tell him I would raise the money by the end of November."

"Oh, Josephina, I do wish you wouldn't. I think it is foolish borrowing money for animals. Why don't you buy yourself some clothes instead? These old things you wear in the house are shameful. Suppose you had been wearing that blue dress you have on now when Lord Venables came today. You are quite a good-looking girl if you would only take care of yourself; otherwise you'll never get anyone to take an interest in you."

"It is neat and clean, and I see nothing wrong with it." Josephina had no wish to pursue Mrs. Trafford's line of thought. "Please pass the bread."

Prudence thought that the ride had improved Josephina's appetite somewhat, but she still looked decidedly pale. She wanted to talk to her sister, for she had exciting news, but it must wait until they were alone.

At seven Josephina announced she was going to bed early again, as she was still not quite herself, and when Pru knocked at her door a few minutes later she found her sister stretched on the bed, fully clothed, staring at the ceiling.

"Do you feel like talking to me, Jo?"

"I must, Pru, because I know I have been acting strangely these past two days and it is unfair to you. I am stupid to feel as I do, so hopelessly emotional, and over such a silly thing. It was my own behaviour that vexed me most, too." And she briefly outlined what had occurred the previous day, mentioning only as little as necessary in order to convey the idea of her distress. Despite the lack of detail, Pru was shocked.

"It was wrong for Lord Venables to take you to the Trummocks' on such an occasion, and he should never have taken such liberties with you on the way back. I begin to think that people must be right in calling him a reprobate, yet it is hard to believe when you talk to him. He seems so kind and solicitous."

To her own surprise, Josephina found herself coming to Venables' rescue.

"But don't you see, Pru, it is my own behaviour that I fault as much as his, even more so. I must have behaved in a manner to invite such attentions—but the worst part of it is that when he kissed me I did not stop him."

"How could you, Jo? If he was determined to kiss you, there was little you could do. He is at fault. His were not the actions of a gentleman, yet even he I can understand, for you are very attractive. I suppose he could not resist the temptation."

"But I also did not resist temptation. It is my own lack of resistance that concerns me. I think I never want to see him again, yet I think it is because I cannot trust myself to be tempted."

"Jo, don't say such an awful thing. You are so strong. You wouldn't give in to mere . . ."

"Mere what?"

"Mere . . ." Pru searched for the word she wanted. "Mere concupiscence."

Despite herself, Jo had to laugh. She sat up on the bed.

"Concupiscence . . . I had never thought of it in such Sunday-sermon terms . . . but that is what I can pray for on Sunday: Lord, give me freedom from concupiscence."

"I am glad to see you laugh again; now you look more like yourself." Prudence looked happy. "I am truly sorry to hear that Lord Venables behaved in such a manner, for he has been most kind to Charles. He has given him the living at Flaxhurst—it belongs to Blenhasset, his Gloucestershire estate. It is a good income and the house is quite large and just outside the estate gates. He says the country there is beautiful and the climate equally as good—even better than ours. It is a wonderful thing for Charles, not that he doesn't deserve it, but it came as a surprise. Lord Venables told him he had been looking for a long time for someone to occupy the living. Since the rectory is so close to the estate, he didn't want anyone whom he might find incompatible living in his pocket. He hates prating clergymen. He is most impressed with Charles, I know, for he told me so last night. They liked one another from the start."

"Pru, that is marvellous. I am so happy for you."

"For Charles, not for me."

"I think it will be for you too, Pru, for I am sure he will propose. I could see it in his eyes the night of the ball."

Josephina continued to stay away from the house for the next few mornings, one day going over to Torbridge to talk to Frank Ridgeway about raising money to buy the merinos, thus missing another visit by Venables, though he stayed only long enough to leave a book of poetry he said he had promised her. No such promise had been made, but rather than protest, she took the book and put it away in a drawer in her room without looking at it.

The visit to the attorney's office had been discouraging, for the interest on the loan would be higher than she had expected. Frank said that since the estate was still in debt it would be no easy matter to find ready money, so that the higher rate of interest was necessary to make the note attractive. He was not at all encouraging, thinking the merinos far too esoteric an endeavour for her undertaking, but his very arguments made her firm in her resolve. It was a risk, she knew it was a risk, and she was intent upon taking it. She was determined to plunge into something that would require all her concentration and energy. So, against her attorney's advice, arrangements were made to procure the money without delay.

In a tone of voice that would brook no argument, she told her mother and sisters of the arrangement when she returned, and then left Prudence to bear her mother's wrathful comments on useless expenditures and rebukes on plunging the estate into debt.

"Your father would never have allowed such a thing. I

know he would never have gone into debt to simply waste all that money on sheep, such stupid creatures. I fail to understand your sister at all, but it's useless for me to talk. She never listens."

There was no way for Josephina to avoid church on Sunday, and she knew Venables would be there. Sunday mattins for the Traffords was as compulsory as prompt attendance at the dinner table, to be missed only in cases of severe illness or catastrophe. Though Josephina was still pale and drawn, she knew her health was not sufficiently impaired to excuse her from church, and in truth, she wanted to go, for she enjoyed the service; the familiar intonations and responses comforted her, and she grew calm in the dim interior lit only by the rays of light shining through the high windows and reflecting on the ancient screens above the altar and on the oak pulpit with its canopied niches holding paintings of the apostles. The high pews gave a sense of privacy, and as she knelt in that which had belonged to her family for over a century, she was aware of a sense of peace. It was not long-lasting, unfortunately, for as she sat down she saw the back of Venables' head in the family pew ahead of theirs. She held her prayer book firmly and resolved to keep her eyes on that throughout the service, a promise which, for the most part, she kept.

The sermon was given that morning by Charles Carew. He took as his subject "Faith in Peace and in War," a topic of personal concern to him and on which he spoke so well and so persuasively that Josephina's esteem for him rose higher than ever. She cast a glance at her sister's face and saw such happiness and admiration there, it was easy to understand her feelings for him. For a brief instance she experienced a pang of envy.

Charles stood by his father in the vestry after the service to receive the congratulations and well wishes of the parish on his sermon and on his new living. As Josephina left the church she saw him in conversation with Lord Venables and determined to save her congratulatory remarks on his sermon until she saw him at dinner that evening, for the Carews were to dine at Westlands. However, as she started to leave, Venables called to her, asking whether she had not found the sermon thought-provoking and profound, and she turned back and extended her hand to Charles, remarking that it had, indeed, been one of the best sermons she had ever been privileged to hear. She was aware of Venables examining her face as she spoke, and when she turned to allow her mother to greet Charles, he caught her elbow and drew her aside.

"You look very pale." His grey eyes searched her face.

"I have not been feeling quite well." She kept her eyes lowered, not trusting herself to meet his gaze.

"I'm sorry, but when may I see you? When will you be home?"

"Please, don't. I would rather not see you."

"I cannot talk to you here, and I must see you," he insisted.

"Later, perhaps, but not now."

And she turned to follow her mother from the church, inadvertently cutting Lady Netherton, who later remarked to her daughter that Josephina Trafford was getting awfully stuck up now she had attracted the attention of Lord Venables, and she couldn't see what he saw in her, she looked so colourless and dull.

The Carews arrived in the early afternoon and a walk was proposed. Mr. and Mrs. Carew decided to remain inside with Mrs. Trafford, but the rest set forth. Charles and Prudence soon outdistanced the others, who were strolling together, Martha and Mildred both extolling the praises of their brother to Josephina, a willing listener, and to Amelia, who had been unusually quiet since the night of the ball. Josephina preferred the slower pace, since she intended to stay within the confines of the park. The girls arrived home first, and Josephina was crossing the hall after removing her pelisse when Charles and Prudence came in. One look at her sister's face told her all she had suspected. Pru was flushed and a little breathless, but quite obviously ecstatically happy. She saw her sister and her blush deepened. Charles, at her side, looked down at her and then came over to Josephina.

"Please be the first to wish us joy. Your sister has just now done me the honour of consenting to become my wife. I am glad that you are the first to hear the news, for I know you are not only her sister but her nearest and dearest friend. I must go now and tell the news to the others, but first I must ask your mother's permission."

Josephina accompanied Prudence to her room and heard her rapturous account of the proposal and of her response and of how she had felt at the time. It was altogether too much, for she broke into tears, as did Josephina, hugging her sister close to her.

"Prudence, I can't tell you how happy I am for you. It is all I could wish for you, and more, for I love him as though
102

he were a true brother to me. He is such a fine young man, I feel there is no compliment you could pay him in which I would not heartily concur. Such happiness will be yours, to have a home of your own and a devoted husband with which to share it, but it is no more than you deserve. To call you an angel is too much, yet I know of no other description for you."

As Josephina descended the stairs, she could hear the congratulatory remarks from the front parlour, where the Carews and her mother were sitting, and she was reminded that Pru, by the terms of her father's will, should receive her marriage portion. Instead of joining the party, she went into her study to think. She could take the money she had borrowed for the merinos and give it to Pru, but without that investment with its possible gain, how could she repay the note when it became due? She could ask the newly affianced couple to wait, but felt that unfair. She decided that evening to lay it all before Charles and Pru and to get their opinion.

As she suspected he might, Charles would not hear of her going into debt for Pru's settlement. He insisted that his living was good and that he had a small amount saved, and promised that when Josephina was able to do so without hardship he would then accept the money, but not before. Josephina, however, would not agree to such altruism. After much discussion, primarily persuasion on Josephina's part, it was decided that upon marriage Prudence would receive one thousand pounds, with another thousand to be paid the following year, and the remainder thereafter. Though Charles and Prudence both protested the necessity of any legal agreement, Josephina insisted that Frank Ridgeway should draw up the arrangement; they only agreed when she explained that to have the matter so settled would help her future planning.

11

Conniston Venables had never been in love, or he had never been out of love—it depended on whose account was being followed. The cause of his leaving home, however, had made him despise the chains of matrimony. Where possible, he had avoided single, eligible young ladies, whose mamas he found both intrusive and pushing, while the girls themselves were shy or boring—worse yet, both—so that their fresh good looks did not tempt him to concede his freedom, especially to one of whom it was possible to discover little in the restrictions of courtship. He had had one attempt made to tie him to one he did not want; he resisted all others.

Soon after he arrived in Jamaica, he became aware that his looks, his manners, and his noble connexions made him desirable to the opposite sex. He also became aware that there were many fascinating women with complacent husbands not altogether unwilling that their wives should take him as a lover. The arrangements with such women were entirely satisfactory, for they were women of experience, in which he was then lacking, and they were women who enjoyed his youth and vigour, yet who were not demanding of his time. The only inconvenience he discovered in such pleasant intrigue was that of putting an end to an affair. He hated tears and recriminations, and though an expensive piece of jewellery helped smooth troubled waters, it did not always prevent a scene. He concluded, however, that these partings were preferable to marriage with any one of those companions, delightful though their hours together had been, and, strangely enough, after the affairs ended, the women he had loved usually remained his friends.

When he returned to England he had resumed his close kinship with his sister, and she, pleased no doubt that her second son was named his heir, assumed the role of intermediary with unwanted paramours. Most of the ladies were, if not close friends of hers, at least those who moved in her circle of acquaintance, and it was not difficult for her to have a close chat at the end of which it became abundantly clear that the affair was at an end. The lady was usually understanding, the parting gift was outrageously expensive and therefore mollifying; the affairs were thus successfully concluded.

Josephina was the first marriageable woman to whom Venables had paid serious attention, and then he had done so because she was unlike other women he knew, so thoroughly independent. Initially he found her charm over him puzzling. She was not above average in looks and her manner was open and simple rather than distinguished. Her dress could by no means be described as fashionable, and to have her on one's arm was not immediately to invite envious glances. Yet she intrigued him. She had a ready understanding and wit and knew when to talk and when to listen, and when she talked, it was with reason. She was well-informed and well-read and her interests were varied. The crux of the matter was that she never bored him. But it was not until he had kissed her and felt her body literally awaken in his arms with a flood of passion, surprising and delighting him, that he knew that he could think of no one else and that he had found the woman with whom he wished to spend his life. He was surprised to find himself filled not only with thoughts of passion toward her but also with great tenderness and a desire to cherish and protect her, emotions lacking from his other numerous affairs.

The solution seemed simple. Though the idea of proposing marriage was daunting, he decided that marriage it must be. But first he had to be rid of Eliza. He had enjoyed her company, she was bright and brittle and very beautiful, but for a long time their affair had lit no spark in him and he resented the way in which she had become increasingly possessive since they had been in Devon. He was spurred to immediate action by his fury at the clandestine invitation her husband had extended to Josephina.

Finding Eliza alone in the saloon on the night following his visit to the Trummocks', he bluntly informed her that their affair was at an end. It was done baldly, without a great deal of grace, and he was aware of it and aware of his own impatience to be rid of her.

She looked up at him with narrowed eyes. "So, the little farmer has finally got you, has she?" she drawled.

He ignored her remark. "I am sorry if I was abrupt, Eliza. We have enjoyed one another and have had good times together, but we both knew it would end, and it is as well now as any other time."

"But it is now because of the little farmer, is it not?"

He stretched out his legs and looked at the toes of his shoes; then, suddenly reminded of Ned Wade, who had found his boots so fascinating at the Trummocks', he looked at her directly and said, "If you mean by that descriptive remark Miss Trafford, then you are right."

"How sweet! How too, too bucolic! I can see you two frolicking in the meadows, bringing in the cows and spreading whatever it is with that machine of hers that she prates about. You will have to change your garb, my dear, perhaps a smock would be more in order. Weston has done so well with your coats, I wonder if he can't be persuaded to run up a few for you. And a staff—of course you will need a staff."

He let her prattle on, and she saw she was not getting through to him as she wished.

"You know, it would really be preferable if you persuaded her to marry that heavyset son of the squire who is always panting at her heels, you know the one, the eclectic dancer. Then you could come back next year and enjoy her company. Undoubtedly she would welcome you. Indeed, after six months with such a husband, I'm quite sure boredom would cause her to welcome suits far less desirable than yours. Such an arrangement would be far less permanent. I know the unalterable laws of the Medes and the Persians have little appeal for you. You abhor constancy."

Had she been a man, he would have hit her, but he recognized, with some sense of shame, that she had voiced a thought that had occurred to him when first he had met Josephina, that it was a pity she had no complacent husband in the background. Now the thought of her living with another man he found unbearable.

He got up abruptly. "I think you have said quite enough, Eliza, and I really have nothing else to add. Go to Gray's when you get back to London—pick out whatever bauble you like, make me pay for my ill manners."

Eliza lost no time in communicating the gist of their discussion to Francesca, who was, indeed, concerned. The depth of her brother's feelings, the seriousness of his intent, were conveyed in the fact that he had himself dismissed Eliza, with not a word to her. Though she did not dislike Josephina, in fact she found her quite frank and unaffected, she had no wish to have her as a sister-in-law. Such a woman was no wife for her brother, especially now that he had inherited

106

land and title. If he wished to marry, there were plenty of choices, all far more beautiful, far more eligible. There was nothing to be gained by the alliance, and everything to lose. She made up her mind to do everything within her power to stop it. It was not that she did not wish her brother happiness, she did, but she could not understand why he could not be just as happy with the daughter of a duke with a handsome fortune as with the penniless daughter of a country gentleman. If that were his choice, she would prefer he remain single and let her son inherit his wealth.

She consoled Eliza as best she could, assuring her that though she did not think the match would ever come about, that it would be preferable if she and Harlan returned to London to await them there.

A tearful Eliza departed the following day with her husband; it was a departure that left Venables outwardly unmoved.

His plans had been upset by Josephina removing herself from his path. Though he could not altogether understand her reticence, he did not consider his suit endangered by it. He informed his sister of his intention of offering marriage to Josephina and was surprised and hurt at the coldness of her response.

"I like Josephina Trafford, Conn, she's a sweet, unaffected woman, but for the life of me I cannot understand why you would want to marry her," she protested.

"I happen to be in love with her."

"Oh, Conn, of all the reasons to give, that is the most ridiculous. Being in love is for children, it's sentimental and foolish," she scorned.

"I have always admitted to being sentimental. I have not before thought of myself as foolish, but perhaps I am," was his laconic reply.

Francesca tried another tack. "But have you fully considered how unfair you are being to her? You see her now on her own ground, where she shows to whatever advantage she may possess. But how will she fit in in London, in our own circles? She will be received as your wife, but will she enjoy it? And if she does not, would you enjoy being confined to the country?"

Her argument was persuasive and one he himself had considered. Josephina had made plain her dislike of town life, but his feelings for her and her own response to him convinced him that was not of great import.

"I don't think it signifies. I believe we shall develop our own way of life."

Despite his assurance, she thought she had gained a point, if only a small one, so she continued. "I had not realized that you had marriage in mind. The Duchess of Danforth approached me before I left London, you know she has a really charming girl who came out early this year and is quite the rage, Daphne. You met her at the Carltons' rout and she is quite fallen for you. The Duchess asked if you were inclined towards marriage, but I told her you were quite set against it."

"And so I am, in that way, but not in the way I feel now. Can you not see the difference, Francesca?"

But she could not, except that she considered the present alternative very much worse.

"I wish you would wait, Conn—you have scarcely known Josephina Trafford a month. That's not very long."

"A month in the country is long enough to become intimately acquainted."

"Perhaps. Nevertheless, I wish you would think it over carefully before you commit yourself."

Venables considered he was having plenty of time to think it over, since it was becoming increasingly difficult for him to talk to Josephina. He determined to see her at the beginning of the week, even if it meant camping on her doorstep. She, in turn, was equally intent on not meeting with him, particularly alone. On Monday, therefore, she set out earlier than usual for Torbridge. There were the papers to draw up for Pru's marriage settlement, and she wished to know whether the money on the note was available.

Her mind was full of Prudence and the happiness in store for her, and so preoccupied was she with the difficulties in finding the extra thousand pounds a year she had promised, that she did not hear her name called until Pandora started to rear and she realized someone was grabbing at the reins. It was Farnsworth, dishevelled and unkempt, clearly the worse for drinking and in an ugly mood.

"Let go of my horse this instant you scoundrel," she commanded.

In reply he gave her an ugly leer and sneered. "Enough of that hoity-toity, Miss Trafford. I'd just like a little word with you, if you please. It's my understanding that it's you I have to thank for losing me my employ. I was doing all right at Venarvon till you came fawning around his lordship, complaining of my services and making up a lot of lies so you

108

could get his ear. I hope you realize what you've done. You've made it impossible for me to get work hereabouts. Me and my family could starve, and it's on your shoulders. Well, you lost me my job and you can get it back for me."

Josephina, though horrified by his threatening manner and the way he was pulling at Pandora's head, made every effort not to show her fear and to keep a tight hold on her whip.

"I'm sorry if you are having difficulties finding another position, but I accept no responsibility for the loss of your job at Venarvon. Your conduct alone was responsible for that. You almost ruined that estate, and if you have not feathered your own nest from the amounts you must have pocketed over the years, more's the pity. I said no more to Lord Venables than I have said for years to your face and what was obvious to any person who cared to see it. You should thank your stars you had such a long and easy time there and not complain. Given your reputation in this county, you had better go elsewhere to seek work."

"With no references, who's to give me work, tell me that?"

"I think you should have thought of that some time ago before you started your underhand dealings. You brought this upon yourself, I didn't bring it on you. You dealt harshly with Venarvon tenants over the years, perhaps now you are getting a taste of how they must have felt. I have no sympathy for you. Let go of my horse or it will be the worse for you."

But far from loosening his hold, he suddenly tugged at the reins with all his might, forcing them from her grasp.

"Worse for me, will it be, or worse for you. You are going to turn this horse around and go up to Venarvon now and use your wiles on my behalf with his lordship, and don't tell me you don't know how. I suggest you do it without further argument, for I know enough about you that you wouldn't want talked of freely around here."

Despite herself, Josephina caught her breath.

"Yes, Miss Trafford, I think you know quite well enough how to get me my job back, you don't need any instruction. If you and your family want to sleep calm at night, I suggest you don't delay about it."

"Don't you dare to threaten me—you know me well enough to realize that's to no avail. Get out of my way before I use my whip to good purpose, you rogue."

"If we're calling names, there are names I could call you. Always acting so high and mighty, lady of the manor, you're no better than any street wench when it comes down to it. I followed you the other morning when you and his lordship went out to the Trummocks'—I followed you there *and* I followed you all the way back. I seen you when you stopped in the lane and carried on like any brazen hussy, kissing and cuddling and—"

He cried out in pain as she brought her whip down hard across his leering face, and she saw a red, angry weal begin to rise before he grabbed at her leg, forcing her down from her horse, struggling with her for possession of the whip. Grasping the hand which held it, he pulled her wrist back until she cried out in pain and the whip dropped from her hand. As he bent to pick it up, she broke away, but he lunged for her, catching her arm and raising the whip with such force that she cringed to shield herself from the blow—a blow halted by a voice from behind her ordering peremptorily, "I suggest you drop that this instant."

It was Venables. In a split second he was upon the burly bailiff, landing a hard left to his jaw that sent him sprawling across the road. He started to get up, but Venables was upon him, raining blows with such force that even Josephina cried out. He looked up, and she thought she had never seen such fury in anyone's eyes.

"See to the horses," was all he said.

As she got hold of Pandora's reins and those of his mount, she heard a torrent of abuse being poured out on Farnsworth's head. She stood with her head leaning against Pandora's saddle. It was a nightmare, it couldn't be happening, but when she looked up again, it was to see Farnsworth heading down the road followed by a trail of blood, and Venables watching him depart, his coat torn almost completely from his shoulders, and a gash above his right eye bleeding profusely. He gave it no heed, however, being concerned only for her welfare, and she hastened to assure him she was unhurt.

"It will never happen again, never, that I can assure you," he said. "I will never let anyone harm you, least of all such a lowly bully. I did not prosecute him before, but now, by God, he'll not get away," he swore softly under his breath.

"Oh, no, not that." She thought of Farnsworth's words. If Venables prosecuted him, what might he say? She could see Squire Ridgeway lapping up all the salacious details. No, it must be prevented at all costs. "Please don't prosecute him ... I would rather you didn't."

"Don't tell me you would plead for a man who has attempted to murder you. I intend to see you home and then ride in and swear out a warrant for his arrest."

"I pray you, don't." She almost gave way to tears.

"Why ever not?" He was astounded. "Surely you don't feel sorry for the wretch."

"Would you not . . . if I ask you not to?" It was the nearest Josephina had ever come to cajoling a man.

He looked at her in puzzlement. "I cannot understand. You must realize that he should be prosecuted. He is a dangerous man."

"He is without work," she pleaded. "He wanted me to help him regain his position. I suppose in his desperation his feelings overcame him. Besides, after the whipping you just gave him, I doubt he'll come back for more. What use is there in hounding him?"

His eyes were still puzzled, but he said, "Very well, if that is what you wish."

He bent down and picked up her whip. "You were very brave to deal with him as you did."

"I did not deal well enough, I'm afraid. I should have used my whip sooner and kept a tighter hold on Pandora's reins. I don't know what might have happened had you not come along. I thank you for your aid." She looked up at him, suddenly shy and awkward.

"Are you sure you are all right? You looked awfully pale yesterday at church, and now this."

"I am quite all right, really I am. It is you who are hurt. You must get immediate attention for your eye before that cut opens up any more."

"That's nothing—I've had a lot worse, I can assure you," he said, mopping with his handkerchief at the blood on his cheek without great avail. "This is a strange way to meet. I've been trying to see you since Thursday, and it takes an attack on your life to make it possible. Why have you been avoiding me?"

Josephina kept her eyes fixed on the whip, twisting it back and forth in her hands. "I've been busy, that's all."

"You've been avoiding me. You know it and I know it. Don't let your honesty desert you now. Why?"

She did not reply.

"Look at me. I want to know why you are avoiding me."

She looked up reluctantly. "I didn't want to face you."

"Why ever not?"

"My behaviour the other day . . . embarrasses me." Her face grew red as she spoke.

Venables laughed. "You silly girl, what a ridiculous thing. Your behaviour the other morning was in no way to blame, it was my behaviour that caused the scene, and I have already, refused, and refuse again, to apologize for it. It is one of the most memorable mornings of my life, and I have no intention of apologizing for it, or regretting it, or forgetting it. If I treasure it, I wish you would too."

She felt he was flirting with her again and saw herself as another of his amorous conquests. "If you wish to be treated like Eliza," he had said, and that was what she was to him, another Eliza. "Let's see," she could imagine him saying years hence, "Josephina, did she come after Eliza or before her? I quite forget."

She squared her shoulders and raised her chin. "I prefer to forget it." Her voice was cold, even a trifle haughty.

"Well, I plan to see to it you never shall," he insisted. "I cannot say what I wish to now, this is not the place, nor is it the time. When may I call on you? You name the day and time, for I want to find you at home when I come. I have had several long sessions alone with your mother. I would prefer to avoid another."

She flinched as he took the whip from her hand, afraid he would hold her again, afraid she would succumb again.

"Don't worry," he assured her, "I shan't make love to you again until you ask me to."

With that he lifted her gently into her saddle, smoothing her skirt and handing up her whip.

"Since you are loath to name a day, will Wednesday at noon suit you? I would say tomorrow, but then you might counter by saying that your plans for today have been interrupted and must be carried out tomorrow. By Wednesday you can have no excuse. Now, I shall see you to your door."

12

The attack by Farnsworth had been beyond credibility, utterly horrifying, but the realization that her conduct with Venables, so distressing in itself, had been observed by another, and that that other was a tyrant of a man who despised her and who now had it in his power to destroy her good name, was far more demoralizing to Josephina. Her cold hands fled to her flaming cheeks as again she relived her actions on that return journey from the Trummocks', but now seeing Farnsworth watching it all, leering. It was beyond belief. She would not think of it, yet she thought of nothing else.

She stayed at home for the rest of the day, silent concerning the morning's occurrences. It was unthinkable to disrupt Pru's realm of happiness, and there was no one else in whom she could confide. She was quieter than usual, paler, but that went unnoticed in the rounds of congratulatory calls on Pru's engagement, where attention was all on the bride-to-be.

The following day, rather than go into Torbridge, Josephina wrote and asked Frank Ridgeway to call upon her. She was, therefore, at home when Lady Francesca Lanyon called to congratulate Pru, speaking most prettily of her liking for her and her appreciation of Charles. Though, she said, she did not personally know him well, she knew of him through his former patron, their neighbour in Yorkshire Sir John Brennan, who had nothing but praise for him, as had her brother's friend Colonel Underwood. She added that she had felt privileged to hear his fine sermon the previous Sunday, such profound thoughts so well-expressed. Nothing could have pleased Pru more.

"I am so happy to have this opportunity to give you my congratulations in person," Francesca went on, "as my husband and I leave for London tomorrow. We must collect our children and make our way to Yorkshire to prepare for Christmas. We always have a large party of friends there for the holidays and there is so much that needs attention before they arrive."

"Is Lord Venables to leave also?" The disappointment in Mrs. Trafford's voice was evident.

"Not tomorrow, but it won't be long before he does, for he is always with us at Christmas. I don't know what the children would do without him around. He spoils them outrageously, of course, but that, I suppose, is an uncle's privilege."

"We will miss all of you when you are gone. It will seem quite bleak without the excitement your visit has caused. When will Lord Venables return?" Mrs. Trafford pressed.

"That I don't know. You must realize that he has now made his home in Gloucestershire, and I know he is much set on staying there, despite his inheritance of Venarvon. I cannot speak for him, of course, but spring brings the London season, and then he will want to spend time at Blenhasset, so that I doubt he will return to Devon before next autumn."

Josephina, sitting by the window with her needlework, found it difficult to reconcile the twin feelings of relief and regret which arose in her breast. They would soon be rid of the presence that had caused her so much disturbance, but she could for once concur in her mother's feeling that the neighbourhood would lack excitement without that presence.

As Lady Francesca was leaving, she asked Josephina to take a turn about the park with her since it was such a splendid day, her last in Devon for some time to come.

The two ladies set off, if not at a brisk pace, at least with a steady stride, and were soon some distance from the house, Lady Francesca chatting of her children and her home in Yorkshire.

"I can't tell you how much we have all enjoyed renewing our acquaintance with your family. It has made our stay here so much more pleasant and endurable. And, too, you have helped us to become reacquainted with the country of our youth. Venarvon has so many memories for my brother and me."

She spoke so feelingly that Josephina, though she had not previously felt great friendship for Francesca, found herself warmed by her words.

"I am glad you have returned, albeit for a short time," she replied, "and I am pleased with the changes being made in your brother's estate. It is sad for all landlords of an area when any estate is allowed to run to neglect, but one such as Venarvon, with its vast and fertile acreage and numerous tenants, should never be allowed to decay."

Lady Francesca gave her an admiring look.

"Miss Trafford, you are an amazing young lady, so capable and yet so unassuming. I do wish you to count me among your dearest friends. I only regret that more time does not remain now for us to become better acquainted, but undoubtedly I shall visit Venarvon again next year."

She paused, then continued hesitantly. "It is because I feel tenderly towards you that I wish to confide in you a matter that has been causing me some concern, and yet I know not how to say it, or whether I should even speak of it."

Josephina was baffled by her words and tone of voice.

"If it is confidential, do not fear that I may talk of it to others, for such is not my wont. However, it may be something truly better left unsaid altogether, in which case I would urge you not to impart a word of it."

Lady Francesca seemed to be struggling with her feelings, but at last she continued. "I do not wish to cause you pain, nor do I wish you to misunderstand what I have to say, but I feel it must and should be said. It has not escaped my sisterly attention that my brother has been paying particular attention to you. He is an attractive man, but you, though charming and perceptive, are not a woman of the world and therefore you may misconstrue his intentions. I love my brother dearly—he was always my favourite brother, and now that only the two of us remain, the bond has grown strong indeed. But love him as I do, I am still aware of his faults, and it is my opinion that his overwhelming failure is in his relationships with those of our sex. It is not altogether his fault, for women give themselves so willingly to him, and he, not being averse to female companionship, enjoys their company for a time. These, however, are ladies who move within our own circles and understand his lack of fidelity, so that when his ardour cools and I acquaint them with the fact, they are not devastated by it."

Josephina, shocked, could not help exclaiming, "*You* acquaint them with the fact—but that is disgraceful!"

"It is indeed, Miss Trafford," she sighed, "but he is averse to hurting their feelings."

"But to get another—and a woman—to perform such a despicable task for him is monstrous!"

"I would never have mentioned it to you unless I feared that Conniston wished to make a conquest of you. He is a man used to having what he wants, and when he finds something unattainable, that is what he desires most of all. I fear you may be that something at the moment. Were I to think

115

that this would be a lasting passion, I would be overjoyed, for you know that I admire you. But I do not wish you to be hurt, and pray you may not be. He has never stayed with any one of them for long, indeed he seems to tire of any long-standing arrangement. When he first returned from the West Indies, I encouraged him to marry, but when I saw his inconstancy, I realized it was preferable that he did not, unless he finds someone able to live with his wandering fancy. I am convinced that you are not such a woman.

"However, he is a formidable man to withstand once he sets his mind upon obtaining something, and I am not sure you could resist him should he set out to conquer you. All I can do, since I leave before he does, is to forewarn you of his ways, in the hope that you will remember my words."

Their pace had slowed considerably during this talk, and Josephina, her hands clasped behind her, her eyes down, had grown more pale.

Lady Francesca, unobserved, examined her companion closely and felt her words had made their impact. For a moment she regretted her action, but then she thought of her son and continued. "Do not think, because of what I have said, that I do not love Conniston dearly. I do indeed, but I love him as a doting sister and can overlook his faults. He is much sought after and cannot be faulted for being devastatingly captivating. My only argument with him is when he chooses someone who could be hurt by his actions."

They had now turned back and were walking towards the awaiting curricle, and Josephina had not yet spoken, but at last as they approached the driveway she responded coldly, "I thank you for your consideration in telling me things that must have given you pain, since they concern someone dear to you."

"I am well aware that you and your brother live in a different world from my own here in Devon and that our outlook on many things is not the same. Nevertheless, country girl though I may be, Lady Francesca, I am not without intelligence and understanding and do not consider that I can be duped by the first prepossessing gentleman to cross my path. Since both you and your brother leave Milvercombe soon, I believe your fears are unfounded, but you may rest assured I shall not forget your visit."

And on this equivocal note Lady Francesca took her leave.

Josephina would gladly have forestalled Venables' visit the next day. It was possible, for the Traffords were spending the day at the rectory to discuss wedding plans. But to send him a note to that effect would only defer the meeting; she knew he was determined to see her, and little though she wished to see him, especially after his sister's visit, she told her mother she would join her later in the day at the Carews', she waited her visitor in the park.

He came, striding across the lawn towards her, and as soon as she saw him her heart sank. He held her hand as he enquired after her health, solicitously studying her upturned face. They talked of trivial matters, Josephina asking whether his sister and her husband had yet departed. He acknowledged that they had, seeming surprised she knew of their leaving, but when she told him of his sister's visit the previous day to wish Pru joy and to bid them farewell, he was gratified.

"I did not know she had come. I am indeed lucky to have such a sister. She attends to so many things and is altogether so thoughtful that I would be quite lost without her."

"So I understand," Josephina replied dryly.

"We are very close to one another now, more than we have ever been . . ." He stopped suddenly and turned to her, and Josephina, fearing an embrace, murmured, "Please . . ."

"Josephina, I have told you that I shall never repeat my caresses of the other morning, not until you signify that you wish me to do so. You may rest assured I shall keep my word."

"And you, sir, may rest assured I shall not ask it." The sharp edge to her voice nonplussed him, but he went on. "There are things I wish to say to you, but I know not where to begin."

"I suggest you try the beginning," she averred.

"Then I will. I have not known you for very long, and yet it seems forever. When I first saw you I was impressed with you as a lady of wit, beauty, and obvious capabilities. I found you different from others I have known, unassuming, with no conceit, living out your own life and allowing others to do the same without interference unless it were to help those in need. I was impressed by you and enjoyed your company, but I did not realize the intensity of my feelings for you until I found you always in my thoughts even when you were not present. When reading a book, I found myself considering what your opinion of it might be; when in conversation, I wondered how you might respond to the topic under discussion—even how you might look in some style illustrated in a magazine. You see, it was a pervasive emotion that overpowered me before I was fully aware of it. Still, I might not have

117

spoken had it not been for our ride last Thursday." Josephina was about to protest, but he held up his hand. "No, I know your feelings on that subject, but I cannot help but speak of it, for it was then that I truly acknowledged my feelings for you as being those of love rather than attraction. The way your body melted in my arms and your response to my embraces aroused in me a feeling far deeper than I had ever known—it was more than passion. I found I wanted to protect and keep you always."

"Sir . . . Lord Venables, I beg you to say no more," she interrupted in a distraught voice.

"But I must. I cannot leave it unsaid. What I have to say is essential to the future happiness of both of us. When I think of the delights that life has in store for us, my heart swells with happiness." He took hold of both her hands. "Josephina, I love you very much—I want you very much. Will you be mine?"

Despite all, she was moved by his words, by the ardour in his eyes, until she suddenly realized they were standing at the very same spot where only the day before his sister had spoken to her of his infidelities. Remembering the words: "he gets what he wants, and you are what he wants," Josephina demanded coldly, "Just what, sir, are you proposing?"

"I am asking you to marry me, of course. Did I not make myself clear? Surely you did not think I would do otherwise. I love you and want to marry you. I am sorry if my proposal was open to any other interpretation." He ran his hand through his hair in a boyish gesture. "I am sorry, but in truth I have never proposed before."

She was silent, unable to speak for a moment. In all the thoughts that had gone through her mind since his sister's visit, she never had expected a proposal of marriage. She knew there were those of far greater beauty and rank than she who would seize the chance of such an alliance, and was human enough to be flattered by it. But did he propose because the only way to attain her was by marriage? His sister had said, "When he wants something unattainable, that is what he most desires." Would he go to such lengths? And if they married, how long would it be before his sister came to her begging her indulgence for his flights of fancy? No, it could not be.

"You have never proposed marriage before, you mean." The harshness of her tone surprised even herself, but he simply answered, "No, not marriage, but I do not deny that there have been liaisons with others, if that is what you mean. It would be hard to reach my age and not be so. I do not deny it."

"It would be impertinent to ask how many of these 'others' are in your past . . ." She broke off. "Anyway, it is immaterial."

"You are right, it is immaterial, for they are in the past and need never concern you. I have done nothing of which I am ashamed."

"No, sir, it is immaterial, though not for that reason but because I do not wish to marry you; therefore, whatever you have done in the past or intend to do in the future is not my concern. I have no right to question your conduct."

He was still, as though not completely comprehending what she was saying. Then the words broke from him. "But why, why, why? Everything gave me to understand that you had some feeling for me, or at least were not indifferent to me, until this morning. If it is the fact that there have been others before you, surely you could not have expected me to have led a blameless life all this time. I have enjoyed myself, but I have never been in love before. I am in love now, in love with you, and I want to marry you. If you reject me, I think I have the right to know the reason why. I do not believe you find me . . . undesirable."

She heard the distress in his voice, she saw the anguish in his eyes, and while she wished nothing more need be said in the matter, she knew he was right, she owed him an explanation.

"You are well aware that I am attracted to you, I will not deny it, but that alone is not enough to make a marriage. I realize also that your life has led you far in the world; you have not moved in my confined circles, and your manner of living is far different from my own. I have been brought up to believe that marriage is a commitment not only of bodies made one but also of lives made one. This hardly seems to apply in the circles in which you move. Only recently I have observed the example of Sir Harlan Coningsby and his wife." She saw a slight flush darken his cheeks.

"You have also seen the example of my sister and her husband. There is nothing wanting in their relationship, is there?" he demanded abruptly.

"No, your sister and her husband well suit one another. Your sister, I believe, married young, and your brother-in-law would not seem to have a roving eye."

"And I do?"

"You do not appear to have lived as a monk since coming to Devon."

"I shall not dwell on the subject of the behaviour of monks, though I suspect on many occasions it has been little different from my own. I presume you are referring to Eliza. I do not deny that she has been, in the past, my mistress, but she is no longer."

"Ah, did you get your sister to send her packing?" It was impossible to measure the contempt in her voice, and it struck him like a whip.

He clenched his fists and turned, as if to leave, then turned back. "If you wish to know, I told her myself. From what you say it appears my sister did more than merely bid you farewell yesterday."

It was Josephina's turn to flush. "She did talk to me . . . yes."

"And I was the subject of that conversation."

"Yes."

"My dear, dear sister. What would I do without her."

"I believe whatever she said was for my good and your own."

"Or for her son's, who is my heir."

Josephina stopped short for an instant. Could that have been the motive behind her visit? Nevertheless, Venables had denied nothing his sister had said.

"Whatever her reason in speaking to me, I believe you cannot deny that our worlds are too different to allow for success of marriage between us. You can expend what to me is a fortune on the lay of a die or whether a woman will wear a bauble to a party, that to you is excitement. You could not long endure the boredom of country living, where the most exciting event in the spring is the opening of the first primrose, and I could not stand the trivia and deceit of your world, with its sordid affairs. Here we marry for a lifetime, not until the passion cools. How long would it be before your sister would come begging my indulgence for your flirtations, asking for my patience, arranging your affairs for you? Would she not fulfill the same role for your wife as she has done in the past for your mistresses?"

The flush on his face had deepened as she spoke, but his eyes had grown dark and angry; still she continued. "The lot of women in this life is not easy, particularly that of married women, who must accept the actions of their husbands without question. Men can do no wrong, they make the decisions, and their wives must abide by them. There are some things,

120

sir, which I could never abide. After your first passion had died, would you not begin to see me, as I believe your sister already does, as a gauche country girl, a little below your touch? Perhaps you might try to educate me to your ways, to a sophistication I do not have and never wish to have.

"I do not wish to marry you, sir. I prefer my single state, in which I am, to some extent, my own mistress. I can have little regard for a man who will use his own sister to discard his unwanted mistresses. I consider such conduct monstrous."

His face had grown exceedingly pale so that the scar above his eye, suffered in his struggle with Farnsworth, stood out sharply red against the pallor of his skin. His head high, the slightest curve to his lips, though it hardly justified being called a smile, he replied wryly, "I have asked for your reasons in rejecting me, ma'am, and you have, as is your style, enumerated them eloquently. You could not have spoken more plainly. In my own behalf I would say I have never used a woman against her will, nor have I done anything of which I am ashamed. If my sister has acted on my behalf, it has been at her own instigation and, I suspect, for the good of her son. I see I was completely mistaken in believing you cared for me, for, indeed, how could any woman care for the monster you describe? Please accept my apologies for troubling you. I shall not do so again. I beg to take my leave of you now, for I, too, depart for London in the immediate future. Please convey my adieus to your mother and sisters. Good day, Miss Trafford."

He turned and strode towards his tethered horse. Josephina did not look round, but moments later she heard the clatter of hooves receding down the driveway. She listened until the sound died and then walked slowly back towards the house. The wind tossed the fallen leaves around her feet as she walked, and the sky overhead was dark and threatening. She felt a large drop of rain hit her cheek, then another, and another, as though the heavens were crying as she was crying inside. The staccato of raindrops hitting the driveway became a downpour, soaking her hair and dress. The long St. Martin's summer was finally over.

13

Prudence and Charles Carew were married the week before Christmas. He was to take up his living at Flaxhurst at the beginning of the year, and they planned to stay in Bath on their way to Gloucestershire.

Pru's happiness was marred only by the knowledge that Jo would not be with her in her new surroundings. While she would have the comfort of one she loved deeply at her side, and the excitement of a new home and a new way of life, her sister would be left at home with no close companion, only her mother for company, for Amelia was to leave for London soon with Aunt and Uncle Mulliner, who would be at Westlands for the wedding. Amelia, delighted that she would be in London a month sooner than had been planned, sewed with unusual vigour, while Pru was also busy with her needle, making her wedding clothes.

Josephina willingly helped, fitting their dresses, adjusting pleats, and pinning trim, until she said she felt capable of opening an establishment of her own after their departure. Though her tone was light, she thought of the days ahead with despair. It would be lonely in the big house. She and her mother had never been close, but open hostility had always been averted by Prudence. Even had Amelia remained, it would have given her mother a companion. She wished that Mrs. Trafford could accompany Amelia to London; it was her mother's dearest wish, she knew, to return to town; but Josephina could not remain alone at Westlands, it was unacceptable and she knew of no one she could invite to stay with her in her mother's absence. Oh, for a maiden aunt who would like nothing better than to sit and nod by the fire, she thought, but no such aunt existed, so it was inevitable that they must rub along together somehow. She would miss Amelia, she realized with some surprise. Her younger sister's frivolity, though sometimes a cause of worry, was cheering and a lively source of entertainment. How would the long winter pass?

122

By the middle of December the Mulliners had joined them, full of news of London but willing listeners to the story of Pru's romance and great admirers of Charles Carew from their first meeting with him.

Isabel Mulliner was four years older than her sister, a tall, stately woman of haughty appearance with an imposing bosom carried before her with all the pride of a figurehead on the prow of a ship. Putnam Mulliner had not been a great catch when she married him; as the youngest son of a baronet whose estate in Hampshire was not large enough for him to bestow much wealth on any members of his family, his expectations were small. However, he had proved astute in the investment of what little money he had, and that, together with the marriage portion his wife brought him, he had built into a comfortable fortune. They lived well on Windham Place and they were received in society, though they did not entertain a great deal. Their two daughters had come out and achieved satisfactory marriages, and Mrs. Mulliner had so enjoyed the experience that she was anxious to repeat it with her niece.

Amelia followed her aunt around the house and was so solicitous of her every wish that Mrs. Mulliner soon pronounced her a sweet, dear little thing and said she could not wait till she introduced her at the Fotheringhams' ball in January. She was sure she would take, with her heart-shaped face and those pretty dimples.

Josephina, finding Amelia gazing at those dimples in the mirror later that day, reminded her tartly that pride is its own looking glass. She hoped the London experience would not make of her sister a flirt and a woman completely lacking in good sense.

Mrs. Trafford was glad to see her sister, though it forced her to reflect on the vicissitudes of fate. When they had married within a year of one another, it was imagined that Mrs. Trafford was the more fortunate of the two, for Mr. Trafford was well-settled on his Devon estate, compared with the impoverishment of Mr. Mulliner. Now, to see her sister dressed in the very latest fashion, attending balls and routs and calling on people in the first rank of London society, while she languished on an estate that was, and always would be, thanks to her daughter's ridiculous investments, indebted beyond relief, situated almost as far from London as was possible, was a humiliation indeed. Nevertheless, she was pleased to be able to show off her daughter's fiancé and gratefully listened to every word in his praise.

123

"It's not more than she deserves, sister, for Prudence has been a thoughtful, sweet girl all her life. There is nothing headstrong or moody in her, as, I regret to say, I find in my oldest girl. Had Josephina played her cards right, she might have been able to catch Lord Venables, for Lady Netherton swears he showed her more interest than anyone else while he was here, but she wouldn't put herself out and he went off without a word."

Mrs. Mulliner laughed. "And a very wise girl she was, too. Lord Venables is quite a notorious womanizer, not that that stops mothers from throwing their daughters at him, and especially now he has inherited the title, he has become more desirable than ever, but he pays little heed to single young ladies of good families. I'm afraid his taste runs to rather more exotic society ladies, married already, for the most part."

"Oh!" Mrs. Trafford's lips parted expectantly. "I had wondered whether there was anything between him and Lady Coningsby; she was a member of his party, but then, so too was her husband."

"My dear, of course there was. It is quite well known that they have been the closest friends for a long time, though I hear it is at an end now."

"Then I do think he was wrong in leading Josephina to think his attentions were directed toward her."

"But I thought it was Lady Netherton who said that, not Josephina."

"Well, perhaps it was, but nevertheless, she would have had her heart broken, and goodness knows she has been moody enough lately, with Pru leaving, without that."

Mrs. Mulliner, accosting Josephina later on the subject, found that although she did not actually laugh at the idea that her heart might have been broken, she gave no indication that she particularly cared one way or the other about Lord Venables.

"I am glad to find your mother was wrong in thinking your affections had been tampered with. I found it hard to credit that Lord Venables had been smitten by you, for you know the women one sees with him are always dressed to the teeth, the more notorious beauties of the *haut ton*. I do not mean to discredit you, Josephina, but you know you have no regard for your appearance. If only you would curl your hair a little, it might help. No, I can see him amusing himself in Devon, but not forming any serious attachments."

Josephina's response was noncommittal and she shortly

thereafter asked after her cousins' weddings and was regaled with all the details, her aunt very much regretting they had been unable to attend. This was shortly followed by every symptom of the morning sickness from which the eldest was now suffering, so that the subject of Venables was dropped.

Josephina was glad, though she had become accustomed to hearing his name without emotion. Her aunt's comments had, however, caused her some pain. She had reflected much about him in the past month, not regretting her action in refusing him, for she still detested his lack of principle, but admitting freely to herself that he was the most desirable albeit unscrupulous gentleman she had ever met.

One day she took her uncle over to examine the merinos she had bought, showing him the quality of the wool and indicating the desirable points of the breed. He admitted the wool was finer than any he had seen but considered livestock far too risky an investment and scolded her for having put so much money into the flock, given other pressing financial needs. She knew he was right, sometimes wondering whether her decision had not been made under an emotional stress, but she was determined, that investment having been made, that it would be a success. It was her opportunity, perhaps her sole opportunity, to free Westlands from debt and to pay her sisters' settlements; she did not intend to fail.

Her uncle had already raised the matter of Amelia's marriage portion.

"Should she receive an offer while in London, the matter is bound to arise, and I must know what can be expected," he explained.

Josephina told him of the arrangement she had made with Pru and Charles, but he looked askance at such an apportionment.

"It would depend where an offer were to come from, of course. In this case, your two families know one another, and so an easy, informal way of making such a financial arrangement is possible. However, it is unlikely those with whom Amelia will become acquainted in London will know more of her than that she is my wife's niece and hails from this estate in Devon. I should hate to make any misrepresentation on her behalf or on my own. I can say that without a portion her chances of making any desirable marriage, despite her pretty face and figure, are negligible. And to offer to pay a prospective suitor in dribs and drabs is not at all the thing." Her uncle's eyebrows met firmly across the bridge of his nose in indication of his abhorrence of such a rackety scheme.

"Well, Uncle, if I succeed, and lambing goes well this spring, I think I can say that Amelia's marriage portion is assured, that is, if she finds a gentleman of whom my mother approves."

"I would not propose any match to your mother which would not meet with her approval," her uncle sniffed.

"No, indeed, I am sure you would not," Josephina mollified hastily. "Let me say that I shall not stand in the way of Amelia's happiness. Should her hand be requested by someone whom she esteems and wants to have as her husband, I shall raise the money. I trust, however," she added with a laugh, "that no suitor will request Amelia's hand until after lambing season."

As they returned together from the meadow where the merinos grazed, her uncle spoke again of his disapproval of speculation on crops or livestock.

"There are too many things that can go wrong, acts of God over which we have no control. I wish you had asked my advice before plunging in so heavily."

Josephina put her arm through his as they walked, and smiled. "Well, I have plunged now, Uncle, and I plan to succeed. Only think, someday I may be able to get one thousand pounds for letting out my ram for the season."

"Letting him out for the season—what does that mean?"

"Stud fees. Mr. Bakewell got as much for his prime specimen."

"Really, Josephina, you really shouldn't discuss such things."

His rebuke reminded her of another chiding she had received for expressing freely her ideas on cross-breeding, yet balking at discussing human relationships. She grew silent at the recollection of that occasion.

Even before her uncle had spoken to her, Josephina knew that the coming months would be difficult. She was deeply in debt again with her merino purchase and the money for Pru, and now, as her uncle reminded her, she might have to raise the money for Amelia. If her sheep-raising endeavour were unsuccessful, she would be in a sorry plight indeed, but she had no intention of allowing that to happen. She had already spoken to merchants in Exeter and had been assured they could handle any amount she could furnish of wool of that quality; if prices were to hold to those of the preceding year, she would have a tidy amount towards Amelia's portion and she could use the sheep as collateral to raise the rest. In the coming years she anticipated the tide of her fortunes to change for the better.

126

Sometimes she wondered how it might have been to have married Venables and never again have had to worry about money, but then she reflected she would probably have had far worse troubles. It saved her from any possible regret.

The night before the wedding, Jo went to Pru's room to bid her good night. She was already in bed but wide awake.

"I don't think I'll sleep a wink all night, there is so much running through my mind."

"Happy thoughts rest easily," said Jo.

"But not all of mine are happy, Jo, for I'm thinking that we will soon be separated for the first time in our lives, and suddenly it seems unbearable."

"How so, unbearable, going off with that handsome man on your arm? If I hear any more of his praises, I think I'll have to imagine some fault he has just so that I can take a contrary view. If God had sat in his heaven and planned the perfect match, he could not have done a better job. For all I know, that is just what he did. Nothing, nothing, can be unbearable for you now, for you will never have to bear anything alone again."

"But you do, Jo, and that is what is unbearable. What are you going to do?"

Josephina, who had consistently refused to dwell on how her life would be affected by Pru's departure, made light of it.

"Anyone would think you were going to China instead of Gloucestershire," she chided. "If I imagined you to be leaving forever, I could see cause to cry, but there are a thousand reasons to bring you back here from time to time—Charles's family and your own, to name but two."

"I realize Flaxhurst is not that far away, but Charles will have the parish to attend to—I expect it may be some time before we can come back, especially as they have been without a rector for so long. But why may you not come to visit us?" Pru's blue eyes earnestly questioned her sister; it was a request Josephina had been dreading she might make. She wished desperately that Charles had any other parish but that of Flaxhurst. She would never feel free to stay there for fear of meeting the patron of that living. Perhaps "never" was too strong a word, for memories must dim, she would grow older and, perhaps, eventually wonder what all her concern had been about—but that was not her present state. She did not wish to marry Venables, his way of life was abhorrent to her, but she was not indifferent to him. Until she could feel such indifference, she much preferred not to see him. But still, she hated to refuse her sister's request.

Gently she replied, "This year will be a busy one for me, Pru. Apart from the estate, there will be the house to be managed now you are no longer here. I don't know how much Mother will be able to or will want to do, but until I find out, I shall not stray very far."

"Is that the only reason you won't come?" Pru persisted.

Josephina looked away at her sister's gown, ready for the morrow's wedding. She wondered how it would feel to get married, to know that for the rest of your life you would forever live with another person. In an instant she knew the thoughts that must have run through Venables' mind when he was being pressed to marry Lucy Ridgeway. It would be intolerable to marry someone without feeling love and esteem. She had never told Pru of the real reason for Lady Francesca's visit or of Venables' proposal, and she still could not.

"It is not the only reason, Pru, but it is a very important one."

Pru hesitated, then said, "Is the other one Lord Venables?"

Josephina nodded.

"I know his actions were reprehensible, Jo, I know that he took liberties with you, and I cannot condone his behaviour except to say that perhaps your attraction proved too strong for him."

Josephina laughed. "Do you mean he, too, suffered from concupiscence?"

"Well, perhaps. But Charles has a very high opinion of him, and I am convinced he could not like a man completely wanting in decorum. I think it was a passion that overcame him and for which he was probably sorry later. Did he never apologize before he left?"

"In a manner, he did."

"Well, you see, his presence should not deter you from coming, and anyway, I suspect he is not there very much of the time. I think he is in London a great deal."

"I expect you are right."

But Prudence knew from her sister's tone of voice that she would prefer not to visit Gloucestershire, and she pressed the matter no further.

The wedding day was cold and crisp. Winter was in the air and the morning had seen a heavy frost on roof and trees. The sun rose to shine on the frost-laden branches, making them glitter like the diadem of Constantine, but it had melted by the time the party set off for the church.

The altar was decorated with holly and evergreens, and

128

there was a hush in the dim interior as Prudence, pale but with her head held high, came down the aisle on the arm of her uncle, looking for all the world like a queen in her white lace gown. Only Josephina was aware of how nervous she was, but this nervousness melted as she met the smile of Charles, who awaited her. Seeing them together, Josephina knew that although she and her sister would always have the greatest devotion for one another, Charles must from that day on be first in Pru's affections.

A wedding breakfast was served at Westlands after the ceremony. Mrs. Cooper had worked for over a week in its preparation and the wedding party did justice to her roast pheasant and goose, tarts and custards, almonds, raisins, oranges and apples, port wine, porter and ale, and of course the wedding cake resplendently iced in sugar and marzipan.

After the meal the bridal pair stayed only long enough to cut the cake and to receive toasts of happiness from their families and friends before they bundled into a post chaise for their journey to the White Hart in Bath. Pru hugged Josephina close to her, trying hard not to cry, and Jo whispered her wishes for their happiness, calling her sister by her married name for the first time; then they were off. Immediately after they left, she excused herself from the party, seeking the solitude of her room.

The following week it was time for the departure of her aunt and uncle and Amelia on their way to London. They were anxious to leave before any bad weather set in, for they had no wish to be confined to an inn on the way, should heavy snow fall. Amelia was all excitement and had little time to spare for either her mother or her sister. Though she frequently said she wished they were coming, she seemed perfectly happy to set off without them on her great adventure. At last all the boxes and bags were strapped to the coach, and with tears pouring from her mother's eyes and Amelia trying not to show her impatience, finally they were off, leaving Josephina and her mother waving on the front steps.

14

The winter following Pru's wedding was long and difficult, worse even than Jo had thought it would be, with she and her mother holding one another at arm's length, attempting to make the best of a situation neither of them relished.

There were interminable days and nights together by the fire in the small back sitting room when, in January, the weather worsened, curtailing Mrs. Trafford's visits to Milvercombe and her cozy if cantankerous chats with Lady Netherton, and leaving Josephina as her only sounding board. As Josephina watched through the windowpanes the leaden skies and the snows continuing to fall, and as her mother's complaints grew louder and more vociferous, she began to welcome George Ridgeway's rides out to Westlands, even though he talked of nothing more than the weather, conjecturing it would become the worst winter on record. Sometimes Fanny Netherton braved the elements to accompany him, and though in his presence she said little except to agree with his every pronouncement, her very deference to him convinced Josephina that her friend felt more than friendship for the squire's heir. Meanwhile, that gentleman's preference for Josephina became so pronounced that Mrs. Trafford, with nothing else on which to speculate, began in earnest to promote a match, unceasingly recounting her daughter's virtues to George Ridgeway while repeatedly asserting to Josephina that the woman he chose for a wife would be fortunate indeed, hints she studiously ignored.

As the weather worsened, she had the merinos brought down from the hilltop meadow, closer to the barn, where she could watch out for them. Despite Mr. Bracewaite's assurances of the hardiness of the merino breed, used to the bleak weather of the Spanish plains, she dared not risk anything happening to them.

The snows continued steadily, completely isolating Westlands, and it became impossible for even a horseman to get through from the village. Then only the click of knitting

130

needles or the rustle of a turning page was to be heard from Josephina's corner of the fireside, while opposite her, her mother kept up an endless dirge against country living.

"I wonder what dear Amelia is doing now? Receptions, balls, and endless pleasant company, I expect." Her mother sighed heavily. "It would be so pleasant to be in town again. You have never lived there, Josephina, that is why you are so set against it. You have never known what pleasure it is to drive in the park and meet friends for the theatre, to make morning calls on a large circle of acquaintances and friends, families of rank, not the type of riffraff we are forced to mix with here, to wear clothes of quality and fashion, such as your aunt brought with her, to give elegant card parties and routs. I know that if you became accustomed to it you would enjoy it every bit as much as I am sure dear Amelia is doing now."

Her mother's strident tones continued in growing discontent. "I do think you are a most unfeeling girl. How you ever came to be a daughter of mine, I'll never know, for you have none of my feelings and my sensitivity. If only Amelia were here, or even Prudence—they understand me, but you never will." And her mother would break into a flood of tears, forcing Josephina to put aside her knitting to calm her. That scene, once begun, would play to its inevitable close, and Josephina, dreading it, yet wishing it to conclude, would end by reiterating her mother's thoughts for her.

"I know you and I differ, Mother. I know you wish that I would sell Westlands, or marry George Ridgeway, or both, but I refuse to do either, nor do I believe either course would ultimately make us happier."

"Who said anything about your selling Westlands or your marrying George Ridgeway, I ask you. I'm sure I never said anything of the kind. I never push my daughters into anything, no one can ever say that of me. I'm sure Prudence made up her own mind, and Amelia will likely do the same, though I hope she will listen to the advice of her aunt and uncle, for if she were to marry well, it would be good for us all. As for you, Josephina, I think you are going to be an old maid, I really do. I hate to say it, but the way you go around, I can't even see what George Ridgeway sees in you—not one speck of fashion about the way you dress, and your hair done so plainly. You wouldn't be bad-looking if you took some pains with yourself. Lady Netherton still asserts that Lord Venables singled you out when he was here, but you did nothing about it. I doubt that she was right, but still, I think if you were to spruce yourself up a bit, George would come to the point. He will be well off one day, for he will succeed his father as squire, and we all know how much his father has and how intent he is on accumulating land. George may not be the handsomest man, nor perhaps the most eloquent, but he is a decent, good man, and you could do a lot worse."

Try as she might, her mother's use of the word "eloquent" in connexion with George Ridgeway would all too often produce a smile; eloquent he was not, nor even loquacious, unless his topic were the weather.

"There you go—I have a serious discussion, and all you can do is laugh at me. You are an unfeeling child." And her mother's tears would begin all over again, forcing Josephina to appease her by agreeing in word, if not in spirit, with her pronouncements.

To escape these scenes whenever possible, Josephina took to retiring to her room earlier and earlier. One day, in searching for a scarf, she came across a book of John Donne's poetry and was unable to understand what it was doing in her drawer until she remembered it to have been the book Venables had left for her one day when he had called. She had not looked at it then, merely throwing it aside in anger, believing he used it as an excuse to see her. Now she opened it and found a marker in a page with a dedication written beside the poem *Lovers Infinitenesse*. It was a piece of Donne's, incredibly logical in structure, that she had always enjoyed. In a bold hand at the top of the page was inscribed "To fair Portia, My dearest, My most beloved, My only Advocate. V." There was a marginal score beside the last lines: "But we will have a way more liberall, Than changing hearts, to joyne them, so wee shall, Be one, and one another's All."

She sat, not turning the page, reading and rereading the poem and the dedication, thinking again of all that had happened, in her mind going over their meetings, the words and the thoughts that had been exchanged. She found that she no longer considered Venables in the same light as she had when she refused him. Realizing his past rejection of the married state, it must have taken courage to propose, and her rejection, as she reconsidered it, had been unnecessarily harsh; she had thought then only of her own feelings, nothing of his. While she could not condone those actions of his described by his sister, towards herself she realized his treatment had not been wholly reprehensible. Nor could she overlook his sister's motivation in warning her against him; provision of an

132

inheritance for a younger son must obviously have spurred her action. She did not doubt that Venables' Christmas in Yorkshire had been more enjoyable than her own in Devon—how otherwise, in company he found congenial? Had he resumed his alliance with Lady Eliza, she wondered, or found another to take her place? That was the thought that saved her from further remorse.

Nevertheless, she kept the book at her bedside and memorized the dedicated poem without intending to do so, merely by continual reading. The feelings it aroused were not altogether salubrious, for she found she often dreamed of the poem's dedicator, dreams she neither would nor could repeat to anyone.

In February, the road from Milvercombe reopened, allowing George to ride out and inform them, with some satisfaction, that it had indeed been the worst recorded winter. The Thames in London had frozen over to such a great thickness that a Frost Fair had been held in the middle of it, with hundreds of people setting up stalls and even printing presses on the ice. Souvenirs of all description had been sold as "Bought on the Thames," and there had been dancing and skittles and all manner of amusement held on the river. They were to hear more of the Frost Fair when Amelia wrote, for she had actually visited it.

Only imagine, a party of us got together on Wednesday and went out on the Thames, not in a boat, but on foot, for the river is completely frozen to an immense depth and they are even holding a Fair right on the water, which is now ice of course. We walked down the Grand Mall, as they call it, that is, from Blackfriars Bridge to London Bridge, and were exceedingly entertained with the swings and dances to be seen everywhere. Captain Rutherford was with us, and he would buy me a locket which bore the inscription "From Frost Fair" across the face of it. I asked whose picture it should contain, and he said no one's but my own would suit for one side, and as for the other, he could only sigh. He is so very gallant and looked so very handsome in his red coat against the white of the snow. We bought hot chestnuts and listened to the funniest sort of music from a band of minstrels. It was all so jolly, I wish you could have been with us. I wish I had a fur muff like the one Louisa carries. I think she said it only cost five pounds, which is not much, considering it is made of marten and very soft and warm. Aunt and Uncle send their love. I must go and get ready, as we are to see Catalini tonight at the King's Theatre.

Though Amelia's letters cheered Mrs. Trafford, they also served to remind her of the delights of London, but with the roads passable once more, she was able to go to Shepton Park and confide her grievances to her friend Lady Netherton.

Amelia's letters did nothing to gladden Josephina's heart, filled as they were with hints for more money; indeed, their frivolous tone was a matter of concern. Attendance at parties, visits to theatrical performances, shopping trips, were fully regaled, yet the details were of whom she saw, and what they wore, with little description of the event itself. Never a letter came, however, without a reference to the dashing Captain Rutherford, who, since he had been introduced to Amelia by the mother of her dearest friend, Louisa, Josephina could only hope was a trustworthy gentleman.

Pru's letters did much to make up for all that was lacking in Amelia's, fully describing her new home and everything in it, the church, and the parishioners of Flaxhurst. It sounded so pleasant and comfortable that Josephina would cheerfully have forgone a whole week in London for one evening at Pru's fireside. There could be no doubt that her sister was happy, but there was also no doubt that she continued to miss Josephina and that had she been close by, her happiness would have been complete. She often wrote of the generosity of Lord Venables, who had attended assiduously to their personal needs as well as those of the church. He had done all within his power to make their arrival a joyous occasion, inviting the entire parish to a festive New Year's celebration with Pru and Charles as guests of honour. Thus Josephina learned, to her surprise, that Venables had not spent the holidays in Yorkshire after all, and try though she might, she could not help but speculate on the reason for the change in his plans.

Spring was come, it was said in Devon, when one footprint could cover three daisies, but for Josephina that year the long-awaited season was marked by the lambing of her merinos—twelve prize lambs, she counted, no, thirteen, for surprisingly for that breed, one ewe had dropped couplets. They were strong and healthy creatures with marvellous long gangly legs and fine curly wool. She visited them daily, and Mr. Bracewaite rode over from Trentor to examine them.

"You've done well, Josephina. I must admit I thought of

you often this past winter, for though I know they like the cold, this was beyond belief. You should be well set now with this flock. The ram I sold you is good, and you should look around now to see the breeds to cross him with; and soon these little fellows will be coming along too. You're going to have a lot of money invested here come next year, and I couldn't be more pleased. I wish your father were here with us to see them."

Josephina did too, but having Mr. Bracewaite to talk to made her feel as if she were talking to her father, for he was always encouraging and enthusiastic about her endeavours.

Even the squire rode out to look the lambs over, and for once he made no derogatory remarks about her wasting money.

"That wool will fetch a good price come shearing time, and the flock looks good and healthy," he admitted. "Come next year, you'll be sitting pretty if they continue this way. Might be you'll be selling some of them, and might be I'd not mind a few. Of course, I'd not be willing to put out as much as you did, but I imagine these small ones would go for a lot less."

Josephina was too happy to do more than shake her head at the squire's acquisitive proposal.

"You took a risk, Josephina, and it looks as though it is going to produce dividends for you," George congratulated her. "Now, I suppose, you'll be more independent than ever."

"I wish I could be truly independent, George, but I'll need a far greater income than I now have before that day comes—but I'm closer than I've ever been to reaching it."

The Carews had visited Charles and Pru in Gloucestershire and returned with glowing accounts of their new home and friends. The parish, though not as large as Milvercombe, enjoyed greater affluence, primarily because of the wool trade. Their son, they reported, had been taken to the hearts of the parishioners, and Pru was also much loved. She did not stay idle, but was constantly occupied in attending to the needs of the poor or giving teas for the altar guild. But the Carews' main item of news was that the newly married couple was expecting a happy addition.

"They waited till we got there to tell us, for it added to their joy to surprise us, but before we left we received permission to give you the news, though Pru is also writing. She had been quite sickly, but that's not unusual at such a time. I don't doubt she'll be over it soon."

"I'm sure she will," agreed Mrs. Trafford. "I well remember when I was to have Josephina how very sick I was for months. Dear Mr. Trafford was so good to me, but no one can understand it unless they have suffered it themselves. How I endured it I don't know, and it was not surprising, for she was such a large baby."

She cast an accusing look at Josephina, a look that went unnoticed in Josephina's concern for her sister.

"But should she be doing so much in the parish if she is not feeling well?"

"I think it is probably the best thing for her," Mrs. Carew averred, "for it keeps her mind occupied and away from her sickness. And, of course, Charles sees that she does not overdo it."

With that Josephina had to be content until Pru's letter came, cheerful as always and obviously delighted with the news she had to impart, though she ended with a wish that her sister could be there with her at that time.

Had Josephina not been so occupied, she would have left immediately, but with spring planting at hand she wanted nothing left to chance that year. Perhaps when it was over she would go. From all accounts received from the Carews, Venables was now settled in London for the season, for they had seen nothing of him during their visit, though they noted he was very highly regarded by the people they had met there.

"He is said to be a very generous landlord and I heard nothing but praise of him. I think we saw something of his abilities while he was with us. He spent some time with me discussing parish matters and seemed to have an amazingly good grasp of them for one who had been away from Devon so long. I only wish he had stayed longer. I was surprised when he called to say good-bye, for I had understood that he would remain at least until Christmas," Mr. Carew commented.

"At least he stopped to bid you good-bye. It was more than he did to us," Mrs. Trafford sniffed.

"Did he not?" Mr. Carew asked with some surprise. "I thought that he had called at Westlands before he saw me."

Mrs. Trafford looked across at Josephina. "He did not call here that I know of. Do you remember anything of it?"

Josephina could not keep from flushing, but she managed to keep an even voice. "He did call, but I had not thought of it as a farewell visit. Perhaps I should have mentioned it."

"Indeed you should have."

The spring days were too full to allow Josephina to become overly concerned about her mother's grievances. The land was prepared and seeded; the lambs grew apace; blossom in the orchard gave way to the nucleus of the apples and damsons soon to grace the Westlands table, all under admirable skies that boded the best possible growing year. Not only was she busy on the estate, but she had taken over supervision of the household as well, for though her mother had assumed Pru's tasks, one by one she found them burdensome and one by one they had fallen to Josephina. By evening she was exhausted and thankful to reach her room and stretch out and sleep, a deep, refreshing sleep that allowed no dreams. She was grateful for the fatigue that produced it, feeling stronger and healthier than she had for many months. Her complexion began to glow with the sun, and her eyes sparkled with the exercise and fresh air. George Ridgeway's gallantries increased, but despite her mother's encouragement of his visits, Josephina made plain she had little time to spare in idle conversation.

In late April, however, her labours were interrupted by a distressing letter from Charles Carew. He begged her to come to Pru, if only for a few days; he asked it of her, realizing full well how difficult it would be for her to leave Westlands. Had it been possible for Pru to travel with comfort, he would have brought her to Devon for a change of air, but the doctor said she should not attempt the journey. She was in low spirits, with the sickness from which she had been suffering increasing rather than abating. He was beside himself with worry and thought that the presence of her dearest sister might help where all else had failed.

I have not told Prudence I am writing to you [he concluded]. Therefore I beg you to make no mention of it, for I know she would not wish me to do so. I fully understand the predicament in which my request must place you, but I only do so knowing that you, like myself, have the welfare of Prudence at heart. But if it is impossible, I do understand.

Should you be able to make the journey, I can send one of Lord Venables' carriages for you, as he has expressly asked me to make use of them during his absence. In this connexion, I should mention that he is, at present, absent from Blenhasset, nor is he expected for some time. From something Prudence said, I felt you might prefer to know that he is not in residence.

If you can spare us the time, dear sister, it will greatly

137

relieve my mind and give joy to your sister. If, however, it is impossible now, please be assured I will understand and will remain, as always,

Your brother-in-law, Charles Carew

Josephina, upset that Pru's sickness was no better, immediately hastened to make plans to leave for Gloucestershire. Her mother, on being apprised of those plans, was indignant that she had not been summoned rather than Josephina, until her daughter reminded her that Prudence was counting on her to be there for the lying-in. That alone might not have prevailed to alleviate her mother's annoyance had not Lady Netherton emphasized the fatigue of two such journeys, remarking that Flaxhurst was almost as remote from London as Milvercombe. For once, Josephina was grateful for her intervention; if Prudence were upset, she was convinced that her mother's presence would worsen rather than calm her spirits. With that obstacle removed, she set aside all concerns at leaving Westlands at that critical time of the year, and relied upon Winslow to carry on in her absence. Pru's health was her only concern.

Though it would not have altered her decision to go to her sister's side, she had been relieved to learn of Venables' absence from Gloucestershire, for a meeting would have distressed her.

Another letter from Amelia, arriving as she was on the point of departure, confirmed Venables' presence in London, and, apart from the usual listing of her sister's social events, it contained the following item:

And only think, the thing which is being most talked of here is the impending engagement of Lord Venables to Lady Daphne Mercer—she is the daughter of the Duke of Danforth, and a great heiress, I hear. She is so beautiful. I saw them together yesterday as I was returning from the plumassier in Regent Street. She was exquisitely dressed in a soft blue muslin gown of a chemise cut, trimmed in broiderie anglais, which set off her proportions to best advantage. Her bonnet must have cost a fortune, for I don't think I've ever seen one as prettily trimmed. I expect she got it from Mlle. Felice's on Bruton Street, for Louisa, who was with me, says she goes there for most of her millinery, and you know you can't purchase anything for under fifty pounds. What it must be to wear clothes like that, I can't imagine. I felt like an absolute dowd after seeing her, I can tell you, and I had to go and buy fresh trimming for my pink silk before I dared wear it again.

I don't think the engagement is official yet, at least it hasn't been printed in the *Gazette,* but they are seen everywhere together. They say her papa is pleased, but that her mama has said he must loosen all his ties before they will give consent, at least that is what Mary Clifton heard her mama tell Mrs. Anderson. But she said that Lady Daphne will have him, so I expect it will be arranged. There is to be a big party in May at Sir Hugh and Lady Francesca Lanyon's, and we are invited. It is expected that the engagement will be announced then. Since he is our neighbour in Devon I was much sought after to tell how he had been when he was among us, and Captain Rutherford has served with his friend Colonel Underwood, so we two were as busy as bees relaying information last evening at the Anderson's rout.

I know you asked me not to apply to you for money, but do you think you could possibly spare me something for a new bonnet? If I cannot buy the bonnet, at least I need new trimming for my Lavinia straw. Botibel's has some luscious white feathers that would serve, and some pink rosebuds, but then, they are a bit jejune. I know Aunt Mulliner would give it to me, but you particularly told me not to apply to her. I have been very careful with the spending money you gave me, but London is such an expensive place, even though I don't spend anything on entertainment, for Uncle pays for all our theatre tickets and for everything else when we go out . . .

Josephina could not ignore the stab of pain that the news of Venables' expected engagement caused her. It was, of course, inevitable; she reasoned that she had no right, having already refused him, to expect that he had any further interest in her simply because her own feelings had undergone a change, and she found herself glad to have the journey to Flaxhurst to take her mind off the event. As she wrote to Amelia, sending her five pounds and telling her that it must last, for she was to be with Prudence in Flaxhurst, she found herself anxious for the change that the visit would make in her life.

15

It was a perfect English May day when Josephine left for Gloucestershire. As she climbed aboard the stage at Exeter, she determined to do nothing except enjoy the journey, the change of scene, and above all, to speed her sister back to health.

The ride to Cirencester, where Charles was to meet her, was without event. She sat by the window looking out on the passing scene, attempting to avoid the wine-laden breath of the fat gentleman who sat opposite and persistently attempted to engage her in conversation, or to listen to the coos of the woman beside her trying to keep her little girl occupied. Josephina thought that if the woman had not been so busy cooing the child would have been a great deal more contented, and when she grew particularly restive, Josephina suggested that woman and child change places and she would take on the task of the child's amusement. Her offer gratefully accepted, the remainder of the journey passed in relative peace, with Josephina's fairy stories punctuated by resonant snores from the rotund gentleman opposite.

When she stepped down at the Fleece in Cirencester, well-named for its situation in a town made rich by the wool trade, she was delighted to be met not only by Charles but also by her sister. She could hardly believe Prudence to have been sick, for after she hugged her and then held her at arm's length to observe her better, she thought she positively glowed, though her face was rather thinner than usual. Charles later told her that the news of her impending visit had produced a complete change in Pru's condition and that though she still suffered some discomfort, she had lost her list-lessness and was quite herself again. He again apologized for calling on Josephina's aid at such a time but assured her that he had been quite beside himself as to what best to do; she could be consoled in knowing that even that much of her visit, hardly yet begun, had produced a most beneficial change in her sister's health. Josephina assured him that she

140

was sorely in need of the change and was grateful for the opportunity to spend time with them in such a delightful place.

Flaxhurst was indeed a charming Cotswold village; it was somewhat smaller than Milvercombe, set in the undulating grey-green countryside with its checker work of roughly hewn stone walls. The parsonage was built of the blond stone peculiar to that country, with a steep stone roof and mullioned windows, the lower ones protruding in attractive bays. Inside, it was spacious enough to be uncluttered, yet small enough to be cozy. The solid oak tables and chintz-covered chairs gave evidence of comfort and taste. The overall impression was that of a home that was lived in, and lived in by people who enjoyed living.

An exquisite pair of Sèvres vases graced the parlour mantel, a wedding gift, Josephina learned, from Lord Venables, who had also been responsible for supplying so many items in which the parsonage had been lacking. Apart from that, no further mention was made of his name.

The sisters seemed never to stop talking. Josephina wanted to hear all that had happened since the moment they had left the front steps at Westlands, and Prudence wanted to know all that had passed in Milvercombe since that day. They discussed Amelia, to discover that Pru's letters from her, though not as frequent as those directed to Westlands, caused the same concern for her welfare in Prudence's breast as they did in Josephina's, that she was too readily succumbing to the blandishments of the world of fashion and that her new life might make her incapable of ever again settling in Devon. Josephina found that Amelia had made just as many references to Captain Rutherford's name to Prudence as she had in her letters home, a fact that made her determined to write directly to her aunt for full particulars of that dashing young officer.

Prudence made light of her own difficulties with her health, putting them down to a ruse to make her sister visit her, and Josephina was assured by the way in which she laughed and joked that she was, indeed, feeling much better. They stayed up until almost midnight that first night, and would have talked longer had not Charles insisted that Josephina had had a long day and that Prudence, no matter how much better she might be feeling, needed her rest. On saying good night to Josephina he pressed his sister-in-law's hand and thanked her again for coming, showing so clearly the gratitude he felt at the change in his wife's condition that Josephina thought it must be enviable indeed to be loved in such a manner.

On Sunday she had another opportunity of hearing Charles deliver an inspiring sermon and to meet many of the people of the parish after the service. In fact, there were so many people who wanted to meet Prudence's sister that there were constant interruptions at the parsonage, and though Pru was delighted in showing her sister off and was pleased to introduce her to her new acquaintances, she resented the time that was taken away from her by these visitors and suggested that the following day they pack a lunch and take the gig to see the Roman villa at Chedworth, not far from Flaxhurst. Josephina was eager to see as much as she could of the countryside while there, but she hesitated, fearing it might be too strenuous an expedition for her sister. Pru insisted, saying there was nothing she would rather do and that it would give Charles some freedom to work on his sermon, which she knew he couldn't while they were prattling and with the constant stream of visitors which Josephina's coming had engendered.

They were in high spirits when they left soon after breakfast, with a tidy lunch of cheeses, fruit, bread, and lemonade packed in a hamper which Charles stowed at their feet. He waved to them as Josephina, taking the reins, solemnly reminded Prudence she merely wanted instructions on the route, not on the manner of handling the reins, and they started off at a sedate trot along the road which bordered the high paling of Blenhasset on one side and a thick hedgerow on the other. The scent of wild honeysuckle in the air and the constant chirping of crickets cast a spell of peace and contentment. They were rounding a bend in the road when Josephina heard the sound of a vehicle approaching at a smart pace and hastened to pull aside to allow room for it to pass. As it appeared, she instantly recognized the matched roans and the travelling chaise of Lord Venables and his tall figure guiding the horses.

"What a delightful surprise," he called out, pulling his team to a halt. "Mrs. Carew, I did not expect to see you up and about so early in the morning, and you, Miss Trafford, I did' not expect to see at all."

Though Venables voiced surprise, he did not show half the surprise or lack of composure that Josephina felt on seeing him. She could only smile, and left it to her sister to respond to his greeting. Prudence expressed her concern at seeing him back in Gloucestershire so soon. "We quite thought you were settled in London until the end of the season. I hope there is no trouble which brings you back now?"

"No, just a little personal matter that demands my attention. And when did you arrive, Miss Trafford?"

"I think it is only three days ago, but we've done so much talking, it seems as though I've been here a month." She flushed as she spoke, and turned away, unable to forget their last meeting. But he showed no embarrassment and merely wished her a pleasant stay, and turning to Prudence, promised to call on Charles on his way in. Raising his hat in salute, he was gone.

As Josephina started the horses again, Pru reiterated her surprise at his return. "We really didn't expect him at this time, Jo. I am glad to see him, but I do wish he had chosen to come at another time, for I know you don't care for him. I must admit, though, he has been very kind to us and he is a good friend to Charles, much more than a mere patron. I think if you see anything of him you will find him quite different. He is at ease here."

Josephina's reply was noncommittal, not wishing to acknowledge that the sight of him had caused sensations in her breast she had thought to have overcome, hoping that now she had seen him again she would be able to face him with equanimity should they meet again during her visit.

"It's quite all right, I assure you. It's been a long time since he was in Devon. I'm sure his actions there are as well in his past as they are in mine. Now, Pru, which fork in this road would you like me to take, for remember, you are my guide."

After touring the amazingly well-preserved villa, with its tessellated pavements and baths that had been heated by underground furnace, causing Josephina to reflect on the ways in which Roman civilization far surpassed their own, they selected a warm yet shady picnic site. Josephina, more herself again, laughed with Pru about her qualities as a guide, for they had, in fact, taken two wrong turnings on their way. They lingered over lunch, enjoying the privacy of their conversation, talking of their mother, their sister, Charles, their old neighbours and Prudence's new ones, of everybody except the man they had met that morning. Josephina sensed an unasked question in Pru's eyes, but she said nothing of Venables, nothing of his proposal, nothing of how much he had been in her thoughts since then. At that time, she had wished to have her sister there to confide in, but now they were alone, she found she could not talk of it, even to her closest confidante. There were some things better left unsaid.

It was almost three by the time they returned to the parsonage. Josephina was concerned that it had been too long a day for Pru, but she insisted she had enjoyed every minute, and to judge by her appearance, she did not lie. Charles was waiting for them with the news that Venables had stopped to see him; they had spent a pleasant morning together, and Venables had invited them to dine with him that evening, but Charles assured his wife, "He left the decision up to you, for he thought it might be too tiring. However, he was quite anxious that we come if at all possible, since he will only be here for a few days. I said I would send a reply on your return."

Prudence looked questioningly at Josephina, who said, "It really does depend on how you feel, Pru. I have no objection to going, but I know your day has been a long one already."

Prudence turned back to her husband. "I think it would be a delightful evening, judging by others we have spent at Blenhasset, and I'm sure that if I rest now it will not overtire me. I'm feeling so happy at the moment, I believe that I could do anything." Her husband, however, insisted on her lying down before he would dispatch their acceptance to Blenhasset.

When Venables' carriage arrived to collect them that evening, Josephina was wearing the same dress she had worn on the occasion of her first dinner at Venarvon, its only alteration being a braid trim in Greek key motif. She had appraised herself critically in the mirror before leaving her room, wondering how she might appear to the man who was escorting the beautiful creature Amelia had described. Was his visit connected with his forthcoming engagement? she wondered, before chiding herself for such thoughts. Those were his affairs; they could not concern her.

The curved driveway of Blenhasset climbed to the great house a quarter of a mile, through great elms and oaks interspersed on velvet lawns covering the rise on which the mansion was situated. To the east was a stream that meandered through the meadows, bordered by weeping willows and poplars, and behind lay the expanse of the Cotswold hills. The sweet smell of honeysuckle still hung in the air as they stopped before the main portico and great double doors of a house built in the classic manner, not overburdened with gables, not ornamental, but striking in its simplicity and straight, clean lines.

The main hall was not as large as that at Venarvon, not as imposing, but it imparted an immediate feeling of luxury and comfort, the floors being covered by thick Persian rugs, with a large Gobelin tapestry depicting the return of Odysseus to his faithful Penelope decorating the wall opposite the entrance.

144

The saloon into which they were shown was again smaller than that at Venarvon, but it was a room of pleasing dimensions, clearly reflecting the taste of its owner. Furnished in blues and soft yellows, colours carried throughout, from the rich Axminster carpet to the heavy velvet window hangings and luxuriously upholstered sofas, it had clearly been designed with ease and utility foremost, with no piece of furniture set in place solely for its appearance, yet altogether it achieved superior distinction of style as well as comfort.

In one corner stood a magnificent pianoforte with gleaming ebony finish. Above the fireplace, where a bright fire crackled, was a large portrait of a lady Josephina recognized as Lady Venables. The likeness had been painted in her youth. It showed a remarkably handsome woman; Josephina saw at once the likeness to her son, the same direct gaze from large grey eyes, powerful, though softened in a female face.

Venables, immaculate in dark grey evening coat and buff-coloured knee breeches, greeted them, apologizing to Prudence for getting her out again that day. "I should have had more consideration, but my time here is limited and I did want you to be my guests before I return again to town. You are, however, looking better than I have seen you for many a day. I think your sister's visit must agree with you."

"It does," was Pru's fervent reply. "We have had a delightful day, and I don't feel in the least tired after it. In fact, I could stay up till midnight again."

"I must tell you that it has been the deuce of a job getting these girls to go to bed." Charles laughed. "Once they get talking, there is no getting them to stop; they treat the hours as though they were minutes."

"We're really not such prattlers as my brother-in-law would have us," Josephina intervened, "but we have been deprived of each other's company for such a long time that no sooner is one thing said than it leads to another and another, and before we know it, it is midnight."

Looking from one sister to the other, Venables' eyes softened at their open and obvious affection for one another.

"And what did you think of the country you saw today? Do you not find Gloucestershire quite as lovely as Devon?"

"I confess to a partiality for my own county, which I believe I would adhere to even were Beatrice to conduct me through Paradise, but I do admit to Gloucestershire being the second-most-beautiful county I have seen."

"Since you have only been through three or four at the most, how are we to take that?" Her brother-in-law laughed.

"You should take it in the spirit in which it was intended, to compliment those who live here, and to assert a great desire to see much more of this country which so closely rivals my own."

"In that case, since I have to drive to Cheltenham tomorrow, perhaps you would all like to accompany me," Venables offered.

But Charles desisted, "Much as I'd like to, I'm afraid I must cry off. Since you interrupted the writing of my sermon this morning, I must set to tomorrow. To leave it until another day may mean having to deliver a sermon already given; as I have been here only such a short time, it is bound to be remembered."

"Then how about the ladies? We could lunch at the Royal, they serve a most excellent duck, and shopping in Cheltenham is a rare treat."

Josephina sensed that the invitation was directed to her and accepted it graciously on the stipulation that her sister feel well enough for another strenuous day.

"It is no great distance," he said, turning to Prudence, "and I promise to go at a sedate rate of speed. I think you will enjoy it, Mrs. Carew."

"I'm sure I shall." Pru smiled in acceptance.

Josephina had crossed the room to examine a hanging that had intrigued her since first she entered. It was of an odd geometric design, done in a roughly woven texture, with bold, bright colours, unlike anything she had ever seen. Venables followed her to explain that he had brought it back with him from the West Indies. It was a native craft not highly thought of there, where things European were more appreciated, but he had found it striking.

"It shows great strength and verve," Josephina agreed, "unlike so much of our art, which is too precise and perfect."

"I'm glad to find we agree on the important things in life."

His direct gaze caught hers and held it for a moment before she turned to survey the rest of the room, remarking, "I find your taste here to be altogether excellent."

"Your approval delights me."

Josephina, unable to determine whether he was mocking her, made to rejoin the others, when he stopped her. "I hear you have embarked upon further experimentation since I last saw you, Miss Trafford. How fare your merino sheep?"

She expressed surprise that he knew of her venture, continuing, "Yes, I have plunged rather heavily, but I am very excited with the results so far. I now have thirteen very sturdy lambs, one of the ewes actually dropping a couplet, which Mr. Bracewaite says he has never seen in merinos before. I must confess the hard winter worried me, but they came out of it well. The wool is magnificent and I am hoping for a good return at shearing time. If they continue to produce at this rate, I shall be able to solve many of my financial problems."

It was hard to disguise her enthusiasm, and for the first time that evening she felt completely at her ease.

"We have a farmer near here, Caleb Dibble, who is crossing merinos with Cotswolds. He tells me he is quite satisfied with the results. Perhaps you would like to meet him. We could stop there on our way to Cheltenham tomorrow if you wish."

"I'd love to! Do you think he could be persuaded to show us his flock?" she enquired eagerly.

"I'm sure he will be delighted to do so. He's only too anxious to have anyone look at them who's in any way interested. My only concern when you and he meet is that we may never reach Cheltenham in time for that fine repast I promised you."

"I won't linger too long," she promised, laughing, "but in Devon no one is interested in innovation. To talk to someone actually experimenting with the breed will be of immeasurable help to me."

That Venables was even aware of the farmer's activities, let alone being willing to discuss them, surprised her, yet she remembered Mr. Carew saying how highly he was regarded in Gloucestershire, and Prudence had spoken of his many friends from all walks of life.

Dinner was announced and Venables gave his arm to Prudence, joking, "I do hope after all this talk of sheep that we shall not have to endure mutton at dinner."

Not mutton, but salmon with fennel sauce, roast loin of veal with beans and peas, chicken cooked in white wine, apricot tart and melon and strawberries, accompanied by a variety of wines, awaited them. Conversation flowed as easily as one course followed another, Venables regaling them with tales of Lady Nugent, wife of the Governor of Jamaica, and her indefatigable entertaining. Though she swore the heat was appalling and absolutely unbearable, and she was terrified of the yellow death that plagued the island, she was ready at any moment of the day or night to dance. Life in Jamaica had resembled life in England fifty years earlier, and though Lady Nugent complained that no one talked of anything but the price of sugar, a strict eighteenth-century etiquette was upheld, with all the pomp that unlimited wealth could command.

After dinner, Venables, who had been explaining the unusual beat of the music of the West Indies, sat down at the piano to demonstrate it and sang some of the native songs, the words of which had them all in gales of laughter. Josephina noticed how well his fingers moved across the keyboard and asked when he was finished if he would play something else for them.

"What would you like?"

"Do you know Mozart's Sonata in A minor?"

"The one he wrote on the death of his mother?"

She nodded.

"It has always been a favourite of mine," he said.

Turning back to the keyboard, he played it as Josephina had never heard it before; the notes, so soft and pliant, seemed to speak to her alone. He looked down at the keyboard as he played, and she watched him; his body moved, at one with the music, and she knew that somehow she was part of that oneness. She wished the moment to continue forever, feeling alone with him and with the reverberating notes, but at last there was silence, broken by Charles complimenting the pianist. "I didn't know you could play that well. Where did you learn to do that? You never cease to amaze me."

"Oh, I use the piano as the receptacle of all my hopes, fears, and griefs. I wonder you haven't heard me pounding away here while you were home composing a sermon. I assure you I have even lost servants because of the din."

Josephina had not spoken, but when he turned to her, she said simply, "It was the most beautiful thing I have ever heard." The sincerity in her voice belied any empty compliment and his pleasure in her response was evident in his face.

They sat long by the fire, sipping brandy and conversing in quiet tones, four people very much in harmony, liking one another's company, at ease with each other. Conversation drifted from Napoleon and Wellington to England and the difficulties under the Regency, then still closer to home to Mrs. Mantree's cow, which, having got loose, had got into the parsonage garden and had eaten all of Charles's cherished daffodils, but before they could dissect Mrs. Mantree's lack of control of her livestock, Charles pointed out that not merely was it past midnight but past one o'clock and that they must get home.

148

It was with regret that Josephina rose from the comfortable armchair, the glow of the fire, and the presence of the companion by her side. An evening she had dreaded had turned into one of the happiest she had ever known.

16

The Dibble farm was neat and well-tended. Larger than most of the Devon farms, it occupied almost five hundred acres of rolling Cotswold hills. The farmhouse itself seemed wedded to the land, harmonizing in colour and form as though it had grown there rather than been built. Mr. Dibble must have been apprised of their visit, for he was awaiting their arrival. He was a younger man than Josephina had expected, probably in his early thirties, broad-shouldered, with a full, weather-beaten face and a sturdy gait. His manners were polite, but he wasted no time upon ceremony. Josephina took an immediate liking to him.

"I'm told, Miss Trafford, that you're raising merinos also."

Josephina told him of her flock and the first lambing.

"You should write to Arthur Young about that couplet, I'm sure he'd like to mention it in his *Annals of Agriculture*. It's the first I've heard of among merinos," he observed. "Come and look at mine and the results I've had crossing them with Cotswolds."

Josephina needed no second bidding, but Prudence said she would prefer to stay inside and talk with Mrs. Dibble, so the three set off, Venables saying little but listening with interest and some amusement to Josephina's eager questions.

Mr. Dibble showed them the change in the build of the sheep after cross-breeding, the greater size and weight and broader form, the increased length of the wool without any loss of fineness or density. Apart from those advantages, he asserted that the animals bred with greater regularity.

"I've had them lamb twice in one year," he finished with pride, "and my wool output has almost doubled. I spent more than I thought I ought in the beginning, but the gains are more than I ever expected."

On Josephina's enquiries about other breeds successfully crossed with the merino, he answered, "Oh, they've tried several. But the person you should talk to is Robert Bakewell's nephew. His uncle passed most of his secrets to him."

"I don't know that would do much good," Venables interposed. "His Leicesters at Dishwell are certainly prime specimens, but he's as wily a devil as his uncle ever was. They say if you go there he'll show you everything on the place but won't say a word about what he's actually doing. Bakewell had half Europe courting him for his secrets—but I suppose he's not to be blamed for his reticence."

Josephina turned sharply to Venables. "I didn't know you knew anything about sheep," she said almost accusingly.

"There are a lot of things you don't know about me," he responded. "But come along. I know Miss Trafford would gladly stay here all day and talk to you, Dibble, but I've promised the ladies lunch at the Royal in Cheltenham, and unless we leave soon we are going to be very late. Perhaps you can come back before your visit is over, Miss Trafford, and continue this discussion."

"That would be delightful," Josephina agreed. "Thank you so very much, Mr. Dibble, for sharing your knowledge. It's really a joy to meet someone actively pursuing improvements in agriculture and livestock rather than carrying on as things have always been done, solely for that reason."

"Come along, Miss Trafford," Venables said, laughing, "I sense you are on one of your hobbyhorses again and I insist on cutting you short now before you get too carried away by it." With that he took her arm firmly in his, and they returned to the house.

It was well past noon when they arrived at Cheltenham and drove into the courtyard of the Royal. The innkeeper came out to greet them, treating Venables, apparently quite well-known to him, with obvious deference. He had expected them and had prepared a private parlour, but the ladies were first conducted to a chamber above to refresh themselves after the journey. Prudence, feeling somewhat fatigued, said she would like to rest for a few minutes. While assuring her sister that there was nothing wrong, she asked her to make her excuses.

Venables was waiting in the parlour when Josephina came down. He had ordered a white wine and he filled a glass for her, suggesting a toast.

"And what is the subject to be?" Josephina asked, fearing for a moment it might be in honour of his forthcoming engagement.

"I would propose a toast to you, but I sense you would prefer that we drink to your sheep."

Josephina laughed, unaccountably relieved, and raised her

151

glass. "I enjoyed this morning," she responded with obvious sincerity.

"And last night?"

"Last night, too, particularly. I don't know when I've enjoyed an evening more or felt more at ease."

"Seeing you among the sheep this morning made me think of Spenser's *Shepherd's Calendar*. Have you ever seen it?" he asked.

"No, I don't think so."

"It is a series of twelve eclogues, one for each month of the year. The best are laments by the shepherd Colin Clout because his fair Rosalind does not return his love." He looked down into his wineglass as he spoke, turning the stem of the glass in his long fingers. "Poor Colin. How he does suffer, but I suspect Spenser knew well love's suffering—do you know the sonnet that begins:

Unrighteous Lord of Love, what law is that
That me thou makest thus tormented be
The whiles she lordeth in licentious bliss of her freewill
Scorning both thee and me.

"I particularly enjoy the part about the 'licentious bliss of her freewill,' an unusual association of ideas, don't you think?" He looked at her keenly but she could not bring herself to meet his eyes, being too painfully reminded of their last meeting.

"Very," was all she murmured in reply. Why did he speak so to her? she wondered. Had she not known he was on the point of engagement to another, she would have thought him once again wooing her. She knew her cheeks were flushed and she had lost much of her cool composure; she turned away as Prudence came in.

"The pillows on the bed were so comfortable I almost fell asleep," Prudence began cheerfully. "They are so much softer than mine at home."

Silence greeted her remark and, looking from one to the other, Pru wondered what could have passed in her absence, for her sister's face was flushed, while there was an air of intensity about Venables'.

Josephina visibly pulled herself together. "I'm absolutely famished—I can hardly wait to try the duck," she asserted.

But when a fine dish of duck surrounded by fresh green peas was put before her, she ate very little, nor, Prudence noticed, did Venables. She alone did justice to the delectable food. Josephina spoke scarcely at all during the meal, leaving Prudence and Venables to carry on a conversation that

152

flagged so often that Pru was convinced his mind must be elsewhere.

After luncheon the ladies set off to shop down the Promenade, where Prudence found a linen draper with just the kind of soft flannel material she wanted for baby clothes and Josephina purchased ribbons for the trim. Next door was a subscription library where they stopped to examine the selection; then they wandered into the pump room to take a glass of the waters, which they drank bravely, hating the taste, but reminding themselves of the good it was doing them.

"My goodness," said Venables on their return, regarding their small packages askance, "I am not used to ladies buying so little when they shop. Why, I even did more than you, though not all of these boxes are for me. This one is for you, Mrs. Carew."

He handed Pru a small box tied with white ribbon, which, when opened, was found to contain a silver feeding spoon.

"It's lovely," Pru thanked him. "No one can say our baby won't be born with a silver spoon."

"And for Miss Trafford, I found this." He handed her a large box. Her eyes lit with pleasure at the contents—Spenser's *Shepherd's Calendar*.

"What a beautiful copy, and such a fine binding." Gently her hand stroked the textured leather before carefully turning the folio sheets. "It's an old copy and so well preserved."

"It is. I didn't think I would find it, but you see what a famous place this is for shopping."

"Thank you," she said simply. "I shall treasure it not only for itself but also as a remembrance of a wonderful day."

They smiled at one another, frankly happy; then he handed Prudence up into the curricle before giving his hand to Josephina.

"I have to leave for London tomorrow afternoon, but I wondered if you had yet seen Birdlip?" he asked Josephina. "It would make for a splendid morning ride."

"Oh, it would indeed," Pru insisted. "I was so hoping Josephina would see the view from there, but I knew I would not be able to take her, and Charles is so busy. It's a lovely place, Jo, you can really get an idea of the Cotswolds. It may even make you reconsider placing Devon over Gloucestershire."

"I have a mare that would just suit you—she's spirited, but I know how you ride. If you would care to come, I'll bring her over in the morning. It takes less than an hour to get there." He looked at her expectantly.

"I'd like it very much," Josephina replied.

"Then it is arranged." He was obviously gladdened by her acceptance.

The next morning Venables arrived with his groom leading a sleek black Arabian of some fifteen hands, a mare of such elegance that Josephina gasped with pleasure. "What a fine animal!" she stroked her mane. "A lovely arch to her neck, and that deep chest—she's a true beauty!"

"This is Patanjali," said Venables, helping her into the saddle. "You're right in saying she's a fine mare, but she's shockingly outclassed today by her rider."

Then they were off, trotting side by side until, beyond the park of Blenhasset, Venables led the way across country at a full gallop. They crossed through woods and jumped streams, but he deliberately led her around a five-bar gate.

"Why didn't we jump that one?" she called. "Patanjali would have taken it beautifully."

"I'm sure she would. I didn't want to take any chances with her rider."

"Then I insist on going back and jumping it."

"Do so by all means, then."

Back she went and, spurring Patanjali to a gallop, she cleared the gate with inches to spare.

"Bravo! I might have known you would jump it with style."

"Anyone who hunts with Squire Ridgeway's pack has to be ready to jump anything," she said, trotting up to where he awaited her.

She saw that the mention of Ridgeway's name had broken the spell of the day and was sorry. She had thought he had overcome his dislike of the squire, but his next remark made her realize that it was the son that ired him.

"How goes the stalwart George?" he asked dryly.

"Well, I believe," and she could not resist adding, "And how goes the beauteous Lady Daphne Mercer?"

"News travels faster than I had realized." From his surprised tone, Josephina gathered that Amelia's speculations had not been unfounded. She became angry that Venables should be dallying in her company while on the brink of matrimony.

"If we are to get there in an hour, we should spur our horses, for you have to leave for London today, I believe."

"That's true. I promised I would be at my sister's gala ball. I'd best not disappoint her."

Josephina, remembering that to be the occasion when Amelia had said his engagement was to be announced,

154

spurred Patanjali and set off at such a rate that Venables had to allow his horse free rein to catch up with her.

"If you wish to race, we can on the way back," he called, "but you'd better follow me now, for the way gets tricky from here."

They rode across an expanse of rolling upland, patterned by stone walls and occasionally darkened by a mass of beech wood, catching now and again sight of a hamlet caught in a fold of the hills with its spare church spire surrounded by clustered grey roofs; then came a panorama of fold upon fold of wooded green. They began to climb, passing barrows and tall standing stones, miniatures of Stonehenge.

At the summit, they dismounted, breathless from the pace. Venables pointed out the distant Severn in one direction and the sources of the great Thames in another. Off in the distance were the Malvern Hills and the Forest of Dean. It was so clear they could see as far as Wales.

It must have been close to noon, for the sun was high in the sky, and in a mood of exhilaration Josephina took off her bonnet and sat down on a low wall, her arms outstretched at her sides, gazing out at the lines of the Cotswolds as they extended in soft green and blue curves all around them. Venables lay on the ground at her feet, resting on his elbow but looking up at his companion rather than the scene around them.

"What are you thinking of?" he asked suddenly.

Josephina laughed. "I'm almost ashamed to admit it, but I was wondering just how my merinos are faring." She noticed his look of disappointment and added quickly, "I'm sorry, but I have so much at stake in this venture, it is hard to forget it even when I'm enjoying myself, and I am indeed enjoying myself. I don't know when I've had such a wonderful time."

Venables' face cleared; then he, too, laughed. "And to think you once berated my habit of gambling. Your venture is even more of a gamble than my casting the die, and probably a lot less predictable. Perhaps now you can begin to understand that all of life is unpredictable, each action has as much chance of coming about as it has of going against you. Life isn't a chess game where moves can be foretold. A winning streak is usually followed by a losing one, but not necessarily so. There are those among us who think we can always come about. The weak quit early; it takes stamina to hold out against odds. I risk my purse on the lay of the die rather than on an obscure breed of sheep. It's less trouble and, I suspect, much less messy, but it's all part of the same game."

Her brow furrowed thoughtfully. "You are right, of course, except that when you risk your purse, should you lose it you have other assets to allow you to stay in the game. My risk is far greater, for I have done what I suspect no good gambler would do, that is to borrow to stake my bid."

"But that is precisely what a true gambler would do," he asserted.

"I have a great deal at stake, not only on my own behalf but also on that of the rest of the family. The gain could be great, but the loss would be disastrous."

"Had I known you for a gambler, I would have persuaded you more vigorously to gamble on me," he said lightly. She could not help but notice his use of the past tense, and she was deeply perturbed by the regret that caused her.

A silence ensued that she broke by asking, "How did you feel the first time you gambled for a large stake, or did you always have enough money so that you could bear the outcome with equanimity?"

"No, indeed. My allowance from my father bordered on the niggardly when I was at home, at least in my opinion. I remember getting into terribly deep water in London and being afraid to tell him of my losses, but a debt of honour is impossible to ignore, and I had no recourse but to make a full confession. Such a tongue lashing I received I shall never forget. But he was right, of course. I should not have gambled money which I did not have . . . nor would I again."

"Perhaps now you understand how I feel, for I have gambled money that is not wholly mine."

"But the estate is yours."

"Except for the provision of my sisters' settlements. I have not yet given Prudence all of her portion, and if Amelia should wish to marry soon, I shall indeed need my wits about me to provide her settlement."

"Do you never think of yourself and your own happiness?"

"Of course, often."

"Will you always be happy to remain as you are, mistress of Westlands, alone eventually, with both your sisters gone?"

"You paint a grim picture. It is not so."

He pulled at the tufts of grass beneath his hand. "Then you are happy in your present state?"

She knew not how to reply. "I am not happy . . . yet neither am I unhappy. I treasure a certain independence, and of that I have more than many women."

156

"You do, indeed. But is there nothing else you want from life?"

His eyes sought hers, holding them in his glance till she lowered hers, afraid that they betrayed her, that he had guessed her changed heart.

She stood up. "We should go if you are to leave for London today."

She did not want to go, nor did she want him to go, yet she could not bear the thought that he might be toying with her as his sister had told her he had done with others.

He stood, brushing the grass from his buckskins. "I wish I did not have to leave, but I promised Francesca to attend. It is my way of burying the hatchet, for as you may guess, we quarrelled bitterly after I left Devon. Perhaps I should not mention it, but I've thought a great deal about our last meeting. Some of your remarks hit home, I'm afraid. I suppose it is time I settled and lived a more purposeful life. There are matters I have to attend to in London, but since I still have unfinished business here, I shall return after Francesca's party."

Could those matters include a proposal to Lady Daphne Mercer? she wondered. He took hold of her hand, but angrily she moved to take it from his grasp.

"Don't, Josephina. Haven't I promised that I won't make any advances to shock your sense of morality? You won't have to defend your virtue from me again, I assure you."

Josephina allowed her hand to relax in his, paradoxically vexed that he was not going to kiss her after all, recognizing, as she did so, her own desire for him.

He raised her hand to his lips and lightly kissed the tip of each finger, and she wished passionately that those lips were upon her own. Raising his eyes suddenly to hers, he seemed to read her thoughts, for he said, "Of course, should you invite my embraces, I should be only too delighted to comply."

Afraid of her emotions, she snatched her hand away and picked up her bonnet, thrusting it upon her head and tying it securely under her chin. What lay behind his laughing gaze? Was he playing with her? she wondered.

"Your affairs in town are undoubtedly pressing, Lord Venables. We really should start our return journey."

"I suppose we should leave. But I trust you will not return to Devon for some time."

"I expect to remain with my sister for another week."

"Good, then perhaps we may ride again when I get back." His tone was light and cheerful.

Would he then continue to tease her, to play with her feelings? Josephina wondered, yet she could not believe it would be so. Perhaps Amelia's speculations on his engagement had been no more than idle gossip.

He lifted her into her saddle, and she bent forward to stroke Patanjali's mane.

"I cannot refuse to ride such a fine animal," was all she said.

"You ride so well, you should always be well-mounted. In fact, you should never have anything but the best."

"Perhaps when I sell my wool you might allow me to buy Patanjali from you."

"You and those damned sheep! Come, Rosalind, Colin Clout will escort you home."

Pru's eyes were questioning when her sister returned from her ride, flushed and windblown, but Josephina did not discuss her companion, though she commented effusively on the countryside.

"I believe that, after all, Gloucestershire may rank quite as highly as Devon scenically. The view of the Cotswolds from Birdlip was spectacular, and the farms we passed equalled many of our own around Milvercombe, in fact some were far better cared for. And those small villages hidden in the hills—they look as though they've been there since the beginning of time. As for Patanjali, she's a real treasure. She stretched out in the gallop, just like the thoroughbred she is."

So Pru had to be content with a description of the countryside and the mare, until she could not restrain herself from asking, "Is Lord Venables to leave today?"

"Yes, I believe it is certain. He is to attend his sister's ball tomorrow." Josephina's voice was expressionless, causing Prudence to reflect that perhaps her conjectures on Venables' attentions to her sister had been without foundation. She questioned whether Josephina's heart was untouched, however, for she noticed that while she would not willingly vouchsafe any information about Venables, she listened in a particularly attentive manner whenever his name was mentioned.

That afternoon, as the sisters sat together preparing clothes for the expected baby, Prudence crocheting a white wool shawl and Josephina embroidering a short coat that would serve equally well for a child of either sex, an express was delivered from Milvercombe for Josephina.

She turned it over in her hands, looking long at the hand, for it belonged to George Ridgeway. A thousand forebodings crossed her mind, but she forced herself to open it calmly. On reading the contents, however, she turned pale and her hand trembled. She sat down, looking at the letter in disbelief; then catching her sister's anxious glance fixed upon her and the letter in her hand, she folded it and put it away in her pocket, saying in as calm a tone as she could muster, "Dear George, he is such a worrier, but really he means so well. He is concerned that Winslow is not carrying out my instructions as he should and feels I should return. I think perhaps Mother is being called upon to make decisions, and you know how traumatic that can be."

"Oh, thank goodness that's all it is." Pru breathed a sigh of relief. "Looking at your face, for a moment there I thought something terrible had happened, that Mother was ill or that something was wrong with your precious merinos."

"I don't believe it is anything to cause alarm, but nevertheless I wish that Charles would arrange for a post chaise for my return. I should go tomorrow early."

"But, Josephina, I thought you would stay at least for the week. Surely Mother can manage a few more days. And I doubt that Winslow is really making such a mess of things as George would make out."

"You are right. However, for the peace of mind of all of us, I should return home. You are so very much better, Pru—I know it is so and Charles has remarked many times on how much improved you are. I am sure your term will go well from now on, and Mother will be with you for the birth. I'm glad I came to see both of you, for now when I get your letters I can picture you in your home, as you sit here now, and it will bring you so much closer to me."

Charles, when told, set off for Cirencester to arrange for a chaise early the following morning. One look at his sister-in-law's face had impressed upon him the urgency of the situation, so that he did not argue with her, nor seek an explanation she did not voluntarily vouchsafe, but, unlike Prudence, he was not wholly satisfied with the reason she gave for her sudden departure. He was not alone with her to discover anything further, and realizing that Josephina wished the evening to pass as pleasantly as any of their previous evenings together, he made light of her sudden departure, though realizing at last how exhausted Josephina was by her effort at making conversation, he insisted she retire early in preparation for the journey.

Her ashen face the following morning bespoke a night without sleep that she excused by saying how sorry she was to leave both of them, hugging her sister close to her and kissing Charles on both cheeks before stepping up into the chaise and waving her last good-byes. Only then did she admit to herself the fears she had gone to such lengths to conceal. Never had she felt such anxiety. Never had she felt so alone.

The journey back to Devon was long and tedious, despite the more luxurious manner mode of travel. She could not delight in the changing scene, nor could she eat anything at the inns where they stopped to change horses. At the *Angel* in Bridgewater, the innkeeper's wife became so deeply concerned at the sight of her pallid face that she insisted she drink a small glass of brandy; that did indeed bring a little colour back to her pale cheeks, but her eyes remained without lustre, dark and deeply troubled.

Despite her preoccupation with the express she had received, her thoughts turned repeatedly to Venables, wondering where he was, wishing that he were there with her in her time of need. She had never wished for anyone before to share her troubles and was surprised by the intensity with which she wanted him by her side at that very moment.

Could he, she wondered, be even then engaged to the beautiful creature Amelia had described? Yet if those rumours were true, surely he would not have behaved toward her as he had at the inn in Cheltenham and on the ride to Birdlip.

Her eyes drifted idly over countryside that became gradually more familiar as the miles passed away. That last meeting with Venables seemed aeons gone, and yet . . . she knew the memory of his words would always be with her. Surely he would not have spoken to her so, looked at her so, and then hastened to London to propose marriage to another. Yet he had said, "You won't have to defend your virtue from me again." Had he meant that he would no longer be a free man? She mulled over his words, believing first one way, then another. No, she decided. He had gone only because of his promise to his sister. The hope that had arisen in her breast, a hope she had attempted to ignore while she had been with him, a hope that he still felt for her as he had during the long St. Martin's summer—only that hope made the despair of that long journey endurable.

18

Late in the day the chaise drew up at Westlands. As she entered the house, her mother hurried up to her, wringing her hands. "Josephina, how glad I am you are back. It has been dreadful, simply dreadful! Squire Ridgeway has been out time and again, and George said he would be back this evening, just in case you are returned. If only you had listened to me. I knew you should not have borrowed money for such foolishness. And now what is to become of us? It has all been so horrible, so absolutely ghastly! And I had to face it alone." And with that her mother burst into tears, so that Josephina was hard pressed to calm her and to appear calm herself.

"I wish you would lie down, Mother. I know it must have been terrible for you, and I am sorry I was not here. But now that I am here, I want you to leave it all to me. I shall talk to Winslow and to George and find out, if I can, exactly what has happened."

"I can tell you what has happened, we are ruined. It is as simple as that. It was such a vindictive act, I can't bear to think of it." Again the tears flowed, so that Josephina had to take her mother upstairs and put her to bed, giving her a little laudanum to quieten her nerves and wishing that she could take a dose herself, but first she had to hear the details of the tragedy, and for that she would need all her wits about her.

By the time she returned downstairs, George Ridgeway had arrived.

"You got my letter. I was sorry to be the one to break the news to you, but I thought you should come back even though there is nothing that can be done now, I fear."

George's face and manner expressed his distress, and she was grateful for his solid presence and long-standing friendship. She led him into the parlour, where he sat down heavily in his favourite chair.

"I suppose you want the whole story?"

She nodded.

162

"It happened on Tuesday night. Winslow had been doing pretty well in your absence, going the rounds and seeing that things were attended to. He had taken on an extra man to watch the merinos, for he knew how much the investment meant to you. Will Meersham was with them most of the time, but on that night he had been invited to drink the health of a friend of his who was married that day—you remember old John Timmons' boy, the one who used to work on the Rawlins' farm. He was married to the daughter of a farmer near Torbridge, pretty good match from what I hear, for her father has no sons."

"Yes, yes, do go on, please. So Will went to drink the health of the married pair, and was the flock left untended?"

"No, there was this extra labourer I told you Winslow had taken on. He was new around here, but he had come around asking for work and he looked a likely lad. He had seemed reliable, and he said he would remain there till Will got back, and promised not to shut an eye. Well, Will swears that he was not gone above an hour and a half at the most, but when he got back he looked around for the fellow and couldn't find him. Then he heard an odd bleating sound, not the usual sound of a lamb seeking its mother, but mournful, fearful, he said it was. So he looked around but could see nothing in the dark. Then, as he was walking, he almost fell over something large and bulky. Leaning down, he put out his hand, to be met with a horrible warmth and wetness, awful, he said. He drew back, realizing his hand was covered with blood, blood from a sheep. He nearly went mad out there, rushing around in the dark trying to see what had happened. Then he came down and got Winslow. The poor old man was terrified, for by that time Will was covered with blood and quite incoherent. Anyway, he learned enough to send someone to inform my father, who got some men together, and I rode out with them to the field. It was dawn by then, and it looked for all the world like a battlefield, blood and dead sheep all over the place. Only two lambs were untouched, and one of the ewes may pull through, but the rest had to be buried, there was nothing else for it. It looked as though a madman had been through, a complete maniac. The men dug a big pit that morning and put the carcasses in; there was really nothing to save. There was blood all over . . . and the flies . . . I've never seen anything like it. I'm glad you were away."

Josephina had sat upright, listening to his grim tale, not moving apart from a slight trembling of her lips. "And the man Winslow had taken on, was he unhurt?"

"Vanished, no sign of him. Of course, my father has people out looking for him, and they should be able to find him. Don't know who he was, though, no one seems to have known him. Winslow shouldn't have taken on a stranger like that, but I suppose he gave him some hard-luck story and he swallowed it. I wish you would get yourself a good bailiff."

"It's not Winslow's fault. Probably had the fellow come to me, I would have done the same. He must have seemed harmless enough, from your description. I can't imagine why he would have done such a terrible thing, if, in fact, he did do it."

"But who else could have done it? Who would have wished to harm you so?"

She put her head in her hands, thinking; then she raised it slowly. "Has Farnsworth been seen around here lately?"

"Farnsworth! Why on earth do you ask about him. Surely you don't think he could be responsible?"

"I don't know. I just wondered." Her voice was tired.

"Well, I haven't seen him, but we can ask around if you suspect him. My father is conducting a complete investigation, I know he'll examine every possibility. He planned to come out to see you as soon as you came back, unless you wish to come in to see him tonight?"

"I am too tired now. I did not sleep well after I received your express. I must at all events try to get some sleep tonight, so that I can try to think clearly what I am to do."

But it was some hours before she reached her room, for she had to endure a long and tearful interview with Winslow, who arrived with Will Meersham, also in an abject state. She assured them that she did not consider them to blame, that it could have happened equally well had she been there, that it was the work of a madman. Winslow would not leave until he had personally checked all the doors and windows to make sure they were locked. Josephina could never remember such a thing in all her days at Westlands, and she protested it as unnecessary, but Winslow was firm.

"Like you said, that was a madman out there that night. I saw it, Miss Trafford, with my own eyes. Someone who would treat animals so is capable of doing the same to people. I don't know why your sheep were chosen, but some-one must have known you had a lot at stake there. It was an act of pure vindictiveness. I can't think of anyone who'd do such a thing, but I won't leave till I know this house is properly locked."

Squire Ridgeway came out early the following morning,

164

adding little to the story she had heard from his son but assuring her of his efforts to secure the villain.

"He won't get away in this county, I assure you, and I've friends over in Somerset if he heads that way. I can't imagine why he did it, but we'll find out when we get him. Beat it out of him myself if I have to."

"Do you know, then, who did it?" Josephina asked quickly.

"Must have been the young scoundrel Winslow engaged. Don't have a proper name, but we've got a good description of him. He won't get far."

"Are you sure it was he?"

"Well, who else could it have been? He disappeared, and all that was left was a bloody knife."

"Was that knife known to be his?"

"No one saw him with it, but that doesn't mean it wasn't his, does it?" The squire was becoming irritated.

"No, but still . . ."

"Well, who else could have done it?"

"I really don't know. The only person I can think of who did not like me was Farnsworth. Has anything been seen of him lately?"

"Farnsworth!" the squire bellowed with incredulity. "Well, Miss Trafford, I know you've had your say about his incompetence, but I didn't expect you to level such a charge as this against him. The man may have been a bit of a rogue, but he wasn't a complete villain."

"I haven't levelled any charge against him, squire," she snapped, her temper beginning to rise. "I merely asked if he had been seen. I am trying to think who might have been involved in such an act, and I know he did not like me."

"Not liking a person and killing off their livestock are two different things. No, no, say what you will about Farnsworth, I am sure he is incapable of such . . . such butchery."

Seeing her continued questioning gaze, he concluded, "Anyway, I've seen neither hide nor hair of him since Venables threw him out. I won't say that Belding isn't doing a better job at Venarvon in many ways, but Farnsworth wasn't the scoundrel some make him out."

Josephina said nothing. She felt numb. What did it really matter who had done it? Her hopes and dreams were shattered, and, worse than that, she was in serious financial difficulty. The note would be due in November, and money for it must be found. Renewal might be possible, but the interest would have to be paid, and she did not doubt that the renewal terms would be even more harsh, in view of what had happened. She felt as though she were sinking in a mire of debts from which there was no escape.

She heard the squire's strident tones continuing, "I wish you had listened to Frank, even if you didn't listen to me. I know he advised you against it, but you are sometimes quite foolhardy, Josephina. I tell you only for your own good. If you had someone to advise you, if you would only come to me before you do these things, I could help, but after the fact it is useless. You were not clear of debt when you started out on this—now look at the mess you are in."

"Squire, I know you mean well, but this is not the time to remind me of my shortcomings. I am only to well aware of them myself. I thank you for all your efforts on my behalf to apprehend the culprit. You have been most efficient. Apprehension will not recompense me for my loss, but perhaps it will provide a reason for such a dastardly act."

The squire rose from his seat, his mouth turned down and the jowls of his large red face positively shaking.

"There you go again. Can't take advice, that's your trouble. I'm speaking plainly now, and if I speak out of turn, I hope you will take it as fatherly advice—"

Before he could continue, Josephina interrupted, revolted at receiving paternal advice from a source so remote from her own father. "Please excuse me, squire. Another day perhaps. I hope you may realize that this has been an awful shock to me. I have not slept well and I would rather delay any further advice you have to offer until I am better able to receive it. I thank you for coming; both you and your son have been most considerate. If you will excuse me now. I shall be available if you need me for a hearing into the matter."

"I plan to hold it on Thursday," he snapped. "I put it off as long as I could, hoping that we will have caught the fellow by then and I can simply send him up to the assizes."

"If he is the guilty one."

"Of course, if he is guilty. I don't send innocent men up for trial." He snapped, making no attempt to hide his irritation.

"I know you don't," Josephina conceded. "I am sorry that may have seemed impertinent. I merely meant that whoever the person is who did it, he is innocent until proven guilty." Seeing the red flush of anger deepen on the squire's face, she hastened to add, "Your reputation as a fair magistrate is well-known. I would not for a moment impugn it. You must

166

excuse me, but I am overwrought, and, I believe, with reason."

"Well," he said, somewhat mollified, "I know you've been through a lot. The hearing is set for ten on Thursday, and I'll see you then unless I get any news in the meantime. Frank said he would come, in case you needed any legal advice."

She thanked him and at last saw him out of the house.

Her next days were occupied with neighbours and tenants coming to express their regret at her loss. Their expressions of sympathy were appreciated, but they did little to help her overcome her despair and desolation, serving more to remind her of the grim business. No one had any light to shed on the matter. Most of the farm labourers had been at the wedding celebration, and at that hour of the night, farmers and estate owners were in their homes, if not in their beds. No one had heard anything extraordinary, nor did anyone mention that Farnsworth had been seen in Milvercombe or in the surrounding countryside. Despite herself, Josephina could not help but feel apprehensive that someone hated her sufficiently to perpetrate such a crime against her.

The only thing that kept her sane during those long, frantic days was Venables. He was not at her side, but the thought of him never left her; it was that which sustained her. He would hear of what had happened. He would come to her, she was sure of it.

But she withheld the news from Prudence, also asking the Carews not to mention it when they wrote, for fear it would upset her sister just when she was so much recovered. Thus, when she received Pru's next letter, it was full only of her recovered health and her joy at the visit, yet the main part of it was devoted to the one whose name Josephina delighted in yet never allowed herself to mention.

We were surprised by the return to Blenhasset on Saturday of Lord Venables. You had not mentioned that he was due to return so soon, but he came here in the afternoon, having just arrived from London, expecting you to still be here. He was quite upset when I told him you had left so soon after his own departure, and asked whether you had left no message or note for him, but of course I had none. I would that I had, for he appeared most anxious. I told him of the letter from George Ridgeway which had necessitated your return, and asked whether I could convey any message to you when next I wrote, but he merely asked the reason for your sudden return home. On that score I was unable completely to satisfy him, because it had come as a surprise to me also. As I had not read the letter you received, I could speak only in generalities. During the conversation I gathered that his sole reason for coming to Gloucestershire in the first place was because he had heard you were to visit us.

Whatever your past feelings, I cannot help but believe that you should be flattered. I think that during those times you met him you must have seen him as we have grown to know him. He can never be accused of any impropriety here; on the contrary he is esteemed as a considerate and gentle man.

Looking back on what I have written, I may owe you an apology, for I seem to be pleading a suit which may not have been rendered. Forgive me if I am reading more into Lord Venables' return than was intended. I miss you, but be assured your visit was the best possible cure I could have had. Now I shall prepare for Mother's arrival and the arrival of my own dear child with good spirits and continued good health. Next time we are together, you will be a brand-new aunt!

The letter left Josephina with turbulent yet triumphant emotions. Venables was indeed free, and he had come for her. She was sure he would now journey to Devon; perhaps he was even at that moment on his way. All of her difficulties seemed surmountable. Nothing that had happened in the past mattered any longer. She would see him. She would tell him how much she needed him. She would seek that embrace she so longed for. She was sure now that he loved her as she loved him. She was sure, also, that that love would triumph.

The people of Milvercombe began to note how well Josephina Trafford was taking her loss.

"She's putting on a good show of it," the squire acknowledged, "but what else can she do? I know to the penny how much she is down and how much she was depending on those sheep. If only she had listened to me, but now it's too late." And he took another glass of port and congratulated himself on his good judgement.

George Ridgeway continued at Josephina's side during those difficult days. Yet even his ponderous statements, mirrors of his father's pontifications, she refused to allow to annoy her. She knew he meant well, and was and would continue to be, come what may, her friend. Though at times he assumed a protection of her, even an intimacy, to which she felt he had no right, yet she knew he feared for her welfare in the light of what had happened. He stayed late in the evening, not wishing to leave her alone, and often arrived so early that she was unable to attend to her routine tasks. Her hints went unnoticed; even her protestations that she felt perfectly secure were unheeded. He strode in her footsteps like a puppy dog at his master's heels.

Just before the hearing, he rode out, his face flushed with excitement. Josephina was sure he must have news—perhaps the young lad had been apprehended—yet he contained himself until he was ensconced in his favourite spot. Then, with obvious satisfaction, he remarked, "I see Venables has at last decided to settle down."

Josephina, finishing her last cup of breakfast coffee, set her cup down with a clatter upon the saucer and then put both of them very carefully on the table at her side. When George made no attempt to elucidate, she was forced to ask what he meant.

"It was in the *Morning Post* received this morning, an announcement of his engagement. Forget the name of the lady now, but it was no one from Devon, of course, daughter of some duke, it said."

"Lady Daphne Mercer." Josephina's voice was so low that he asked her to repeat the name.

"Yes, that was it, I remember now, the Duke of Danforth's daughter. Well, I'm disappointed, you knew of it all along, and here I thought to surprise you. But I suppose you learned of it in Gloucestershire. No one here knew anything of it, I can assure you. Father thought Venables should have at least informed him, for he is squire, after all, but I suppose he doesn't think as much of us here in Devon as he does of his new Gloucestershire cronies."

Josephina wished that she would wake suddenly to find it was all a terrible nightmare, but George's stalwart shape before her, heavy boots outstretched, was all too real.

"I must say I'll be glad to have him married and settled and not scurrying around and upsetting our lives again. I can say now that I thought he paid far too much attention to you when he was here, and I must admit I was concerned when you said you'd seen him in Gloucestershire that he would continue those attentions. I see now I need not have worried, he had other things on his mind."

Josephina's mouth felt dry; a lump had arisen in her throat. The horror that had awaited her on her return seemed slight compared to that she was now forced to bear.

"There was never any cause to worry, yet indeed, George, you have no right to do so."

He ignored her comment, asking only, "Did he mention his forthcoming engagement to you when you saw him?"

"No, he said nothing of it, but I had heard of it from another source."

"Well, if she's of the Danforth family, she'll bring him a pretty penny," George mused, loudly sipping the coffee she had handed him on his arrival.

"I don't believe money would concern him," she observed bitterly.

"That's a romantic view, not a practical one. Money draws money, you know. Like any other man, he undoubtedly thinks it a good commodity to accumulate. Then, too, I expect he is anxious to produce an heir, now he has the title. And a duke for a father-in-law is not to be sneezed at."

Josephina could no longer bear his conjectures on Venables' motives. Abruptly she got up. "I'm sorry, but I must ask you to leave. There is much to do, and with the hearing on Thursday I shall be forced to lose yet another day. I shall see you then, and not before."

He started to protest, but she was insistent on his leaving, conducting him to the front door herself. When at last he was gone, she seized her copy of the *Morning Post* from the hall table.

There could be no mistake; there it was, the notice of the impending nuptials of Lady Daphne Mercer, daughter of the Duke and Duchess of Danforth, and Conniston Avery Glendenning, sixth Earl of Venables. For the first time since, as a child, she had dropped her china doll and it had shattered into countless unmendable fragments, she put her head in her hands and cried in utter defeat. Then she had refused all offers to replace the doll, for to her that doll was irreplaceable. Now she had even more irrevocably lost the only man she had ever wanted, the only man she would ever love.

19

Josephina sat between the solid forms of Frank and George Ridgeway, her eyes resting on the large bronze paperweight in the shape of a bulldog that reposed in the middle of Squire Ridgeway's desk, listening to Will Meersham repeat his testimony at the hearing. It followed the same lines as the testimony already given by Winslow earlier that morning, but there was no numbing the intensity with which the grim details sickened her.

She tried not to look across at Farnsworth, who sat between the two hefty men who had brought him in the night before. Could he possibly hate her enough to have done this dreadful thing?

She had not expected to see him there, nor had the squire. When she had arrived that morning, Squire Ridgeway had been awaiting her, his face flushed and angry. He called her aside as soon as she came.

"Josephina, since I am Justice of the Peace of this parish, I think it is only courtesy to inform me when you decide to take matters into your own hands. Hiring Bow Street runners is going to cost you a pretty penny and will not bring back your livestock."

"Hiring Bow Street runners!" She looked at him as though he were mad.

"I'm speaking of the two men who brought Farnsworth in last night. A fine fool I felt, I can assure you, having to tell them I knew nothing of it. They had no warrant with them, said it would be here today, so I presume you have it."

"I have no warrant, nor do I know anything of sending runners after Farnsworth," she retorted.

"Yet it was you who mentioned him the other morning. He says he has nothing to do with it, and I know of no one who has seen him here. They picked him up down in Cornwall, says he's been there all along. It'll be a pretty kettle of fish if there's no warrant forthcoming. Can't hold a man like that,

171

just on inclination. Besides, I never thought he was involved anyway."

"I know nothing of it, squire, I assure you," Josephina insisted. "But since he is here, it will be as well to get his sworn testimony as to where he was that night. That, presumably, can be corroborated; then, if there is no warrant and if nothing incriminates him, I presume you'll have to let him go."

"I know that," the squire expostulated. "But who sent the runners after him, if not you?"

"I have no idea. Perhaps you should have asked the runners themselves."

"I did, but I got nothing out of them. Insolent fellows. Londoners! Think they can come down here and throw their weight about. Refused to leave their man all night. Said they were paid to bring him in for the hearing and they would do just that. I was hard put to find a place for the three of them at a moment's notice. Farnsworth is mad as a bull, and frankly I don't blame him, especially if it's found he was not involved, as I suspect will be the case."

"Perhaps we should get on with the hearing, then, and get it over with." Josephina turned to go. She was tired and felt sick. Farnsworth reminded her of the last time she had seen him, and their ugly scene on the road. She thought of the names he had called her—hussy, wench—his leering laugh. Would he repeat it all at the hearing? she wondered. She could deny nothing if she were under oath. The emptiness, the affliction that had been hers since hearing of Venables' engagement increased in her loneliness.

She realized, with a start, that Will Meersham had completed his testimony and stepped down and that it was her turn to take the oath.

She gave the squire the details of the purchase of the sheep, their number, including the newborn lambs, and the details of those surviving, only the two lambs, for the ewe had died two days after her return.

"Where were you on the night the killing took place?" the squire asked.

"I was in Gloucestershire, staying with my sister."

"Where in Gloucestershire?" His voice was testy.

"At Flaxhurst. My brother-in-law, Charles Carew, has the Blenhasset living there."

"I know, of course, but I have to ask this for the record," the squire explained.

She nodded.

"And how did you hear of it?"

She started to reply when the door opened and all turned to observe the newcomer. It was Lord Venables. He had obviously just arrived from a journey, for his usually immaculate clothing bore signs of road dust, his linen lacked its accustomed crispness, and his normally mirror-finished boots were quite muddied. All eyes were fixed on his tall and commanding figure as he walked in, apologizing for the intrusion.

"Well, Lord Venables, this is a surprise. I did not expect you." Squire Ridgeway's astonishment was evident. He half-rose from his chair and then sat heavily down again.

"I had intended to be here for the start of the hearing, but one of my horses threw a shoe in Bridgewater, which delayed me." Venables appeared far more at ease than the squire. "You must excuse my appearance, but I felt it more important to come here immediately and to present my testimony than to change my linen."

"I was unaware that you had any knowledge of the event or that you intended to testify." The squire's voice was puzzled.

"I was not here at the time, as you know, but I believe I may be able to throw some light on the motivation for the crime."

"If you can do that, we shall all be relieved. No one has been able to understand anything whatsoever in any of this business." The squire showed some vexation, as though his role were being usurped, but Venables appeared oblivious of his discomfort as he seated himself in the chair Winslow proffered, after the merest glance and bow to Josephina. Farnsworth, whom he had ascertained was there as he entered, received no acknowledgement.

"Yes, well, let me see, where were we?" The squire turned to his clerk, who was keeping a record of the hearing.

"You were asking Miss Trafford how she came to hear of the killing."

"Ah, yes, that's right. Well, Miss Trafford?"

"An express arrived for me at my sister's house. It was from your . . . from George Ridgeway. He explained to me what had happened, and of course I immediately arranged for my return."

For the first time she looked directly at Venables as she spoke. The look he returned puzzled her. What was it—sudden understanding, remorse, despair? She could not tell, but the squire's questions continued as she turned back.

"And what did you do when you got back?"

"I talked with my bailiff, Winslow, and with Will Meersham, both of whom told me essentially what they have told you here this morning. I also spoke with George Ridgeway and yourself."

"Did you issue a warrant for the arrest of Farnsworth in connection with this crime?"

"I did not."

"Do you know who might have done?"

"I do not."

"Do you have anything else to add?"

"No, I don't believe so."

"Then you may step down."

Josephina returned to her seat between Frank and George without looking again in Venables' direction, but constantly aware of his eyes on her. George turned and whispered something to her, and she nodded. She had not heard what he said, for she was still in a daze, wondering at the meaning of Venables' arrival, and she had no wish to enter into a long, involved conversation.

"Well, now, let's see." Squire Ridgeway scratched his chin. In all the years since he had been magistrate in Milvercombe, this was the most difficult case he had had to handle, and finding himself under the scrutiny of Venables, he did not wish to make any mistake. "I think perhaps that you, my lord, should give your testimony next, and then I'll hear from Farnsworth."

"Very well."

Venables' tall figure rose, and he strode over to the squire's desk and placed his right hand upon the Bible, repeating the oath, before he seated himself in the chair facing the assembled group, his head high, fixing the squire with his penetrating gaze.

"Your name, for the record, my lord?"

"Conniston Avery Glendenning, sixth Earl of Venables, of the parish of Milvercombe."

"And your age?"

"Thirty-two."

Squire Ridgeway scratched his chin again. Now that he had the preliminaries out of the way, he was not sure how to proceed with this unexpected witness.

Venables came to his aid. He reached into his coat pocket. "I believe I should give you this. It is the warrant I had issued for Farnsworth's arrest in connection with this crime. I believe he has material evidence of his part in it, and should he be unwilling to give it voluntarily, I expect that definite

174

proof will be brought in before the day is out. I know that as yet all the evidence is circumstantial."

"So, it was you who sent the runners after him?"

"Yes. I heard of what had happened from my bailiff, and suspected Farnsworth to be involved. I did not want him free to do possible harm to people as well as animals, so I swore out a warrant and sent runners after him. I have another runner still out searching for the young lad I believe he hired."

Farnsworth, who had worn a pugnacious expression throughout the hearing, narrowed his eyes to stare venomously at Venables, but his look missed its mark, for Venables completely ignored him.

Yet Squire Ridgeway's worried frown continued. "But I fail to understand the connexion with this matter, my lord. You were not here, and it was not your livestock which was harmed. As far as I know, no damage was reported from Venarvon, nor from any other place, for that matter."

"Precisely," said Venables. "It was for that reason I immediately fixed upon Farnsworth as being involved. He has an abnormal hatred for Miss Trafford, and has, on at least one occasion of which I am personally aware, threatened her life."

Farnsworth gripped the arms of his chair while Squire Ridgeway stared at Venables in disbelief.

"This was never reported to me. I cannot believe that he would have done such a thing and Josephina . . . Miss Trafford would not have told me of it."

"I came upon him attempting to strike at her with her own riding whip, which he had wrested from her after pulling her from her horse. Had I not arrived at the scene, quite by chance, there is no saying what the outcome might have been."

"But this is impossible," the squire sputtered. "What could possibly have been his reasons for such unholy conduct?"

"I presume you will find that out from him. My understanding of it was that he held her responsible for the loss of his position on my estate, a suspicion that was quite unfounded. I had come to Devon to examine the condition of the place on the death of my brother. Within half an hour of my arrival it was painfully apparent to me that he had been bilking Venarvon unmercifully for years. Whatever Miss Trafford said—and she spoke purely as a close neighbour who had borne firsthand testimony to the difficulties suffered by my tenants during his tenure—merely corroborated what I had already learned. I had made up my mind to get rid of

175

Farnsworth, and I did. My mistake was in not pressing charges of fraud and embezzlement against him. I regret today that I did not."

The look of incredulity had still not left the squire's face. "But why did Miss Trafford not press charges, or at least report the incident when he attacked her?"

"I should not speak for her; however, I know that he had told her he was having difficulty finding employment, and I believe she felt sorry for him."

"Sorry for him, after he struck at her! It's incredible!" The squire fixed his gaze upon Josephina, who returned it without flinching, though dreading Farnsworth's testimony yet to come.

"Well, I can see why you would suspect him after that. And I know Miss Trafford mentioned to me that she thought he bore her some ill-will. If you have nothing further to add, sir, I think we should hear from him now."

"I have nothing to add for the moment, but I hope the other runner may come in with the witness I want before this hearing is over."

"That is my hope also, for we need some solid evidence to corroborate your suspicions." The squire fidgeted at his desk, resenting Venables' high-handed manner but fearing him at the same time.

After being sworn, Farnsworth sat belligerently in the witness chair, no longer looking at Venables, but glowering at Josephina before turning all his attention to the squire.

He began quietly enough.

"Squire, you have me here under false pretences. I have nothing to do with what happened to Miss Trafford's sheep. I now live in Cornwall, and my wife can testify that I was there at the time this event took place. I have neighbours there also who will be willing to testify. It is cruel the way I am being treated; having ruined my good name, now they are tracking me down like a dog every time a crime is committed here. I've had a hard enough time of it since leaving this parish without being persecuted in this manner. I have a wife and family to support, and you are taking me away from my livelihood."

"Which is?" the squire enquired.

"I have a small farm near the coast, just a little house and a few acres, you understand."

The squire looked at him with some sympathy. "You have heard it said that you abused Miss Trafford. Did you, in fact, strike her, as has been reported here by Lord Venables?"

176

"I didn't exactly strike at her, but we did have an altercation, I admit to that."

"Was it over the loss of your position as bailiff at Venarvon?"

"No, it was over a matter which I don't suppose Miss Trafford will want me to discuss here."

Josephina lifted her eyes from her hands and stared directly at Farnsworth for the first time. Venables stretched his legs out in front of him and leaned back in his chair, surveying his former bailiff critically.

The squire regarded his witness with interest.

"What do you mean, something Miss Trafford doesn't want you to discuss."

"It's a personal matter of hers. I had promised not to mention it, but now that my neck is on the line, I see no need to keep such promises."

Josephina kept her eyes upon him, though her hands were clenched tightly together.

"Well, out with it man." It was obvious that the squire's curiosity was fully aroused.

"Well, squire, I had always regarded Miss Trafford as a lady, even though she goes around doing man's work, and I treated her as such, that is, until I found myself forced to speak to her about her conduct. It was for her own good, I assure you."

He paused, and Venables leaned forward, while the squire's eyes widened in anticipation. Josephina did not flinch, but continued to keep her eyes on Farnsworth.

"Well, I seen her one day, her and his lordship, driving back from the Trummocks' place they were. I just happened to be in the lane when they stopped, and then she carried on in such a manner, just like a hussy. I never thought to see a lady behave so, especially one like Miss Trafford, who gives herself such airs and graces, always holier than thou." He paused again to let his words sink in.

"Carrying on?" The squire raised his eyebrows.

Venables' eyes were steely, and he jumped to his feet, addressing Squire Ridgeway.

"Your honour, if you intend that this witness should be allowed to besmirch a good lady's name in front of us all, I must strongly object. He is deliberately trying to detract from his role in the matter with which this hearing is concerned by bringing salacious accusations against a person who is above reproach. I find it totally disgusting to sit here and listen to it, and I should think you, as presiding justice, would be of the same mind. I also find in what he says evidence that there is nothing he will not stoop to in order to harm Miss Trafford, further corroborating his ability to have committed the heinous crime of last week."

Turning to Farnsworth, his face white with anger but his voice steady and cold, he continued. "After this you may be assured I will not let a stone remain unturned until I learn everything of your role in the slaughter of that valuable livestock."

Squire Ridgeway's desire to know more of what Farnsworth had seen struggled with his knowledge that Venables' objections carried weight. It might not be relevant, but he tended to agree with Farnsworth's opinion of Josephina,

"I think I should at least call upon Miss Trafford to ascertain why she did not press charges when this attack, or argument, or whatever it was occurred."

Venables looked at Josephina's tense, pale face and again intervened. "Has not this lady suffered enough? You ask why she did not press charges or report this person, well, she is not one to flaunt her own virtues. Most of us in this room are aware of her serious and responsible attitude toward her own tenants and to others who come to her in need. Though I have not until lately returned to this parish, I am aware of instances where she has come to the aid of those in difficulty." He looked over at Will Meersham as he spoke. "I know there are those here who can vouch for her unfailing wish to help those in trouble or those less fortunate than herself. In this instance Farnsworth was out of work and had a wife and family to support, and he approached her to get his job back. Had he done so in a proper manner, the incident might have ended differently. Instead, he used threats and force, tactics anyone at all acquainted with Miss Trafford would know to be fruitless. But despite that, when I suggested to the lady that charges be pressed against him, she argued he was already having enough difficulty finding work, that if he were to be incarcerated, his wife and children would be thrown upon the parish and their situation would become even more perilous. Her motivation in not pressing charges against him was entirely altruistic, I can assure you."

The battle was now between the squire and Venables, and Farnsworth sat back, crossing his arms across his chest, feeling he had a champion in the squire. But he was doomed to disappointment, for the squire was unwilling to carry the point further.

"Well, my lord," he conceded slowly, "in that event I suppose we must press on, though where to press on to, I cannot say. He says he was not here, and no one has seen him. Motivation there may be, but hard evidence there is not."

"I have statements"—Venables spoke slowly and deliberately, his eyes fixed on the squire unflinchingly, even arrogantly—"statements which will be put into your record, showing that Farnsworth was in Torbridge the day before the crime was committed. I have a statement from the man who sold a knife to him, a knife very similar in description to the one found in the field, and I also know that he was seen at the Wayfarers Inn there with a young man who sounds remarkably like the fellow who disappeared after the crime."

"Well, that's something, but I'm not sure it is enough to send him up for trial at the assizes, especially if his alibis prove sound."

Venables walked over and gripped the edge of the squire's desk.

"I warn you that if you let him go free you are deliberately placing Miss Trafford's life in danger." Venables' voice was still controlled, but there was no concealing his anger.

Squire Ridgeway sighed heavily. Venables was entirely too arrogant, but he was too powerful a man to ignore. If he were to prove right, there would be the devil to pay and no pitch hot. It looked as though there had been something between him and Josephina after all. Lady Netherton had told his wife all along that there was. He would have liked to hear all Farnsworth had to say about that scene in the lane, but the chance was gone. What these men saw in Josephina Trafford was beyond him. And there was his son and heir making a fool of himself over her; well, perhaps this would serve to open his eyes.

It had been a long time since breakfast, and the squire was hungry. More than food, he wanted a glass of wine; perhaps that would give him some ideas on how to proceed.

"I'm going to call for a recess now. Perhaps, my lord, you would care to join me in some refreshments."

"I should be delighted," Venables responded, glad also to gain time.

Venables bowed distantly to Josephina as he left the room in the wake of the squire. George did not look at her but suggested somewhat coldly that they might also partake of refreshments, and they, too, followed the squire into the dining room, where cold meats and cheese had been set out on the massive mahogany table.

"Well, my lord," said the squire, assuming a jovial expression as the wine was served, "had I known you were to be here today, I should have called for a finer wine in order to drink the health of you and your good lady. Only yesterday I wrote to you expressing my felicitations on your forthcoming marriage. I read of it in the *Morning Post*." His tone was reproachful, but Venable merely thanked him with an expressionless face, dutifully raising his glass in response to the squire's hearty toast. He kept his eyes assiduously on his host, as did Josephina, who maintained an outer calm in drinking a salutation to an event for which she could feel only dread.

"As I say"—the squire's joviality was heartened by the wine's smooth flavour—"it caught all of us by surprise, except for Miss Trafford, that is, but I expect that was because she was so recently in Gloucestershire and heard of it there."

It was Venables who looked surprised as he turned to ask her forcefully, "But it was impossible for anyone in Gloucestershire to know of it, particularly at the time of your visit, for I had not then . . . I was not then engaged."

"No, it was not there I heard of it, but before I left Devon. My sister Amelia is a constant harbinger of London gossip now that she is having her season there—one of the *on-dits* in her letters had been rumours of your forthcoming marriage." Her voice was as steady as her pounding heart would allow in discussing a matter that hurt her so deeply—particularly with the one who had caused that hurt, particularly surrounded by those who could in no way sympathize or empathize with her distress.

"But that was pure conjecture then, nothing more than that. I assure you," he insisted, his expression making her believe he wished to say much more.

"Well, conjecture it may have been, but obviously where there's smoke there's fire." The squire laughed heartily at his own witticism, then gave Josephina a sharp glance, remembering Farnsworth's comments.

"I understand your good lady is the daughter of the Duke of Danforth?" he went on.

"She is not my good lady yet, sir, but that is so." Venables made no attempt to hide the annoyance that the discussion was causing him, but if the squire noticed, he paid no heed.

"And when is the wedding to be?"

"The date is not fixed."

"June is a fine month for weddings," the squire offered.

"I can assure you it will not be that soon."

Mrs. Ridgeway entered and bade them sit down, allowing

180

Venables to steer the conversation to the difficult life of a justice of the peace, a subject dear to the squire's heart, and the difficulties of this particular hearing, but not before her voice had been raised in further felicitations.

Josephina sat beside George, who spoke little, not an unusual occurrence when food was on the table, for that always demanded his first attention. She was aware, however, that his attitude toward her was unusually distant; for that, at least, she felt relief. Humiliating as Farnsworth's words had been, if they had removed her as an object of George's attentions they had not been totally without benefit.

While they were still at the table, a message came for Venables, who immediately excused himself. It was some time before he returned, but he then appeared to be in better spirits.

"Well, squire, your calling a recess at this point was a matter of excellent timing," he affirmed diplomatically, "for it has allowed my man to bring in the fellow who was Farnsworth's accomplice."

"Oh, he's here," the squire responded in some excitement.

"He's here and spilling out the whole story at this very moment. I asked your clerk to record it. Once there is a confrontation between those two, I believe we shall know everything. There can be no doubt, now, of Farnsworth's part in this. I think the young lad was primarily sent there for the purpose of seeing that the field was clear, and in that he had no difficulty because of the wedding feast that night, but I suspect from the amount of carnage he may also have taken part in the butchery. Anyway, it should now be a simple matter to send them both up for trial and let the judge and jury at the next quarter sessions make that decision. The important thing is that Farnsworth should not be loose, for there is no telling what he might do. I am sure you can understand that after his venomous talk today."

"You may be sure I know my duty, my lord. There seems no question now that he'll be sent up." Turning to Josephina, he added, "I do wish that you had come to me when he threatened you in that manner. It should have been reported. Had it been, this misfortune might never have befallen you."

"You are perfectly right, squire," she acknowledged. "I was at fault. Had I had the gift of foresight, I should certainly have done so."

"Had any of us the gift of foresight, many things might be different today." There was an emotional tone in Venables' voice, and his eyes sought hers as he spoke, making Josephina feel his response was directed to her.

"I had thought myself a better judge of human nature," she said, only partly to the squire.

"I'm afraid your judgement in that regard has erred on more than one occasion, Miss Trafford," Venables added in a low voice.

"Perhaps," she assented, turning back to the squire for fear these remarks might again pique his curiosity.

"Squire Ridgeway," said Venables, "I feel a great personal responsibility in this tragedy. I know that Miss Trafford had invested heavily in this breed of sheep and that a great deal depended upon it. I believe I am at fault in not having pressed charges against Farnsworth earlier for the civil crimes he had committed against me and my estate. Had I done so then, Miss Trafford would not now be suffering her loss." He turned to her. "It would greatly relieve my mind, Miss Trafford, if you would allow me to make good that loss."

She looked at him for a moment before slowly shaking her head. "I thank you, sir, but no. It is in no way your fault, and I cannot accept it."

"But, Josephina," Frank Ridgeway intervened, "you should reconsider. I am well aware of your circumstances. If his lordship wishes to make reparation, I think you should deliberate his offer before refusing."

"Of course, he is not legally bound to do so," his father intervened.

"Morally, rather," interposed Venables.

"Morally, perhaps, but not even that, I think, in view of Miss Trafford's failure to press charges against Farnsworth of an even more grievous nature."

"We are splitting hairs," Venables interjected with some irritation. "I shall instruct my solicitor to contact you, Miss Trafford, to ascertain the amount needed to replace your livestock."

"I am sorry, sir, but I refuse your offer. I gambled and I lost. I cannot expect someone to bail me out because my scheme failed, whatever the reason. I have found out the hard way that speculation is not my forte, but at least I have discovered that now rather than later. I have come through difficult times before; undoubtedly I shall come through this also. I beg you not to concern yourself on my behalf. I would, however, appreciate it if care could be taken to keep news of this from reaching my sister. Her health is still delicate and I do not wish her to be upset any more than is necessary."

"You need have no fear on my account, I shall not mention it," said Venables gravely, "but may I not talk to you later about my offer?"

"I think not. I thank you for it, but there is nothing more to be discussed on that matter or any other." She turned to the squire. "If you do not need me any more today, I should much appreciate being allowed to return home."

"Well, of course, Josephina, you have had a difficult day, I don't doubt it," the squire agreed. "If all goes smoothly this afternoon, along the lines that Lord Venables predicts, there will be merely the matter of the complaint to be signed, but I can bring that out to you."

"No, I'll ride in tomorrow if it can wait until then, but I shall be at home if you need me."

"I'll take you back, Josephina," George offered, though without his usual enthusiasm.

"No, thank you. I came with Winslow, and since he has given his testimony, I presume he is free to go. We can return together."

She turned and left the room without a backward glance. The next day Venables left Devon for London without making any attempt to see her.

20

The end of June was to bring Amelia back from London, but prior to her arrival Mrs. Trafford received a letter from her brother-in-law, Putnam Mulliner, conveying the information that Captain Derek Rutherford had made an offer for Amelia's hand. Mr. Mulliner's praise for Captain Rutherford, if not overwhelming, was sincere. He described him as the younger son of a Lincolnshire baronet, now serving with the First Foot Guards under General Sir Peregrine Maitland; he was a man of good character, anxious to advance in his profession, though, unfortunately, deterred by a lack of means. It was obviously a love match, Mr. Mulliner noted, for otherwise it would have been to Captain Rutherford's advantage to fix his attentions where there was money, a possibility entirely feasible, given his bearing and family background. As it was, Captain Rutherford did not wish to make a formal proposal for Amelia's hand until he was assured that her marriage portion would be forthcoming. Mr. Mulliner hastened to point out that he did not consider Captain Rutherford at all mercenary in this stipulation, merely practical. As a younger son of a baronet himself, he could understand the difficulties faced by Captain Rutherford and hoped that his sister-in-law would adopt an equally understanding attitude. He knew this would place a financial burden upon the family and was willing himself to lend up to two thousand pounds towards the amount if they could promise the rest. Captain Rutherford was to rejoin his regiment, but if all arrangements were concluded by October, he would then get leave to return for the wedding.

Isabel Putnam had included a short note to her sister saying that she was very much taken with Captain Rutherford and regretted his lack of fortune. She thought, however, that the young couple would do well, both of them being gregarious in nature and adaptable to the ways of society.

Mrs. Trafford carried the letter to Josephina, thrilled beyond measure at the thought of the match.

"Isn't it exciting! He sounds such a nice gentleman, the son of a baronet no less, even though he is a younger son. Isabel says he has such perfect manners and that he is so handsome. I knew Amelia would make a good match, she's such a pretty girl and, as Isabel says, she has a talent of making herself liked wherever she goes. Isabel is going to be sorry to lose her, I'm sure. But how are we to raise the money, Josephina? I'll have to leave that in your hands, for you've always managed these things. I'm sure I wish you hadn't wasted it on those foolish animals, but if you can raise money for sheep, you can surely raise it to ensure that your sister has a good husband."

But Josephina knew that money would not be available from the same source. She was aware she could not cover her note, due in November, and given her present circumstances, it was doubtful whether it would be easily renewable; to ask for another five thousand or even less was out of the question.

"Well, Josephina, what am I to say when I write? Uncle Mulliner is going to want to know what to tell Captain Rutherford, and I expect Amelia will want to be thinking about wedding clothes, for October is not far off, you know."

There could be only one answer, and that was to sell Westlands. Squire Ridgeway had hinted on several occasions recently that he would be willing to buy those parts of her land which adjoined his, but she was averse to splitting the estate. She was proud of the fact that, though it was not large, it had been preserved with its original boundaries for over a century. To sell a portion would make it into one of those piecemeal affairs she deplored, neither estate, nor manor, nor farm. Similar small holdings were to be found all over the country, estates hardly worthy of the name. Such sales often forced the tenantry from land they had long farmed to accommodate others willing to pay more for its use, or their houses were converted into cottages for people from town. It was a change in the countryside that Josephina deplored. If she were to sell, it must be the entire estate or nothing, and she would insist that the tenants be allowed to remain.

Her mother stood before her, waving the letter. "Well, Josephina, I must write immediately. What shall I say?"

"Tell my uncle that we wish them happy and that by October the money for Amelia's marriage portion will be available. I trust we shall not need to borrow the two thousand pounds he offers, but thank him anyway."

"It will be a splendid wedding," her mother enthused. "October is such a pretty month. We can decorate the altar with autumn leaves and chrysanthemums and Amelia can carry a bouquet of the same colours, which will set off her fair beauty so well, and Captain Rutherford will look so handsome beside her in his Guards' uniform. It will be such an event, only wait till I tell Lady Netherton. I do think Amelia should purchase her wedding clothes in London before she leaves."

To this Josephina strongly objected; Amelia must make do with their dressmakers. She could see her sister scouring the London shops, running up accounts to add to her financial miseries.

"But, Josephina," her mother wailed, "it won't do. He is the son of a baronet, after all. She can't be sent off just anyhow, and the cut of London clothes speaks for itself, it can't be reproduced in the provinces."

The scorn her mother managed to convey in that last word was vitriolic.

Josephina looked at her mother's petulant face, her lips pursed in contempt, her cheeks puffed in disapproval, wondering whether it was worth making a stand over a few hundred pounds. With thousands to be found, did it really make any difference? At least it would keep Amelia from under her feet for a little longer. She resigned herself.

"Very well, but tell her I will pay nothing over two hundred." With this figure Josephina hoped that the bills would total no more than half as much again, and her mother, after wondering whether to press for more, decided against it, leaving it to Amelia to fight that battle when the time came. She went off happily to write her letter and to hurry in to Milvercombe to carry the news to Lady Netherton. Only think, two daughters married, and poor Fanny still at home.

The summer dragged on at Westlands. It was warmer than usual, but without the drought of the preceding year. Crops were abundant and farmers hastened to get them in, fearing early rains might again spell their ruin. Despite the abundance, Josephina was unable to rejoice with them. It could not provide the money she needed; only the sale of her estate could do that.

The announcement of Amelia's engagement duly appeared in the *Morning Post*, and a short time later her mother received, among other congratulatory messages, a note from Lord Venables felicitating her on her daughter's forthcoming marriage.

"Fancy him noticing it. I must say I was surprised. Of course, I know he is our neighbour and I think Prudence and Charles are quite friendly with him, but I'm surprised that he took the time to write." And she set his note aside to show to Lady Netherton.

Josephina had read, from time to time, in those news columns devoted to social activities, items concerning Venables and his bride-to-be. A number of receptions had been given in honour of the engagement, though no wedding date had been announced.

Prudence rarely mentioned Venables in her letters, but Josephina gathered that Lady Daphne and her parents stayed at Blenhasset occasionally. Prudence said only that she was very beautiful but somewhat distant in manner. Josephina tried not to think of their impending marriage. She still kept the two books of poetry Venables had given her by her bedside, but she no longer read from them, for to do so increased her sense of loss.

George Ridgeway's attentions had cooled for a time following the hearing. Josephina did not doubt that he had mulled over Farnsworth's words, but since he never mentioned the incident to her, she vouchsafed no explanation. She was, in fact, rather glad to see less of him, for she valued her solitude. She suspected, from sly glances she received, that Farnsworth's insinuations had gone further than the hearing room, but since any speculation that may have arisen was never discussed in her presence, she never spoke of it. As the summer months wore on, however, George gradually resumed his visits, dropping in unexpectedly and sometimes staying for hours. She wished he had something else with which to occupy his time.

Squire Ridgeway asked her several times what she planned to do with her note so soon due, causing Josephina to curse the fact that his son was her lawyer and that her affairs were freely discussed in that family. She had vowed more than once to change her legal representative, but it was not a matter easily undertaken without cause. The squire renewed his offer for her land, but she refused, having made the decision to sell the entire estate. Frank Ridgeway was unhappy when he learned of the conditions she was imposing on the sale.

"We're too far from London to bring a high price, and it is preferable to make the conditions as attractive as possible to the buyer in this case. To saddle him with a parcel of tenants will make it difficult. I know that my father is interested in your land, but he wouldn't accept those conditions, even if

187

the asking price were lower. I don't know why you didn't accept Venables' offer to make good your loss on the sheep. At least now you wouldn't be in such difficulties, though I don't know how easy it would have been to raise money for Amelia. Still, we might have done it."

There were times when Josephina wondered why she had let her pride stand in the way of accepting an offer she knew was well-intended. The sum would have been infinitesimal to Venables, while it had ruined her. He had presented her with a practical solution, and she, usually a practical person, had allowed her emotions to stand in the way of its acceptance. But she could not be indebted to him; it would be difficult enough to face him again after his marriage—and their paths must cross either in Devon or at her sister's in Flaxhurst—without adding to that burden the knowledge that she owed him money; she would rather be indebted to a stranger than to the man she loved. For, to herself, she frankly acknowledged that love—now that he belonged to another—and she pondered on her own perversity. Did she desire him because she could no longer have him? she wondered. But, recalling those days in Gloucestershire, seeing him at the piano or strolling beside her on the Dibble farm, she knew she had loved him then. Had he proposed to her there, rather than in Devon following that disastrous conversation with his sister, there could have been no doubt of her answer. Had she only stayed at Flaxhurst until his return . . . But it was futile to pursue that line of reasoning.

Within the week, Westlands was put up for sale, and almost immediately an offer came in from Squire Ridgeway, such a paltry offer, so far below the price, Josephina refused to consider it; she was, in fact, infuriated that he had dared to make it. The squire, however, considered himself generous, for, at church the following Sunday, he raised the issue.

"I see you are selling Westlands after all, Josephina. I always said it would come to that. But Frank tells me you will part with only the whole, you refuse to subdivide the property. That's not what I would do in your place, but of course you know your own mind."

Josephina mustered a smile. "Indeed I do, squire, and on that point I am determined."

"I cannot see why you didn't like my offer," he said, his annoyance showing through his joviality, "but perhaps you did not realize that I planned to settle Westlands on George." He looked over at his son, engaged in conversation with Lady Netherton and Fanny.

"You know, Josephina"—the squire took her arm and led her aside—"if you agree in this matter, it is possible that you may not have to leave Westlands. I know how you feel about the estate, and what it has meant to you. Even though you are a woman, you have done a good job at that. I give the devil his due. But you must agree, it's not woman's work. You would be far better off concentrating your efforts inside the house and leaving matters outside to a husband. Now, I hope I am not speaking out of turn, but despite my own wishes for George, you must realize that he—"

"I'm afraid you *are* speaking out of turn, squire," Josephina snapped, feeling angry and trapped.

"I am sure George plans to talk to you, that is why I mentioned it. He is shy, you know, and I thought I should prepare you for what is in store."

"Sir, it is preferable that he should not mention it, for it is a matter I could not agree to. He is a dear friend but—"

"Marriages between dear friends are the very best, I can assure you. I don't hold with this romantic nonsense you hear so much of now from these poets. Utter balderdash, if you ask me; they don't know what they're talking about. That's not for us country folk, and I can assure you it's not what a solid marriage is based upon. Take my lady and myself. Why, when we were young, these things were arranged as they should be, and I'm sure a better or more solid marriage is not to be found."

Josephina remembered Squire Ridgeway's attentions to Lady Eliza at Venables' ball. The marriage was solid, all right, but he could not convince her it was the best, and that was what marriage with his son would be, solid and deplorably dull.

George joined them and nothing more was said, though the squire continued to give Josephina meaningful looks. He felt he had behaved magnanimously towards her, for he would so much have preferred Fanny Netherton as a daughter, but George was stubborn in his choice. The squire had thought that Farnsworth's statements at the hearing had changed his son's affections for a time, but now George was back where he had always been, glued to her side. Well, she came from a decent family, though not prudent, he feared; otherwise she wouldn't be in such financial straits. If she'd stayed out of debt, George could have had her and the estate without his having to buy it, but it was worth far more than he had offered—it would still be a bargain. Anyway, George should settle down and marry soon to provide an heir for his holdings. With Westlands in his pocket he'd now be coming a close rival to Venables as the largest landowner. There was no reason that a title might not be in the offing after that.

When George came out the following day, Josephina noticed a change in his manner, a determination to press his suit to its conclusion. She wondered whether it was better to hear it out or avoid it. Since she had no intention of accepting his father's offer on Westlands, she resolved to avoid a proposal and made sure she was never alone with him when he called. Often she invited Fanny Netherton to spend the day at Westlands, and George, more often than not, found himself addressing his remarks to Fanny rather than to Josephina; she certainly provided a more appreciative audience. Josephina was sorry to resort to these measures, for she was fond of George; she hoped that he would desist, but despite all her lack of enthusiasm, his determination to press his suit seemed to increase.

With Frank Ridgeway informing her that he could find no other buyers for the estate, Josephina felt that the whole Ridgeway family was combining to force her into an unwanted sale and an unwanted marriage. More than ever did she regret that she had not earlier changed her lawyer, but her fury knew no bounds when one day she received a letter from Mr. Thackeray Smithers, a London solicitor, who said that he had been in correspondence with Frank Ridgeway regarding the sale of her property, but since he had received little satisfaction from him he wished her to confirm whether or not the estate had already been sold, as he had a client interested in its purchase.

Josephina stormed into Frank's office that same day and flung the letter on his desk.

"Is this how you represent me? For weeks you have told me that there is no buyer for Westlands except your father, and now I find you are not responding to offers on my behalf, nor even informing me of them. Is this the ethical behaviour to be expected from one's lawyer? Whose interests are you looking after, mine or your father's? I hesitate to denounce you publicly, for I know your family too well, but be assured you will no longer handle my affairs."

The flush that had arisen in Frank's cheeks on seeing the name of the London solicitor on the letter before him did not subside during this tirade.

"Josephina, let me explain. I know it sounds as though I have kept this from you deliberately, but if I did, it was for your own good, believe me. Father has told me that George

190

plans to offer for you, which means you can remain in your own home, you will not have to leave it. Besides"—he threw the letter aside, gaining strength in his argument—"I have reason to believe this fellow may represent someone we would not wish to have in this neighbourhood, at least in the position of owning an estate here."

"What on earth makes you think that," Josephina expostulated, "and, anyway, what concern is it of yours? That is for me to decide. Furthermore, I see no name of his client, and whoever he is, he could not be represented by a more reliable firm, for if I am not mistaken, Smithers, Royd, and Fernald are legal advisers to many noble families."

"That is true, but that is not to say all their clients are of the nobility. They work for money, as we all do. There is something strange about this offer which led me to disregard it. You see, it was five thousands pounds above your asking price. Now, you know, no one in their right mind would offer more than was asked unless he had a particular wish to move into an area which might otherwise be denied him."

"Five thousand pounds over the price!" Josephina could not keep the astonishment from her voice.

"Just so. It is my belief that this man's client is Potter—Stanley Potter, who used to be a shopkeeper here—that is why his name is not mentioned, and that is the reason he made such a ridiculous offer. We don't want these cits moving in here, and particularly a man like Potter, who would attempt to make himself one of us just because he has money. We know where that money has come from—trade. Be assured he would not be received by my family, nor by most others I know. It would be an embarrassment to us all, and it could provide him with little happiness. I am sure now you see why I did not refer the offer to you."

"Yet you had no hesitation in forwarding that of your father, which was almost as much below my price," she snapped.

"Nevertheless, it would be money in your pocket. If you marry my brother, you can stay there and be mistress of your mansion as you have in the past."

"That is irrelevant. My matrimonial plans, should I have any, which, by the way, I have not, have no bearing on this matter. Whoever made an offer for my estate, you were honour-bound to forward it to me as my legal representative. Westlands does not belong to your father, or to your brother yet. *I* have no objections to Potter. His money may have come from trade, but it is honest money. I believe he would take as much care of Westlands as anyone else."

"Your father would turn over in his grave at the idea of having a cit usurp his place. Westlands has been Trafford property, gentleman's property, for over a century. Now, to sell out to a cit . . ." It was the mention of her father rather than the scorn in Frank's voice that made Josephina's face colour in anger as she reached over and took the London solicitor's letter from his desk.

"I shall handle my own affairs from now on, and when I need legal advice, you may rest assured I shall not ask it of you. Will you please ensure that all my papers are turned over to me without delay. Good day to you, sir." And she swept from his office, leaving him furiously shouting for his overburdened clerk to turn out the Trafford papers and bundle them up and deliver them immediately to Westlands.

21

Josephina replied to Mr. Smithers informing him that since Frank Ridgeway no longer represented her, she would be pleased to consider his client's offer for her estate. A courteous response was soon received, noting that Mr. Smithers would personally journey to Milvercombe to discuss the offer with her the following month.

That month took Mrs. Trafford to Flaxhurst to be with Prudence at the birth of her child and brought Amelia back to Devon to await the arrival of her bethrothed for the wedding. A change had been made in the wedding plans, however, for Amelia was to be married from her aunt's London home instead of Westlands, the sale of the estate making it uncertain whether it would still be in Trafford hands on the wedding date. Amelia much preferred the arrangement, for, she said, she now had more friends in London than she had in Devon.

The change in Amelia from child to woman was immediately apparent to Josephina as she stepped from her uncle's coach, clad in a smart turquoise-blue pelisse over a gown of a lighter blue, an elegant straw bonnet topping her newly styled curls. There was a self-assurance about her, an air of fashion and authority that had not been there before, but what pleased Josephina least, there was also an air of contempt—contempt for the home and the village she had left.

Though Mrs. Trafford had left for Gloucestershire the previous day, it seemed to Josephina that her mother spoke as Amelia said, "My dear sister, how dusty the roads are here, and how bumpy. I had quite forgot. The village looks smaller than it ever did, and goodness knows it was never more than a dot on the map, but now it looks quite seedy and ill-kempt, at least that is the way it seemed as I came through just now. Everything is much the same as it ever was, I suppose, I just hadn't realized before how dreary Milvercombe really is."

From that beginning, matters went from bad to worse. Though Josephina was a willing listener to the delights of

London life and her sister's affianced husband, after the third day of nodding her head and exclaiming periodically on how grand it all must have been, she grew weary, particularly when the paeans of praise for London were followed so swiftly by denigrations of the life Amelia had formerly led. Josephina was relieved when Fanny came to provide an appreciative ear to Amelia's monologue, and since she had had a London season, she could more readily share in Amelia's enthusiasm for the people, places, and events of the last few months. Not that Amelia needed any prompting, for she prattled on unceasingly with her continuing chronicle of the joys of town. She was happy to have another admirer to view her clothes, though she assured them that she had left her best dresses in London for the wedding trip. As Josephina suspected, she had far exceeded her allotted amount in purchasing her wardrobe, but she decided against speaking of it. The damage was done, and relations between them were already becoming strained, for Josephina found her sister endowed more with frivolity and less with good sense than she had ever been. Still, Amelia would soon be married, so she endeavoured to keep peace between them for the short time she would be remaining at home.

The only time she had given her undivided attention was when Amelia described a ball she had attended given in honour of Lord Venables' engagement.

"I was so surprised to receive the card, for though my aunt knew Lady Selford, who was the hostess, they are not close friends. My aunt is not very social, by that I mean that though she moves in the best circles, she herself does not entertain a great deal and Lady Selford had never been a guest at Windham Place, so I think it may have been because Lord Venables had seen the announcement of my own engagement in the paper that she invited us, for Mama said he wrote a very nice letter about it. Anyway, he came up at once when he saw me with Derek and congratulated us. You should have seen the dress Lady Daphne was wearing, sheer white silk interwoven with gold threads and a design of gold fleur-de-lis around the hem, I have never seen anything so beautiful and her engagement ring is simply enormous, rubies and diamonds in heavy gold, it gleamed so on her white hand that I was conscious of my own being so much smaller, but Derek says that when our ship comes in he is going to replace it with a diamond as big as the Matterhorn, I don't know where that is, but Derek has seen it and it's huge.

"Lord Venables asked me whether you were in good

health, and I said as far as I knew you were the same as ever, but he said that the last time he saw you that you were unusually pale. I said it must have been the light, because you have always had the brightest colouring of any of us, I think it is because you are out and about so much, but you should take care that your skin doesn't get coarsened on that account. Anyway, he said it was because of that that he was concerned. You certainly look well enough to me, though I think you have lost a little weight. What you need is a season in London, there's no chance of getting thin there with all the delicacies that are offered. At Lady Selford's ball they served the most exquisite lobster canapés, I sent Derek to get some for me immediately.

"I thought Lord Venables seemed quieter than when he was here in Devon, or more thoughtful or something. He only stood up for half the dances, and those were with Lady Daphne and the hostess and her daughter. I heard he had lost a huge sum at White's the night before in playing piquet with Lord Cansfield, but Cansfield said it was about time he got some of his money back."

A week later Mr. Smithers arrived and put up at the Blue Boar in Milvercombe, an inn not noted for its appointments, but the only establishment the village possessed. Mr. Smithers made no attempt to disguise his obvious discomfort at being so far from town and was anxious to conclude his business without delay. He was a stately man with iron-grey hair and a beaked nose which he fondly looked down, assigning the rest of the world to its due position. He was, however, all courtesy when he visited Josephina to discuss the sale. His client, he informed her, was willing to pay a higher price for the property than she asked, for he considered it an estate that had received great care and because innovative use had been made of the land. He was also hoping it might be an inducement to encourage Miss Trafford to continue there with her experimental agricultural pursuits, since he would not be taking up residence, his interest in the property being as an investment rather than a residence. If she had no other future plans, and if she would consent to remain and run the estate for him, there would be an annual amount of five hundred pounds to recompense her, and any additional funds she needed for machinery, repairs, or upkeep would be forthcoming. Miss Trafford and her mother could live in the house as though it were their own, and she could count on the arrangement for as long as she wished.

The terms amazed Josephina in their generosity, and she

could not help exclaiming, "But this is too much, Mr. Smithers, I simply can't believe it to be so. Who, pray tell, is your client?"

"My client, ma'am, wishes to remain nameless, at least for the time being, but I can assure you that you have nothing to worry about in that regard, It is merely his wish to remain anonymous, and I, as his legal representative, must respect it. On this subject may I say, Miss Trafford, that I am glad you dismissed Mr. . . . Mr. Ridgeton as your lawyer. I considered his conduct in this affair deplorable."

Despite her own feelings, Josephina upheld Frank's name before this eminent member of his profession.

"Mr. Ridgeway did not act wisely, but I believe he had my interests at heart. He disliked the fact that your client hides behind anonymity. For my own part, my main concern has been that my tenants would not suffer in this transfer. Your client shows a generosity which can only come of great wealth or an understanding of what it means to be poor."

Mr. Smithers sniffed, but gave no reply.

Josephina felt sorry that Mr. Potter, despite his obvious wealth, felt so unsure of himself that he would not let his ownership of the estate be known. Since she was not opposed to him as purchaser, she made an effort to convey that fact to Mr. Smithers by turning to the subject of those in trade and of money honestly earned, concluding, "Those in trade provide a valued service to all of us."

Mr. Smithers stared down his long nose and looked even more arrogant. "Ah, Miss Trafford, that is all very well for you, living here in the country as you do, and so far from it all. We in the city see quite a different side of it, I can assure you." With that he appeared to catch himself short, for he concluded, "But, you are right, they provide valued services, and many among them are worthy."

His attitude made Josephina wonder why Potter had ever chosen him as his solicitor, but she decided it must be because he was the best. She was beginning to think that Mr. Potter was a man who wanted the best and would accept nothing less. But whatever faults he might have, he was a generous man, as the terms clearly showed. It all seemed too good to be true: to be able to remain at her dear Westlands, to have money to rethatch the roofs of the buildings on the north boundary that so badly needed it, money for another seed drill, perhaps even that thresher she had heard of—and she had wanted to try a new method of irrigation on that land which sloped so and caused the water to run off, carrying away everything she planted. It would all be possible. Of course, Westlands would no longer be Trafford property, but perhaps she could get Uncle Mulliner to invest her money for her so that she might be able to buy it back eventually. She could not wait to tell her mother.

"I must insist," Mr. Smithers was continuing, "that you have a solicitor go over the terms of this agreement before you sign it, but once you have agreed to the terms, I can assure you that you will receive a bank draft within a matter of days."

Josephina thanked him, promising she would get Mr. Flint in Ilchester to look over the papers before returning them to him.

Before she could despatch a letter to her mother telling her the good news, she received one from her in that day's post announcing the birth of a son to Prudence.

Little Gerald was born about two in the morning. It went very well for both mother and son, despite being a first birth. Prudence was very brave, as I had expected, and is overjoyed with her little charge. He is very much like her, though I think he has his father's eyes. He quite reminds me of my own dear Gerald, but I must not think about that now, for it makes me grow sad, and this is such a happy occasion.

Lord Venables surprised us with a visit this morning. He called with Lady Daphne to congratulate Charles, though how he heard so soon of the birth, I don't know. She is such a beautiful young lady, so fragile and delicate-looking and so exquisitely dressed. She was rather silent, but I think that is her way. He remained for some time talking to me about Devon and the time he spent with us. I'm afraid he quite bored his betrothed, for, of course, she knows none of the people yet of whom he was speaking. I asked whether we could expect to see them at Venarvon soon, but he was unsettled about the future, and when I enquired about the date of the wedding, he said it was not yet fixed. I cannot understand why, for the match is so eminently suitable on both sides. I told them I wished they would marry in Devon and described the church to Lady Daphne—wouldn't it have been a splendid thing for us? She seemed enthusiastic; the idea, however, did not appeal to Lord Venables, so I suppose nothing will come of it. Her parents are here, and they all leave at the end of the week for Yorkshire to visit Sir Hugh and Lady Francesca Lanyon. I think it is a shooting visit for the gentlemen, for Lady Daphne did not seem at all keen on going to Yorkshire, saying she would rather be in town even if it were an unfashionable time to be there.

The references to Venables still had the power to pain Josephina, though she could not keep herself from listening whenever his name was mentioned. She wished he would hurry and marry and live as far away from her as possible; it came as a relief to know that they were unlikely to settle in Devon.

In her reply, Josephina was able to convey the news of the sale. It would mean that Prudence could now have her marriage portion, and she was sure it could not have come at a better time. It also meant that there would be no delay in Amelia's settlement, and papers were being drawn so that the wedding could take place as scheduled in October.

The final settlement of the sale and her mother's return to Westlands occurred at the same time the following week. Mrs. Trafford's pleasure was evident, but Josephina was disturbed to discover that she considered it an accepted fact that they would all move to London to live.

"Did you not understand, Mother, that we may stay here as long as we like, and that in addition I can draw a handsome sum for managing the estate for the new owner? We do not have to move anywhere, that is the beauty of it."

"My dear girl, it is all too demeaning, to act as an agent on your own property. I don't know what your father would say."

"But it is no longer my own property."

"Exactly so, that is precisely what I mean. To stay here on property which does not belong to you is out of the question. London is the place for all of us. Amelia will be there while Derek is on the continent with his regiment, and we can all set up house together until he returns. And there is nothing to stop you coming out, and I don't know why you might not be married. You are still quite pretty, you know, if only you would dress properly and stay out of the barnyard."

"Mother, I'm twenty-six now, to talk of my coming out borders on the ludicrous. And what would I do with myself in London? Here I have duties which I can continue to perform, but even better, Mr. Smithers has assured me that I need only write for the sums I need to institute repairs and buy more livestock and machinery. I can get all those buildings rethatched on the Trowes' farm and—"

"There you go, Josephina, back to your cows and sheep, as though those creatures haven't caused us enough harm already. I think it is time you lived a civilized life for a change. London is full of shops and amusements; you need never have a dull moment, I can assure you. Isn't that so, Amelia?"

"Indeed, Mama, I have been telling Josephina about it all. There is no place like it. I would not live anywhere else, unless Derek's duty requires it, but then I would hope it would not be for long."

"There, you see, if you will not take my word for it, listen to your sister. The trouble with you, Josephina, is that you have never moved in society and do not know its pleasures. I have already written to Aunt Mulliner from Gloucestershire asking her to look out for a place for us, so that when we go next month for Amelia's wedding we can simply stay there. I know we can stay with your aunt and uncle until a suitable house is found. It must be a good address, of course, that is so important in London, I can't overemphasize that. And we will all need to refurbish our wardrobes, for I know I haven't a single thing I can be seen in. Amelia can now get a few more things, for, poor girl, she has skimped and saved all this time. I think it is about time we all started to live for a change, instead of the kind of drab existence we've endured these past years."

So that was it, Josephina thought; they were to move to London and squander the money from the sale of Westlands and live a life of endless morning calls and evening routs; well, she simply refused to do so. She would make her mother an allowance, but she herself would stay. But first she must find someone to live with her, she could not remain alone; she had flouted many conventions, but even she balked at breaking that one. But who would come? She knew of no single, unattached woman except Fanny Netherton, and she would not wish to leave her mother. Perhaps she could advertise for a companion, but she wondered whom she might find in the short time remaining; it would be awful to be saddled with somebody completely incompatible. No, she would rather marry George than that.

Marry George! She had never seriously considered it until that moment, but it would be a solution to her problem. She did not stop to consider whether he would consent to the idea, thinking only that it was ironic that after all the time she had spent preventing him from speaking that now she would welcome his offer. He had not been to see them as often since it was known that Westlands had been sold. His father had been furious and had forbade him to visit Josephina, but he continued to call, anxious to know what her plans were for the future. Having made up her mind now to accept him, she heard her mother out with calmer feelings.

"I have never enjoyed country life, and well you know it. I tried to make the best of it, but I was not made for it, tramping in the mud, jogging around in a gig—you wouldn't even let us keep the carriage. I'm tired of economizing, and for what?—so that you can buy silly creatures and let them get cut up and buried with nothing to show for it. If the money is to disappear, let us at least enjoy it. I am determined to go back to London, it's where I belong. If you do not choose to come with me, you can stay here."

"Very well, Mother, I shall do just that. I shall stay, and you may have an allowance and live in London with Amelia until her husband returns, and then you can decide what you wish to do. I can see no other way for all of us to be satisfied."

Her mother was clearly astonished. "Do you mean you will really stay on here? But you can't live on your own. Even you are not that eccentric."

"You are right, even I am not that eccentric. No, I shall not live alone. I shall marry George Ridgeway."

"George Ridgeway! But I thought you were determined not to have him."

"So I was, but now he seems the lesser of the evils, and he is at heart a good man. I expect we shall get along. At least there will be no surprises, unpleasant or otherwise. I know what to expect of him, as he does of me."

"But does he still want you, now that you have sold the estate? His father wanted the property . . ."

"I'm well aware of what his father wanted, Mother, and I shall have to wait till George calls again to find that out."

George did call, the following day, and Josephina hastened to remove him from the watchful eyes of her mother by suggesting they walk back to the orchard.

"I remember how we played here as children, Josephina, and I can't believe you will be gone, for your mother has told Lady Netherton that you will all leave for London and settle there after Amelia's wedding."

"My mother will, George, but I have decided to remain here. The new owner wants me to continue to manage this estate and is willing to pay me handsomely to do so, so I have decided to remain."

"Remain here!" George was dumbfounded. "But you cannot remain on your own, and if your mother leaves and Amelia is married, who will be with you?"

"Just so, George. It is a matter which I have been pondering." There was a pause during which they walked together toward the orchard without speaking, one wondering how to broach the subject, the other dimly aware that he found himself in a predicament, for only that morning he had promised his father, in response to his repeated entreaties, that he would offer for Fanny Netherton; yet if Josephina were to remain, that was out of the question.

At last Josephina broke the silence. "I was wondering, George, if you are still of a mind . . ." It was more difficult than she had imagined; the words did not seem to want to come out. "I wondered whether you still felt . . . that is . . . Oh, George, what I want to know is whether you still want to marry me, for if you do, I accept."

In all his days, George had never imagined that Josephina Trafford would actually propose to him. He had often wondered how he would feel if she consented to be his wife, and here, in one moment, she had not only consented but had made the proposal as well. He regarded her with consternation and wonderment, and she, after waiting for some minutes for his response, began to feel she had made a terrible mistake. Perhaps all along he had not intended to propose to her at all.

"George," she began, "I'm sorry if I have misinterpreted your feelings, but I thought that you wished me to be your wife. If I was mistaken, please forgive me and disregard what I have just said. I was under the impression that you wanted to marry me, but—"

"But I do, Josephina, of course I do. It was just that you caught me by surprise. Of course I want to marry you, I can't think of a time when I wanted to marry anyone else."

And completely disregarding his father's advice and his own promise to offer for Fanny Netherton, he turned and took Josephina into his arms, planting a kiss firmly on her lips to seal the betrothal, His father be damned; he had always wanted Josephina Trafford, and now he would have her.

Josephina, for her part, was horrified to discover that rather than feeling excited at his bear hug and rough kiss, she felt a distaste that almost amounted to revulsion, and was glad when he released her.

"Josephina, you have made me the happiest of men." It was said with great sincerity, but Josephina could not help but wonder whether it was a phrase gleaned from one of his

201

mother's novels, it sounded so unlike him. "I think I should go and ask your mother's consent to our marriage, and then tell my father. We should hurry, for although the rooks flew straight in the sky this morning, a sign of a good day, I noticed on my way over that they were screaming more than usual, and that, you know, portends a change in the weather. I'd just as soon not be caught in a rainstorm, for this is my new coat I'm wearing. Do you like it?"

Josephina had, in fact, observed the bright blue superfine coat he was wearing, it suited him rather less that his usual brown worsted, she thought, but she merely said it was very nice. She looked at his red, open face and light blue eyes, now gazing skyward for signs of the predicted rainstorm, and wondered whether she could, indeed, spend the rest of her life with this man. Should she not withdraw now?—it was not too late—but even as the words rose to her lips, he turned and took her hand.

"Josephina, you don't know how happy I am. I have imagined this day so often, but I never really thought you would have me. When Venables was here, he made me so jealous. I thought at first that you liked him, and I knew he was only flirting with you. I know, now, it was stupid of me, but I longed for him to go away and leave us as we were before. That is why I was pleased to learn that he is to marry."

Josephina wished heartily that he had not introduced Venables' name into the conversation, but, strangely enough, it firmed her in her resolve to marry George after all. Venables was the only man she wanted, and she knew there was no longer any possibility of such a match. In that case, George would be as good a husband as any other. He was kind and steady and he loved the country. They had much in common. There was no reason it would not work. She tried not to think of his kiss, consoling herself with the belief that he would not often enforce those rights.

Her mother received the news with indifference. Josephina had always been a willful girl, and she considered this just one more example of her obstinacy. When she wished her to marry George Ridgeway, she would not hear of the match; now that she was sure she could find her a far better husband in London, she would have him. But if she preferred this miserable place over the delights of town, that was her affair, and at least George would inherit his father's property, which, given the squire's saving and acquisitive nature, would be considerable.

If Mrs. Trafford was less than enthusiastic at the news, Squire Ridgeway was apoplectic.

"Only this morning, George, you told me that you were going to offer for Fanny Netherton, a fine, genteel sort of girl, an only child with a tidy amount to bring with her. I know she likes you, for Lady Netherton has told your mother as much. But you wouldn't listen to me, and the next thing I find is that you deliberately disobey me and ride over and propose to Josephina Trafford, whom you know I cannot stand and never could. She's a willful, obstinate girl." On this point at least, Mrs. Trafford and Squire Ridgeway were in agreement.

"But, Father, I didn't do it deliberately. I just went over to see Josephina, sort of for the last time, to tell her I was going to propose to Fanny, and then she let me know that she would like me for a husband."

"Do you mean to tell me she actually proposed to you!" His father's shout could be heard all the way down in the kitchen.

"Well, in a manner of speaking, she did."

"Well, if that doesn't beat all. I always said she was a brazen girl, and you yourself heard what Farnsworth had to say about her that day at the hearing—"

"Father," said George in offended tones, "you are speaking of the woman I am going to marry. I would prefer you consider your words more carefully. I won't hear her maligned."

"Yes, I think those were Venables' words also, wouldn't hear her maligned after he'd been playing around with her."

"If you're going to speak in that fashion, I'll stay to hear no more of it. I am marrying Josephina Trafford, and you may as well get used to the idea."

"We'll see about that, my boy," were the last words George heard as the squire left the room, slamming the door behind him.

22

They set out for London at the beginning of October, Mrs. Trafford and Amelia overflowing with excitement and anticipation, Josephina quiet and resigned.

The last week had not been an easy one; in fact, it had almost made her break her resolve to stay in Devon. Squire Ridgeway had made no bones of his dislike of the match, but George had held firm in his decision to marry Josephina, so that at last his father had given a begrudging and conditional consent. He had, at first, attempted to make a stipulation that Josephina give up the idea of managing Westlands, but she was adamant in her decision to remain there, it being her only reason for the marriage. She had written to inform Mr. Smithers of her impending marriage, asking that he get the approval of the estate's owner that she might remain there with her husband; she informed him that as she would be in London she could receive his answer there. It was settled that they would be married in Milvercombe when Josephina returned from her sister's wedding, but the squire insisted that the banns not be read, nor the engagement announced, until she returned, hoping perhaps that she might be persuaded to remain there. George, possibly under the same apprehension, had announced that he would come to London for the wedding and escort Josephina and her maid back to Devon.

As Josephina gazed out of the carriage window at the passing scene, the leaves a brilliant orange, yellow, and red; the rich red soil of the dormant fields, cleared of their crops, a lush reminder of past fertility and yield yet to come, she was reminded that it was at that time, St. Martin's summer, that Venables had returned to Devon, and of all that had happened since. With George's farewell kiss still on her lips, she dared not look ahead another twelvemonth. She wondered, almost aloofly, why she found him actually repugnant. It was true that in the past she had not had to endure his embraces, but though she did not love him, she had always thought that she liked him. Now she found herself critical of his appearance, his manners, his conversation or lack of it, in fact, everything about him. She knew she had made a mistake in promising to marry him—no, in proposing to marry him—but she found it far more complicated to release herself from that vow than it had been to make it. George spoke only of the future and their life together, while she concentrated on not thinking about it at all. Perhaps she would stay in town, she thought, but as they neared London and she saw row upon row of red and brown chimney pots, while Amelia pointed excitedly to the shops and pleasure domes and her mother exclaimed on the changes made since she was last there, with fashionable London beginning to move northward towards Marylebone Park, for which John Nash had outlined such grand plans, Josephina became convinced it was not a place where she would be happy. Try as she might to share her mother and sister's enthusiasm, where they saw opulence, she saw litter and overcrowding, and where they admired the monuments and splendour, she deplored the poverty and squalor that existed side by side with such immense wealth.

Their arrival at Windham Place was greeted with jubilation and the news that Captain Rutherford was expected to be in town within a few days, for Mr. Mulliner had seen Colonel Underwood, who had served with him in Spain, and he had had news that he had already sailed for England.

"And whom do you suppose I ran into last week?" Mr. Mulliner concluded. "Just imagine, he wanted to be remembered to you."

Josephina turned expectantly. "Lord Venables?" she asked quickly.

"Don't be silly, Josephina, he's in Yorkshire—don't you remember that he told me so when I was with Prudence."

"Nobody like that, no indeed!" her uncle riposted. "It was a man from your own village—Stanley Potter—he owns a large linen draper establishment on Bond Street now, done very well for himself, extending into textiles and I don't know what. He puts his money to good use, and I've nothing against that. Nevertheless, I fear it's given him a swollen head, he's getting above his station."

"Oh!" Mrs. Trafford mused, casting a conspiratorial glance at Josephina.

"Yes, indeed. He'd heard of Amelia's wedding and sent congratulations on that—that was perfectly in order. But then he insinuated he might call upon you and pay his regards. I let him know in no uncertains terms that that would be quite unacceptable. You know, my dear, that's the trouble with these people who come up in the world, they think their money will buy everything, not only material assets but social connexion as well. Just because he is from your part of the world is no claim to acquaintance, and I let him know that in no uncertain terms. After my little setdown, I doubt he'll darken the door."

"No, indeed," Mrs. Trafford agreed faintly, leaving Josephina to conjecture how Mr. Potter, who had been so generous in every way, must have felt. But she said nothing; after all, she was scarcely at liberty to reveal the name of the new owner of Westlands, not having had it officially disclosed to her.

When Mr. Smithers did not call, nor send a reply to her letter, she wondered whether her uncle's little setdown of Mr. Potter had made him look with less than favour on her request for George Ridgeway to live on his property. As long as he did not renege on the sale, that could prove a welcome relief from the predicament of her engagement.

Each day was filled with calls and callers, and with visits to dressmakers, milliners, mantuamakers, and shoemakers. Mrs. Trafford insisted that Josephina's wedding clothes be every bit as fine as Amelia's, and put aside the sombre colours she selected in favour of jonquil yellow and rose pink. Josephina took no great interest in the selection. The only items which she personally chose and which she would let her mother have no hand in selecting were two serviceable riding habits to replace those that had grown shabby beyond belief in their daily use. However, when she tried on the first outfit to be sent from the dressmaker, a yellow muslin overdress with silk below, with a white Norwich shawl around the neck and shoulders and a Dunstable straw bonnet with matching trim, she had to admit that her mother had chosen well, for the jonquil shade clearly set off her brown hair and hazel eyes to perfection, heightening her colour and banishing any tint of sallowness from her slightly tanned skin. She examined herself in the mirror, turning this way and that; then, suddenly realizing that it would be George who would be seeing her in it, she tore it off and flung herself across the bed, not crying, not sighing, scarcely breathing, feeling trapped beyond measure in a web she herself had constructed.

Captain Rutherford arrived at last, to be entertained handsomely by the Mulliners and their many friends. He was, indeed, a bold figure, wearing his uniform of the First Foot Guards to perfection, his figure tall and impressive, with only the hint of a swagger in his walk. Mrs. Trafford was elated beyond measure and continued to thank her brother-in-law and sister for arranging such a fine match, disregarding that that match had caused the sale of the family estate. Josephina had to admit that she had never seen her mother happier, and thought, for the first time, that she had been selfish in depriving her of living where she most desired. She liked Captain Rutherford, finding him and Amelia well-suited to one another; neither having great depth of character or being given to intellectual pursuits, but perfectly pleasant and amiable, enjoying the changing scene around them, loving the nightly entertainments and the morning calls and deploring those days when they were forced to spend their time at home. Josephina liked him, but she could not believe he warranted the sale of Westlands, yet again she had to admit she had never seen Amelia happier, and she paused to consider her selfishness in concerning herself with the property rather than the happiness of other members of her family, for that, also, had been entrusted to her under the terms of her father's will.

One morning, as Josephina and her mother sat in the morning room waiting to see Amelia in her wedding dress, which had just been delivered, Mrs. Trafford, who had been cursorily scanning the *Times*, cried out, "Well, I never! What on earth can be the meaning of that? I'm sure I never saw a better matched pair in my life, and so in love. He was so changed, so quiet when he was with her, and she hung on his every word. What ever can have happened! Well, I never!"

"What is it, Mother? Whom are you talking about?"

"Why, Lord Venables, Josephina—Lord Venables and Lady Daphne Mercer. I saw them, you know, when I was at Flaxhurst, but do look at this."

And she passed the newspaper to Josephina, who read, in equal amazement, the announcement of the termination of the engagement of Lady Daphne Mercer and the Earl of Venables.

Amelia arrived, but apart from glancing at her sister, who immediately commanded her mother's attention, Josephina turned back to read and reread the announcement. What could it mean? From all she had heard, Venables had been perfectly true to his betrothed; there had been no whisper of his former philandering; in fact, as her mother had noted, it was said his behaviour was quite changed. She could only think that since the lady had broken the engagement, he must, indeed, be suffering, and she found herself with conflicting feelings in her breast, of sorrow at his hurt but happiness that he was not to marry. She had little time to reflect on the matter, for George Ridgeway arrived that day to be introduced to her aunt and uncle and new acquaintances as her affianced husband, a term she detested but bore with composure. She was encouraged in not having heard from Mr. Smithers; it was a straw to which she clung as an excuse for terminating her engagement.

However, the following day, as she sat waiting for George to call, the rest of the family having taken themselves off on their last round of morning calls before the wedding, the footman announced a gentleman to see her. From his manner she guessed the caller was not George, and became agitated, thinking it to be Mr. Smithers; that agitation only increased at the sight of the gentleman who was shown in,

"Lord Venables," she murmured, her heart pounding against her ribs.

With long and easy stride he crossed the room to where she stood and took her hand in greeting, his glance taking in her new yellow dress.

"I did not realize you were in London," she said at last, seeing in his face a sternness she had not before known. His eyes seemed bleaker than usual; his mouth was set in a more harsh line. There could be little doubt that he had received a crushing blow.

"I just came from Yorkshire. I hear your sister is to be married this week."

"Yes, Captain Rutherford is now arrived, and the wedding is set for tomorrow."

It was an unfortunate subject to be discussing, in view of his own so recently dashed hopes, and though loath to do so, she felt some mention should be made of it.

"I was sorry to read that your engagement is broken off."

"Oh, that." He shrugged, before demanding, "And your wedding, ma'am, when is that to be?"

She flushed, equally loath to discuss that event, only answering quietly. "When we return to Devon."

He turned away, and then turned back angrily. "I hope you do not expect me to felicitate you on such an unholy match. What were you thinking of, Josephina? What on earth made you have him? Why did you accept—are you quite mad?"

The torrent of words, fast and furious, that broke from his lips took her aback, and she replied quickly, with equal ferocity, "What right have you to speak to me in such a manner?"

"I intend to have every right after you have explained to me what made you have him."

208

"As a matter of fact," she retorted, "it wasn't so much a case of my having him as of him having me. You see, I asked him to marry me."

The look of sheer incredulity that crossed his face made her forget her anger.

"That is the most unbelievable thing I have ever heard. You asked him to marry you . . . in the name of heaven, why?"

She was about to remonstrate that it was not his concern, but a look in his eyes made her give a factual explanation of the sale of the estate and the conditions under which it had been made.

"But those conditions allowed you to be independent. Why on earth would you offer for Ridgeway?" Then, as though a thought occurred to him that he could not bear to consider, he ejaculated, "You're not . . . you can't be . . ."

"No, I assure you I am not." She was unable to contain herself from smiling at the look of relief on his face.

"Forgive me," he said, "but I was unable to think of any other plausible reason for your act."

"It was because I could not remain at Westlands alone. My mother is determined to come and live in London, and with both my sisters married I would have no one there to live with me. Even I cannot face the censure that would cause in our village."

"I see. That's something I hadn't thought of." His response puzzled her. "You do not love him, then. I knew you could not."

"I respect him. He is a very . . . solid man."

"Solid, yes, that he is. But these are not, I believe, the words of a woman in love, nor of a woman about to enter into married bliss." His voice had assumed a new strength and assurance, yet it was much lighter in tone. "I knew you could not love him."

"Sir, I hardly feel it is for you to decide whom I should or should not love. Your own affections, I know, have been engaged elsewhere."

"My own affections are engaged where they have been engaged ever since I first saw you, and if I have half the power which you once claimed was mine, I intend to use very bit of it to prevent your marrying George Ridgeway."

"But why—why are you so set against it? Because your own love affair is broken?"

"It has taken me months to break off from that insipid creature. She was driving me to despair, but I thought I could gradually prevail and make her wish to break away from me. Then I found you were engaged, and I had no option but to be brutal. I took her to the most decayed estate I could find in Yorkshire and told her it was the very place for me and that I was decided to settle there and that I thought we should marry immediately and start our married life there. I had to buy the place to prove I was in earnest, and I feared for the moment that she might agree and that I would have to be the one to break the engagement, an undesirable thing for her or any woman, but as luck would have it, as we were examining one of the decayed towers a large rat ran across her path and terrified her—she ran from the place and me back into the arms of her doting parents. I have never felt such relief in my life. No, my dear, my own love affair was broken only when you refused to marry me. I was wrong in proposing to Daphne, and did so only in a fit of pique on finding you returned to Devon when summoned by Ridgeway. When I found out the true reason for your departure, it was already too late, I had proposed and been accepted, and I felt absolutely wretched. It's been a dismal time, but I deserved it for attempting to use another person to suit my own ends."

"As I have done with George." Suddenly she looked at him speculatively. "But how did you learn of my engagement? Squire Ridgeway is against it, and he would not have it announced."

"For once I find myself in agreement with that worthy man." He grinned.

"But how did you know?" she pressed.

"Mr. Smithers, my solicitor, wrote me of it."

"Mr. Smithers is your solicitor also?"

"Does he represent someone else you know?"

"Why, yes, Mr. Potter, the new owner of Westlands."

"Mr. Potter the new owner of Westlands! That is impossible, for I purchased Westlands, did you not guess it? I did it because you wanted your independence and I thought I could give it to you. The last thing I expected was that you would shackle yourself to Ridgeway. I did not want it known that I had purchased it, for fear you would refuse. You had already refused my earlier offer of recompense. Why did you do that?"

"I could not be indebted to you," she said hesitantly.

"Why ever not?" he demanded.

She hesitated for a moment before looking at him directly and declaring, "Because I love you."

He did not immediately reply, but they stood looking at one another for a long moment before she held out both her hands to him.

"Conniston, I love you very much. Will you please kiss me?"

He pulled her gently to him, murmuring, "Darling, I thought you were never going to ask," before brushing his lips against hers softly and tenderly, then ardently, demanding her to give all of herself to him. She felt her body melt into his in that passionate embrace she had thought never again to enjoy. The thrill of his strong arms around her, the smell of his newly shaven cheek against her own, the sensation of his hands caressing her, combined to drive every thought from her mind except that she was where she belonged and where she had always wanted to be. So lost were they both in each other's presence that they were unaware that someone had entered the room until a shocked voice bellowed, "Josephina, what on earth do you think you are doing?"

Josephina drew back abruptly and turned, but Venables did not completely release his hold upon her, keeping one of her hands tightly within his.

It was George Ridgeway.

"It would have been polite to have had yourself announced or at least to have knocked before you entered." Venables' tone was as insolent as his words.

"I'll be damned if I will. You take your hands off my promised wife."

"She has no intention of ever—"

"Conniston," Josephina interrupted firmly, "this is my affair. I must talk to George."

"Conniston!" George shouted. "What kind of familiarity exists between you? It looks as though Farnsworth was right after all."

In a second Venables was upon him, seizing him roughly by the collar and shaking him.

"Conniston, don't," Josephina cried. "Please don't. I insist on explaining this to George on my own. Please understand it is something which I must do."

He released his hold, and George straightened his collar and cravat with a shrug of fury.

"Give me half an hour," Josephina pleaded. "I insist upon it."

"It is against my better judgement, but I will give you ten minutes and not a second more." He turned to George, saying abruptly. "You know where to find me if you want me, I presume."

George turned upon Josephina as the door closed behind Venables.

"I owe you an explanation, George, and an apology," she began.

"I should say you do." His voice was belligerent. "We are engaged to be married and I find you being embraced and, I might say, embracing another man. It's not to be borne."

"Of course it is not to be borne, you are exactly right, and it is as well we found out before we married that we are unsuited to one another."

"But I didn't say we were unsuited, merely that you can't behave so with other men."

"But it is the same thing, George; we are unsuited because you, quite naturally and quite rightly cannot stand by and watch a feeling which I have long had for Lord Venables and which I have been unable to overcome, nor could I promise to restrain myself from feeling as I do in the future. I was wrong to have consented to marry you."

"You did not consent to marry me, you asked me to marry you," he exploded.

"So I did. Well, that makes my conduct even more abysmal, and therefore I demand more of you in begging your forgiveness. But I know you to be a gentleman in the truest sense of the word. The fact of the matter is, George, that I am unworthy of you. Now, someone like Fanny Netherton could appreciate a man of your calibre."

"That is just what my father has been telling me for ages. I should have listened to him." George's voice was bitter.

"You should, indeed, George," said Josephina, finding herself in the strange position of espousing the cause of the squire. "But it is not too late. No announcement was made of our engagement, and I know your father feels too strongly against it to have voiced it abroad; therefore no damage has been done. We can both forget that it happened."

"But I cannot forget, Josephina. I love you despite all. But I must insist that you never see Venables again."

"That is just what I cannot promise you, and it is for that reason we must not marry. Living in the same village as Venarvon, it is impossible that I would never see him again, and if I did, I cannot promise you that I would stay away from him."

George's face turned ashen. "Do you mean to stand there

and tell me you would commit adultery?" His voice was shocked beyond recognition.

The word shocked Josephina also, yet she replied quietly, "I might be forced to it if you insist on keeping me to my promise to marry you."

"Farnsworth was right, you are a hussy!"

Josephina resisted the impulse to voice the rebuke which rose to her lips, reminding herself she had won her argument, and she gave no hint of the anger she felt as he turned and strode from the room without a parting word. She was beginning to feel she had indeed behaved like a hussy when Venables came in and drew her to him.

"I saw him leave; now let us begin where we left off."

"But he called me a hussy."

"So you are, my love."

"Oh, you wretch."

"You see, now you are calling me names."

"Well, you deserve it."

"Let me see if that is so," and he drew her close to him again.

"You know," he said later, "there is something I am still waiting for."

"And what is that," she said, trying to make some order of her loosened hair.

"I am waiting for you to propose to me. I'll be damned if I'll make another offer. Two within twelve months is quite enough, and both of them turned out to be perfect debacles. I'm afraid to try my luck again, but the special licence I have is positively burning a hole in my pocket."

"Well"—Josephina laughed—"I haven't been very successful either, but I'm willing to try again."

With that she took both of his hands in hers and earnestly studied his face before entreating, "Lord Venables, I have long admired you. At first I was attracted to you by your wit, then I must confess I desired you more than a maiden should, now I find I love everything about you with all my heart. Will you do me the honour of becoming my husband?"

He looked down at her, his eyes soft and loving. "My darling, I believe one is supposed to say that this is so sudden, yet all I can say is I have never desired anything more in my life. My heart is filled with a deep, enduring love which promises only to increase in our years together. You do me the greatest honour in asking me to be your husband and thus agreeing to be my wife."

As he put his head down to kiss her, again the door

opened and a horrified voice shrieked, "Josephina, what *are* you doing?"

It was Mrs. Trafford.

Venables greeted her calmly by saying, "Your daughter, ma'am, has just proposed to me and I have accepted her. May we ask for your blessing?"

Mrs. Trafford was speechless.

"I trust your silence does not mean that you disapprove, for we are shortly leaving for Gloucestershire, where your son-in-law is to marry us, and then I plan to carry my wife off to a fine estate I have recently purchased in Yorkshire which is quiet and secluded and much in need of her talents as an organizer."

"But, my lord, my daughter is already engaged," Mrs. Trafford stuttered.

"To me, ma'am."

"But, Josephina, tell him . . . tell him . . ."

It was all too much for Mrs. Trafford. She fainted.

"Oh, no," cried Josephina, and together they helped her mother to a sofa.

"Now, my love," Venables insisted, "if you wish to leave here with your mother's consent, you must go and find the vinaigrette, and please make haste if we are to at least make a start for Gloucestershire today."

"But Conniston, there is Westlands . . ."

"Mr. Smithers has arranged everything, my love, it is all taken care of."

"Then you knew I would come with you?"

"I knew that if you did not come voluntarily, my dear Portia, that I was prepared to kidnap you. I was determined you would not slip through my fingers a third time. Now, please hurry and get your maid to put together some things for the journey. Your mother is coming round, and I shall talk to her while you are gone, but let it not be too long, for we don't want further intruders demanding to know what you are about."

"Oh, Conniston." Josephina put her arm around his waist and laid her head on his shoulder. "Is this really happening, or is it a dream?"

Once more the door opened, and Aunt Mulliner entered, followed closely by Amelia. She saw her niece embracing a tall, elegant gentleman who was certainly not the man who the previous day had been presented to her as her future husband. Beyond the embracing couple, stretched out upon the sofa as though she had received a mortal blow, was her sister.

Her morning room had never been the scene of such a contretemps.

"Josephina!" she exclaimed in sepulchral tones. "What, pray, is the meaning of all this?"

About the Author

British-born Diana Brown has lived and worked throughout Europe and the Far East. Ms. Brown, a librarian, now lives in San Jose, California, with her husband and her two daughters, Pamela and Clarissa, who are named after Samuel Richardson's heroines. Two other Regencies by Ms. Brown, *The Emerald Necklace* and *A Debt of Honour*, are also available in Signet editions.